"We'll find them and straighten out this whole mess."

"We will," Kristine agreed with obvious determination.

He couldn't help it. He bent down and kissed her gently on the mouth.

Within the space of a moment, they stood still on a secluded path and he kissed her once more.

Hell, Quinn didn't just want to share kisses with her. He wanted to touch her everywhere.

That wasn't going to happen now. Probably wouldn't happen ever. It *shouldn't* happen.

Reluctantly, he pulled back. "Guess that was for luck," he said, making a joke of it.

"Yours or mine?"

"Both."

Dear Reader,

Even honeymooning members of Alpha Force can get into trouble, and it takes both family and friends—shapeshifters or not—to help them out.

In *Undercover Wolf*, the protagonists of the preceding Alpha Force story, Lt. Grace Andreas Parran and her new husband, Lt. Simon Parran, have gone missing on their honeymoon. Simon's brother, Lt. Quinn Parran, and Staff Sergeant Kristine Norwood, Grace's Alpha Force aide and good friend, go undercover, unofficially and against orders, to find them. It's hard enough ignoring their own growing attraction but their undercover identities require that they pretend to be honeymooners! Kristine must also act as Quinn's aide for shifting into wolf form, which means she keeps seeing him naked!

I had great fun writing *Undercover Wolf*, the fourth novel about Alpha Force—a highly covert military unit partly comprised of shapeshifters. I hope you enjoy the story.

Please come visit me at my website, www.LindaO Johnston.com, and at my blog: http://KillerHobbies. blogspot.com. And, yes, I'm on Facebook, too.

Linda O. Johnston

UNDERCOVER WOLF

LINDA O. JOHNSTON

MILLS &
BOON

Linda O. Johnston loves to write. More than one genre at a time? That's part of the fun. While honing her writing skills, she started working in advertising and public relations, then became a lawyer…and still enjoys writing contracts. Linda's first published fiction novel appeared in *Ellery Queen's Mystery Magazine* and won a Robert L. Fish Memorial Award for Best First Mystery Short Story of the Year. It was the beginning of her versatile fiction-writing career. Linda now spends most of her time creating memorable tales of paranormal romance and mystery.

Linda lives in the Hollywood Hills with her husband and two Cavalier King Charles spaniels. Visit her at her website, www.LindaOJohnston.com.

I've been visiting a number of national parks lately and enjoying them immensely. Acadia National Park, near Bar Harbor, Maine, has been one of my favorites, so I had to set a story there. But as always, I have invoked poetic license—this time to make sure those who investigate the fictional crime that happens there handle it the way I want them to, not necessarily as real law enforcement folks might operate. But real law enforcement folks might find problems with having Alpha Force members shapeshift in their jurisdiction!

Those who read my books will expect that this one, too, is dedicated to my husband, Fred, who enjoys travel even more than I do and has fun visiting national parks.

Chapter 1

Why do I feel so unnerved?

It wasn't as if Staff Sgt. Kristine Norwood hadn't seen a lot of naked male bodies during her years as a nurse, before she'd become a member of the covert military unit Alpha Force.

Maybe it was because she had foolishly allowed herself to notice exactly how good-looking and sexy her new but temporary superior officer, Lt. Quinn Parran, was when they'd first been introduced a few days ago.

They had just reached the test mission's planned location—a woodsy area at the far end of Ft. Lukman, on Maryland's Eastern Shore. Clad in her usual camo uniform and boots, Kristine had hurried in this direction with her heavy backpack over her shoulders. She stopped now and could sense the presence of the man who had kept up with her along the path through the most remote area of the military base where Alpha Force was headquartered.

She ignored that niggling uneasiness, embarrassment—and something she didn't even want to think about, lust—as she turned toward him.

"This the place?" He glanced around at the pin oak trees looming around them.

"Yes, sir."

She caught the sardonic raise of his dark brows over his golden-brown eyes.

"Stop calling me 'sir,'" he said. "You called me Quinn when we were introduced at Simon's wedding."

"Yes, sir, but we weren't on an official exercise then." And she hadn't felt so uneasy at the wedding of her regular superior officer, Lt. Grace Andreas, to Quinn's brother Lt. Simon Parran, who had also just recently joined Alpha Force. Kristine had been maid of honor and Quinn was best man.

He had undoubtedly been the best-*looking* man there.

Grace and Simon were on their honeymoon now, which was why Kristine and Quinn were temporarily assigned to work together.

He was right, though. She usually called other

Alpha Force members by their first names from the time she met them, no matter what their rank. She was friendly enough with Grace and others to joke around with them. But this was different. Way different.

"You want to play military?" he asked. Hell, they *were* military, even if he chafed at it. "Here's my next order, Kristine. Stop considering this an official exercise."

Kristine couldn't help herself. She smiled both at his words and at his exasperated expression. His military haircut hadn't compelled him to do a great job of shaving, and the hint of dark stubble on his face emphasized the razor-sharpness of his cheekbones. She ignored the sexiness of the look and how it caused her insides to churn and simmer, and responded, "Can't do that, sir. But I'll call you Quinn."

"But this is only quasi-official." What, did the guy just love to argue, or was he serious? "It's a test, both for me and your oh-so-secret military unit. *Our* military unit." He'd obviously seen her scowl and was reacting to it. That was a good thing. "We both want to see how I do during my first time using the Alpha Force elixir that my brother Simon has described so glowingly to me. He wants to know, too."

Quinn was a new recruit. He had obtained his rank because of what he was, not because of training or achievement. At least not yet. And so far,

Kristine's impression was that he had joined the military not because he wanted to—as she had—but for some very unusual benefits he would not have received otherwise.

Like this—using the elixir.

He obviously had some issues with it all, though. She, on the other hand, was perfectly happy following military protocols…most of the time. Tonight, though—well, she would obey orders notwithstanding how uncomfortable she was.

And that meant acting as Quinn's aide for this very special session. Mission. Official mission.

Quinn was taller than his brother, with wide shoulders and a devil-may-care stance he affected even now that he was a soldier. His uniform was similar to hers—much crisper, though. Probably never worn before. It displayed the bars showing he was a commissioned officer. And now, he was about to remove it….

Orders or not, how could she stay completely remote and objective as she did all the things necessary to assist Quinn?

She simply would, because she had to. Having her temporary commanding officer naked in front of her was not beyond the call of her very special duty. After all, she'd seen Grace naked a lot when her superior had shapeshifted into wolf form and back.

Now it was time for Quinn to do the same.

Yeah, but Grace was a woman, argued Kristine's logical mind. She'd seen nothing different from what she saw in the mirror, just in the unique configuration that was Grace's instead of her own.

But Quinn? He was all man. Well, almost all man, except for what she knew about him and what he was about to accomplish here.

After she saw him naked...

"Tell you what," he said. "Let's do it all backward. You give me some orders. What do we do next?"

"I assume this won't be your first time shifting outside a full moon," Kristine said, buying a little time. Plus, she was curious. This would be his debut shifting as a member of Alpha Force, but he'd had other resources before.

"That's right. I've taken some of the shifting pills that Simon developed, so I've already changed now and then at different times. I've even taken his medication during a full moon because it helps to keep us from changing automatically then. Mostly. My bro's a smart guy, but his pills need work."

"You probably know that some of what he did has been incorporated into the new Alpha Force formula," Kristine said. "It was already good stuff, but now it's better."

That wasn't her area of expertise, of course. But

she, like all Alpha Force members, knew that the basis for what Quinn would be drinking here was the most current version of the Alpha Force elixir that had first been developed by one of its commanding officers, Maj. Drew Connell, even before he had helped to form the very unique, very covert military unit composed partly of shapeshifters.

The formula had been modified over the few years of Alpha Force's existence, improved by development and experimentation.

And now, Kristine had heard, they had also made some initial modifications to the elixir that were triggered by the formula first developed by Quinn's brother Simon. That blend was still in experimental stages and not yet in common use. Simon's prior version was not as sophisticated in most ways as what Alpha Force was using—but it contained some very desirable qualities.

"Bring it on," he said. "I've been waiting to try it."

Kristine inhaled deeply. "Okay, then." She kept her tone crisp. "I'll give you a dose of the elixir. You remove your clothes, then I'll shine the light on you."

"It's supposed to mimic the intensity of a full moon, right?" Quinn asked. He didn't even comment about the fact that he was to completely strip in front of her. Maybe it was no big deal to him.

She wouldn't let it be a big deal to her.

"That's right," she said.

"Fair enough."

Kristine removed a vial of elixir from the back-pack where it had been carefully stowed. As he drank it, she also extracted the moderate-size battery-operated light.

She pretended not to be especially aware of what he was doing as he removed his shirt, then his slacks. But she did sneak a glance in his direction. Damn, but his body was as buff as she had anticipated from seeing him fully clothed.

Then he removed his black boxers. She felt her face redden as she turned the light on and aimed it toward him. She had no choice but to look then. Oh, yes. His male parts were as large and enticing as she had imagined, too. She quickly lifted her gaze toward his face.

He obviously was aware of her discomfort. As she bathed him in light she could see his masculine expression that clearly said, *Like what you see?*

And then, as anticipated, his shift began. Kristine watched, as always amazed yet accepting of the miracle she observed so often.

Quinn's body writhed, and he dropped to all fours on the ground. His limbs contorted as fur erupted from his skin. His grimace elongated into a canine muzzle.

Soon, he would be, for all intents and purposes, a wolf.

*   *   *

Standing still, paws grounded on the soft dirt of the earthen path, he stared at the beautiful human who had aided his change. She had turned off the bright light and stood watching him in the darkness, eased now only by the distant lights of the military base. She remained unmoving. Her head was tilted, as if she studied him. Wondered about him.

Except for his family, he had never had any company while shifting.

The fact he could think about that now was astounding. Always before, even when using Simon's treasured pill that helped to control shifting nearly anytime—at least somewhat—his thoughts while changed had been as wild and uncontrolled as his wolfen body.

But this Alpha Force formula allowed him to keep all his human awareness. He loved it!

What else was different now? He had to know.

He would not find out by remaining here.

He dragged his gaze from the wide blue eyes watching him, bared his teeth for an instant to convey his intent to be on his own and began to run.

The late summer nighttime breeze wafted around his long silver-black pelt. Smells of trees, of large birds of prey, of small squirrels sleeping in branches above, filled him with a sense of belonging.

He circled the vast area inside the fence, remaining within the confines of Ft. Lukman.

He had an urge to run and never return. But his alert mind acknowledged the wish while ensuring that sensibility and caution governed all.

Wise or not, he had taken an oath to become a soldier. With his new ability to think as consciously as a human, he remained aware of the penalties for a soldier's going AWOL, no matter what his assignment. Or the form of his body.

Besides, he wanted more access to the formula.

For a long while, Quinn ran in loops, circling the perimeter of the military base, staying far from the buildings. He watched for people to ensure he got nowhere near them—though he was fully aware that many among this group of humans, more than any other, would understand what he was. Accept it. Accept him.

Yet he preferred being on his own, absorbing every nuance of the sights and sounds and smells utilizing his enhanced senses and his maintained ability to understand.

He didn't feel he would ever grow tired. But he had not taken a large quantity of the changing formula for this, his first experiment with the medication that was so new to him.

For the first time since reluctantly agreeing to

join his brother and enlist in this unique military force, he started to believe it was not a mistake.

Yet would this new environment, this new job, ever feel important enough to quell his natural curiosity? Would he ever be comfortable acting like a soldier, taking orders, especially if there were any he felt to be needless or ludicrous?

Could he, as he had been promised, ever use all the prized abilities that he had carefully honed over his years as a private investigator?

He would have to wait and find out.

Eventually, he began to feel tugs beneath his skin, a sure signal that he would soon change back. Reluctantly, he turned in the direction from which he had come.

The woman who had helped him remained there, sitting on the ground near where he had left her, a softly lit electronic reader on her lap. She was reading. Waiting for him.

He wanted to greet her. Thank her.

Instead, what poured from his throat for now was a soft growl.

She immediately looked at him as if startled.

And then she nodded.

"That's great stuff," Quinn said. "The shifting formula." He had hardly stopped grinning since changing back from his wolf form.

He looked entirely human now. He was also fully clothed. Kristine, walking beside him on the path to the center of Ft. Lukman with her backpack again over her shoulders, resisted glancing toward the private areas of him that she had glimpsed—and considered potentially *great stuff.* They were all hidden now anyway.

And staring wouldn't be professional.

Of course, the heated stirrings inside her, being close to this man again, were anything but professional.

"Once we're back at the main building, I'll conduct a recorded interview with you and enter your description into our computer database."

"I'll have a lot to say," he responded. "All of it complimentary."

Her thoughts, too—about him—but of course she didn't mention that. She would be a lot more comfortable when Grace returned and she could get back to being her regular charge's aide. She didn't know who would be there for Quinn, but at least it wouldn't be her.

Ft. Lukman was a fairly large base, but it didn't take long to return to the building where they had started their trek earlier. The aboveground portion held quite a few dog kennels for the canines that acted as partial cover for the wolfen shapeshifters headquartered here.

Quinn and she immediately headed for a stairway down to the lab areas, clean rooms and primary Alpha Force offices. This, Kristine knew, was
where those supposedly magical formulations of the
Alpha Force elixir were mixed and changed and
improved. She sometimes wished she knew more
about how they worked, how they acted to enhance
the process and conditions of shapeshifting.

But she never wished that she were a shapeshifter. Oh, she admired them. Liked working with
them. But when all was said and done, she preferred
being…well, herself.

At the bottom, Quinn reached around to open
the door for her. She appreciated the gentlemanly
gesture. Maybe there was hope for him to be a real
soldier yet.

Not that it really mattered to her.

She gasped as a backlighted body clad in a camo
uniform loomed before them in the hallway. It was
late, and she hadn't expected to see anyone there.

"Glad you two are finally back," said Maj. Drew
Connell, commanding officer of Alpha Force.
"Come with me. There's something important going
on that I need to brief you about."

Kristine had thought it interesting and fitting that
a shifter had been designated to command this covert unit. At first she had wondered whether she
would accept taking orders from those who were
so different from her. Now, it was second nature.

If Drew said something significant was happening, that meant it was definitely critical.

He ushered them into the small office off the main lab facility where he and others worked on the shifting formulation. He was not only the one who had developed the prototype, but he had also stayed closely involved with its modifications.

"Sit down. Please." It was an order, but people around here tended to give orders more politely than the rest of the military, as if Alpha Force was different.

Which it was.

"What's up?" asked Quinn, as he settled his large frame into the designated seat across from Drew's desk. "Sir," he added when Drew's suddenly chilly golden eyes reminded him where they were and who outranked whom.

Was this some kind of alpha thing, too, among male shifters? *Interesting,* Kristine thought.

"Yes, please tell us what's going on, sir," she added in a respectful tone, one she hoped Quinn would use himself in the future.

"A couple of people were killed two nights ago in Acadia National Park," he said, his face grim.

That had been a night when the moon was full, Kristine realized.

Before Drew could continue, Quinn interrupted. "That's near Bar Harbor, Maine. Where Simon and Grace went on their honeymoon. I haven't been in touch for a couple of days—didn't want to bother them. Are they okay?" He had stood abruptly, and Kristine empathized, although she remained seated. She was worried, too.

"Unknown so far," Drew said. "The victims have been identified and aren't Grace and Simon, so you needn't worry about that. They were apparently attacked by some kind of wild animal, and the first assessment indicates the wounds could have been caused by canines."

"Are there wild wolves in that park?" Quinn demanded.

"Used to be, a long time ago, but not now," Drew said.

The three of them were silent for a long moment, staring at one another.

"Could the attackers have been…werewolves?" Kristine asked quietly.

"That's not been proposed officially, even by those who know about Alpha Force," Drew said. "But—"

"Has anyone talked to Simon?" Quinn demanded. "To Grace?"

"Several of us have tried to call them on their cell phones and at their hotel," Drew replied. "We haven't been able to reach either of them."

Chapter 2

The time was 0930. Kristine was surprised that this group of people, which included both brass and nonmilitary honchos, could come together so quickly here in such a remote location, but it had happened. Around twenty people were gathered in the assembly room on the first floor of the building at the heart of Ft. Lukman, where the offices of the commanding officers and others were located. Of course most were familiar Alpha Force members, including Lt. Autumn Katers, a shifting hawk, and her aide, Sgt. Ruby Belmont, who had been on a mission with Kristine and Grace in Arizona when Grace had met Simon.

There were also some relatively new recruits, like

Lt. Colleen Hodell, a cougar shifter, and Sgt. Jason Connell, a wolf shifter related to one of the unit's commanding officers.

Then there were the others.

Kristine had entered the room fifteen minutes before and taken a seat out of the mainstream of the Alpha Force group, on one of the theater-style chairs mounted on the concrete floor. She had left a chair empty beside her in case Quinn decided to join her.

Quinn had just come in with Maj. Connell and Lt. Patrick Worley, the hands-on commanding officers of Alpha Force, whom he'd probably waylaid in the hall. He stood with them now at the front of the room, apparently attempting to pump them in advance for information. But he didn't seem overly pushy, at least not from Kristine's perspective. His expression seemed interested, his nods deferential. Had he decided to accept where he ranked in the military, or was he just acting that way to get what he wanted? Or was she entirely wrong in her interpretation from this distance?

Damn, but she wanted to join them.

She glanced at her watch. The meeting was scheduled to begin in about two minutes. The officers wouldn't appreciate her interrupting them—that would only delay the assembly they'd thrown together so quickly.

She couldn't help feeling a bit riled. Quinn should

have contacted her, involved her in his discussion. They were a team, at least for the moment. He ought to recognize that. Live by it.

Even so, she recognized that though they had similar interests in what was about to be discussed, his interest was even greater than hers. She was a buddy and comrade-in-arms with Grace.

He was Simon's brother.

Apparently Quinn and she weren't the only ones worried about what was happening with the two missing Alpha Force members. The concerns of most of these people, though, might be more about the effect of the current situation on the unit than on the individual members involved.

Okay, call her cynical. She gave a damn about Alpha Force, a lot more than, say, Quinn did. And, most likely, more than those now in an apparently intense discussion with Gen. Greg Yarrow near the door at the side of the room, including a couple of suits and a higher-ranking general.

But the people involved, and what was happening to them, were important, too.

That was why she had tried calling Grace's cell phone. Three times.

And left three messages, each more urgent than the last.

None had been returned.

"Okay, let's get started." Drew broke away from

his discussion with Quinn and Patrick and stood at the front of the room in front of the U.S. flag to address the whole gathering. Quinn did not look pleased, but he moved quickly toward her, beyond the couple of rows filled mostly with others in camo uniforms—both shifting and nonshifting members of Alpha Force. Kristine had already noticed that among them was Dr. Melanie Harding-Connell, a local veterinarian and Drew's wife. They'd had a baby a few months ago, and the little girl, Emily, was sleeping in a nearby stroller. Melanie was not a member of the military and was also not a shifter, although her husband was both.

More than once, Kristine had wondered what little Emily's shifting abilities might eventually be. Her understanding was that the gene was dominant, so the baby would grow into a werewolf.

Interesting, that Melanie would choose to marry and have an unusual child. Kristine was aware that most shifters were the result of mixed marriages. She loved working with shifters, but marrying one? Giving birth to a baby shifter?

How would a nonshifting parent cope?

Maybe she was too traditional, despite being part of Alpha Force, but give her a nice, calm, loving marriage someday, preferably to another soldier, and a home filled with regular kids. Kids who were loved. Well cared for. A family that was way different from her own disastrous childhood.

Hell, she'd risen above all that. It had brought her here, where she belonged.

Quinn sat down beside her on the aisle seat, nodding grimly. She, too, remained silent. She knew he had a close relationship with his brother and could only imagine what he was feeling now, with Simon the center of a situation that could only be bad, whatever the explanation. She had an unwelcome urge to reach over and squeeze Quinn's large hand, now resting on his leg, in a gesture of comfort, but that wasn't appropriate.

"I think you all know why we're here," Drew said. He stood in front of the group, speaking without a microphone since everyone had gathered at the front of the room. He probably hadn't gotten any more sleep than Kristine had after their quick briefing last night, but he looked alert, his golden eyes sweeping the crowd. "Even so, I'll describe my understanding of the situation."

He briefly went over what he had said to Quinn and her last night. There'd apparently been no further information gathered since then. Two tourists were fatally mauled. Simon and Grace, who had been honeymooning in the area, were missing. The news had been picked up by local media but national coverage was minimal. So far.

"Are you certain the two things are related?" This came from one of the two men in suits seated in the first row near the generals. The speaker was now standing. Kristine recognized him from the wedding: Darren Olivante, team leader for domestic projects at the Defense Special Projects Agency— the agency within the Department of Defense that had assisted in the creation of Alpha Force and now helped monitor it.

As Olivante turned to glance around the room, Kristine noticed that his salt-and-pepper hair was longer than the traditional cut of the military members he worked with. He wore glasses and a challenging expression on a round and flabby face.

General Yarrow rose and walked to the front of the room beside Drew. He, too, had been at Grace and Simon's wedding. Although he was headquartered at the Pentagon like the Defense Special Projects Agency, he also maintained an office at Ft. Lukman. Kristine hadn't seen him around here lately, so he must have dashed here for this meeting.

The general was in his sixties but well preserved, and his hair, although behind a receding hairline, was still black. The wrinkles on his face seemed to show up mostly when he scowled, and he maintained a strong-looking physique.

"We have received no evidence that the killings and the disappearance of our two officers are related, but it's a potentially logical assumption," the general said. "Of course, given the special nature of Alpha Force and its members, we're hoping the Parrans weren't involved in mauling those tourists, but the information we've been given indicates that the wounds appear to have been caused by at least one wild animal, probably canine. That could indicate—"

Quinn stood beside Kristine. She tried to grab him, to warn him not to interrupt, but it was too late. His otherwise handsome face had turned an angry shade of red, and he shouted, "If you're insinuating that my brother and his wife attacked some humans for no reason while shifted, forget it. Isn't this Alpha Force organization intended to be a pack of sorts? Pack members have each other's backs. We don't level false accusations at one another."

The DSPA official had remained standing. He glared at Quinn, then turned toward General Yarrow. "I think this is a good example of why the plans we've been discussing are the way to go, General," he said. "And why it's been so difficult to ensure that funding for Alpha Force stays intact." Even from several rows back, Kristine could hear the ice dripping from his words.

But what was he talking about? What plans?

And was Alpha Force in jeopardy? Without adequate funding, it could disappear. What would happen to its members?

"My suggestion, sir, is to approach the investigation in a two-pronged way," General Yarrow said. "And to make sure it's successful. That will convince the powers that be to appropriate funding. But this isn't the place to discuss it all." He turned from the civilian to face Quinn, who remained standing with his hands clenched into tense fists. "Lt. Parran," the general said, "we will have a private briefing as soon as this meeting is over. For now, you are dismissed."

Drew Connell, who stood beside the general, gave a curt nod toward Quinn, seconding the order.

Quinn didn't move, except that his gold-tinged brown eyes narrowed. Kristine half expected him to erupt in a heated volcano of protest and fury.

But he was now a member of Alpha Force. Of the military. He had taken an oath that involved following orders. He'd spoken of the pack mentality of Alpha Force. Surely, he would at least bow to that, to Drew Connell's authority—wouldn't he?

In any event, she was his acting aide.

She reached up and grabbed his forearm. As she had anticipated, tension had turned it into a steely rod. "Don't protest," she whispered up at him. "We'll talk to the general and the major later and get this all sorted out."

He glanced down at her. She almost winced under the barbed anger in his gaze. But in moments, he relaxed. Closed those eyes for an instant.

Then he called to the ranking officers, "Yes, sirs." The tone was sardonic, and the salute he flashed after Kristine released his arm was a parody. He turned and started down the aisle toward the door.

Kristine remained worried for him. He was her charge, after all, at least for now. She had an urge to follow him.

But she needed to know what was said here. He needed to know, too, whether or not he realized it.

She remained seated while Drew and General Yarrow described the situation in Maine and the Alpha Force position.

Then Olivante joined them and commented.

Kristine was afraid she knew how the investigation was going to be handled. And it wasn't the best way for Alpha Force.

They sat in a small room outside the general's office waiting for Major Connell and General Yarrow to call them in.

"I take it that my attitude—even though I was right—didn't help my brother's position," Quinn said to Kristine with a shrug. He had stayed outside the assembly room, pacing back and forth, until the meeting had disbanded and Kristine joined him.

Despite his keen wolflike hearing, even in human form, he hadn't been able to make out much of what was said.

Since the meeting had been short, he didn't expect that there'd been much of substance anyway.

Only speculation.

While waiting, he had tried texting, then calling Simon and Grace again. Both calls had gone straight to voice mail, and he had received no responses to any of his attempts to reach them.

"Probably not," Kristine answered. Sitting in a stiff military pose in the chair beside him, she raised her head, jutting her chin out in a characteristic motion he had noticed before. It showed her determination. Her stubbornness. Her beauty.

All right, maybe it wasn't her most beautiful feature, but he liked it. Enough that he had an urge to touch that strong chin with his fingers. Better yet, cup it and pull her forward so he could test her stubbornness with a kiss...

He stopped, mentally punching himself. Where had that come from? He had just met her a few days ago, at Simon's wedding. Yeah, she was a looker, and she'd seen him buck naked—and the thought of her eyes on him started his privates stirring even now.

But she was also all military. His assigned aide. A nonshifter. Not someone to get all hot over.

Was worry for his brother turning him into some kind of nutcase?

Maybe. He'd have to be careful. "So the powers that be, people I don't even know who can send orders down the pipeline to me, think that my brother and his wife just went on some kind of shifting rampage and killed a couple of innocent folks right out of the blue?"

Kristine ducked her head, causing the cap of her dark hair to feather around her face. "You could say that." She grimaced. "*They* did."

Before Quinn could express what he thought of that, the door opened and Drew appeared. "Come on in," he said.

Quinn had been in the general's office before—when he'd been interrogated about whether he really wanted to join Alpha Force, and also what he could do for it.

It was quite an office. Not that Quinn had any idea what military offices were supposed to look like, but he figured this might be the epitome. The desk was made of a dark polished wood that looked like mahogany. There was the usual U.S. flag, but the brass pole was anything but ordinary. Then there were the worn classic books on shelves behind the general, written by some of the English-speaking world's most renowned authors, like Robert Louis Stevenson and Bram Stoker.

There was a slight scent of brandy that Quinn could smell with his enhanced senses. He glanced toward a closed wooden cabinet behind the desk. The general might fortify himself in here for what he faced while commanding Alpha Force.

Drew had told Quinn after the last time he'd been here that the general had subsidized all the office furnishings himself just because he wanted to, and this was a getaway from the Pentagon.

Quinn waved Kristine through the door before him. He might as well act like a gentleman here, since he was committed to being a soldier.

Damn it.

Where are you, bro? his mind shouted silently. *What the hell's going on?*

Quinn liked his new sister-in-law, Grace. Had been glad that his brother seemed so happy.

But he hadn't been thrilled at being the best man at the wedding, wearing a monkey suit. Being in the middle of a bunch of fawning people, most of whom he didn't know. Military types. Even a couple of Department of Defense guys, including the one from the DSPA.

At least he'd never have to do it again. Wolves mated for life. Even shifters.

Grace was part of their pack. He was as concerned about her as he was about his brother. Almost.

Drew, Kristine and he sat in the chairs facing the general's desk. Greg Yarrow stood, then glared at Quinn. "I should strip you of your rank for insubordination," he growled.

Quinn closed his eyes for just a second. He had a role to play here, and he'd better do it right if he wanted any chance at helping Simon. And Grace. "I understand, sir," he said quietly. "I would like to apologize and—"

"Let's not lay it on too thick." Greg smiled grimly, causing divots to form in the cheeks of his aging face.

"Okay." Quinn smiled briefly, too. Then waited.

"Here's where we are," Drew said from beside him. "Acadia is a national park, so the feds are involved in the investigation into the deaths of the tourists. So are the local police. Since the disappearance of Simon and Grace is assumed to be related, both are looking into that, too."

"So we go as members of Alpha Force and find out what the hell happened," Quinn predicted.

"No." The general stood. "That's what I hoped for, in the multipronged investigation. But I've been told in no uncertain terms that since members of Alpha Force might be the perpetrators of a crime here, we need to let other agencies take the lead."

"No!" Quinn almost stood but felt Kristine's restraining hand on his arm again. He took a deep breath, then another. "Sorry, sir," he managed. "But my brother wouldn't have killed anyone, whether he was shifted or not."

He would probably have been shifted under the full moon, on the night of the killings. He might have taken the new version of the changing elixir even then, because of its benefits. As Kristine and he had discussed, some of the modifications resulted from incorporation of parts of Simon's shifting medication, now that he had joined Alpha Force and turned over his formula.

But the combined new version might not have been tested adequately....

Yet Quinn had felt fine after taking it. Once. A reduced dose. Still, he wasn't about to mention even a hint of concern about that.

Besides, he didn't know for certain whether Simon had brought any of the Alpha Force elixir with him, or his own medication, or any shifting formula at all.

"We hope you're right," the general said. "But suspicion otherwise is partly what Team Leader Olivante's dig was about. There's a faction in the DoD that doesn't know details of Alpha Force's special abilities but even so doesn't trust a unit that's different. They'll potentially shut Alpha Force down if it's proven that any of its members have gone rogue."

"I can help as much as anyone to find Simon and

Grace. Maybe better." Quinn struggled to keep his tone controlled. Of course he felt frustrated. Why the hell hadn't Simon responded to any of his attempts to reach him? "And with that attitude in the organization...well, I don't trust anyone else to find them safely. To find the truth. You know my background, sir. I'm a private investigator. You've got to let me..." He stopped, hazarding a glance down at Kristine who nodded encouragingly. "Okay. I enlisted. I get it. You don't have to do anything I say. But I do have investigative skills I've developed over time. I've got to at least try to find Simon and Grace and figure out what happened. Please, sir."

That last was a real effort, but he intended to do all he had to, to help his brother and new sister-in-law. Even act the role in which Simon had cast him.

Before either Greg or Drew responded, Kristine spoke up. "You know, sirs, I haven't taken a leave for a long time now. I realize that Lt. Parran is too new a recruit to be entitled to one, but...well, I think he and I both need to take some time off. Maybe even take a trip. To Maine. And if we happen to end up in Bar Harbor just for the fun of it, who knows what we might uncover?"

General Yarrow's laugh was a bark of humor. "I wasn't exactly going to approach it that way, but I had something similar in mind." He looked toward Drew. "What do you think, Major? Could you give these two Alpha Forcers a little time off to have some…fun on their own?"

"Sounds like a workable situation to me," Drew said.

"Can our leave start tomorrow?" Kristine asked. "I just can't wait to take my vacation as soon as possible."

"Ditto that, sirs," Quinn said. Was he laying it on too thick?

Most likely, there was no such thing.

"Then you've got it," Drew said. "Although your leave will have to be short. We need answers fast, and we'll have to disavow any knowledge of what you're up to. And you'd better not plan on a military transport to Maine."

"No, sir," Kristine said. "For this leave, we're going to go civilian all the way."

"But you'll still report to me," Drew said.

"Absolutely, sir."

And Quinn forced himself to imitate Kristine's smart salute without a grimace.

Chapter 3

"We need to plan this."

Kristine walked at Quinn's side after the meeting, working hard to keep up with him. He hurried along one of the walkways at Ft. Lukman that led away from the building where the meeting had just been held. His stride was purposeful, his face grim.

Two other soldiers, also dressed in camo, approached from the opposite direction. They must have seen something in Quinn's expression, too, since both seemed to do double takes before hurrying past.

Kristine didn't slow down. She wondered what Quinn was thinking. Well, he needed to tell her, at least some of it.

"We have to figure out where and when we're going," she continued, trying not to sound out of breath. "How we'll get there, how we'll play it when we're there, how—"

"Yeah, I get it," Quinn finally grumbled. "In fact, I'm working on it."

"How?" she demanded. "I need to know. I'm in on it, too."

He stopped dead beside her and she had to make an effort to stop alongside him. "You don't need to be," he said in a tone that edged too close to threatening. "I can handle this myself."

"Sure you can." She leaned closer, looking up so her chin edged belligerently toward him. She kept her voice low but equally gruff. "You'll be trying to figure out what happened. Maybe shifting. Maybe needing to shift by using the elixir you just tried for the first time. Without help? Maybe, but I don't think so. Besides…"

She let her voice trail off, staring straight into those harsh golden eyes. Lord, but the guy was good-looking, even when he appeared grim and determined and angry.

He reacted the way she wanted him to, at least. "Besides what?" he demanded.

"Your new sister-in-law, Grace, is not just my commanding officer. She's my friend. I intend to help her. Period."

She continued to stand her ground and glare straight into his return glower.

He was the one to flinch. Well, not flinch, exactly. He smiled. And if she'd thought his rugged features to be a turn-on before, now he was absolutely the hottest man she had ever seen.

Her recollection of seeing him naked only reinforced the current of heat that passed through her. But she shrugged that off. She had to.

"Okay," he said. "And you're right. I'm sure I can use the help. But I want to think this through before we rush up there. And we are going to rush up there. No later than tomorrow."

"I'm game," Kristine said. "Let's find somewhere private to discuss this."

They crossed a wide driveway, passing the main gate into Ft. Lukman.

Quinn was leading Kristine to someplace they probably shouldn't go: his apartment in the Bachelor Officers Quarters. If anyone saw them inside the building, it might appear as if they were fraternizing, and that was a military no-no. She wasn't a commissioned officer. He was.

In a world where things were fair, their roles should be reversed. She had told him she was career military and had planned it that way forever. She had trained to become a nurse, then had enlisted. She had been in the service for a few years and was now a staff sergeant.

She should be his superior officer.

He was the newcomer, and yet because of who he was—no, what he became when he shifted—he'd come into the service as a ready-made officer, outranking her.

As a result of all that, she could be his aide but not—officially, at least—his date. Let alone someone he snuck into his quarters. Not that he gave a damn about that kind of prohibition, but she would.

And she was right. He needed her help—as much as he hated to admit it, even to himself.

"Glad to see things are quiet around here," Kristine remarked as they started up the sidewalk in the direction of the BOQ. He glanced down at her. She'd slowed a bit, and he figured she, too, was thinking about the military taboo they might be about to violate.

Fraternizing. That suggested more than holding a meeting to plan their approach to Bar Harbor and learning what happened to Simon and Grace.

Not that he intended to seduce Kristine—although the idea was far from repulsive. Instead, while alone in his quarters, they would discuss what they'd do to help find Simon and Grace.

To start with, Quinn needed to do some more online research, using some of the resources already programmed into the laptop computer in his room.

"Here we are," he told her softly, using a key to open the BOQ's side door nearest his apartment. Good thing they could get in through a side door that was relatively remote and sheltered by its nearness to the next-door parking garage. They would definitely give the appearance of fraternizing later, if the plan that had been forming in his mind reached fruition. But it would be worse if they were caught around here, where others could see.

Soon, they were inside his unit with the door closed. As far as he knew, no one had seen them.

He had an urge to take the lovely, determined Kristine into his arms and kiss her. Only out of relief, of course.

But that was a bad idea. And she was already checking out his place. It was filled with government-issue furniture and not much else. He hadn't been there long. He'd never been sure how long he would stay in the military, even if he hadn't been about to undertake this unofficial mission. A lot depended on whether his appreciation for the shifting elixir outweighed his unease at being a soldier and following orders.

But one thing he did know. They would head to Bar Harbor tomorrow—and before they left, he had a lot of online investigating to do.

* * *

Kristine pulled a chair from the kitchen into the well-lighted alcove that Quinn used as an office in his small apartment.

She had been in BOQ units before—mostly Grace's. It was larger than this. But Grace had been in Alpha Force for a while, had proven herself as excellent military, as well as a shapeshifter. She'd clearly been entitled to a comfortable place to sleep.

Sleep? Kristine had purposely not even glanced through the door that apparently led to Quinn's bedroom. Sleep—and what else people did in bedrooms—weren't why she was here.

Even though her body throbbed just a little at the idea of joining Quinn, with that amazing body of his, in bed.

That wouldn't happen.

Instead, she sat determinedly beside Quinn, who had already booted up the small computer that lay on a shelf that acted like a desk in that alcove.

First, though, he pulled out his smartphone. "I've tried this before," he said, "but I'll call each of them again, just to see if they answer."

They didn't. Nor did they respond even now to any of the many text messages and emails he'd sent. He had even resorted to trying to contact them through Twitter and Facebook. Nothing.

Quinn and she had asked both Major Connell and

General Yarrow if they'd continued to try to reach Simon and Grace. They had—also to no avail.

The last anyone had heard of them—or so it seemed—was a call Simon had made to Quinn while sightseeing along the Mount Desert Island coast just after they had reached the Acadia Park area.

Which made Kristine fear the worst. Were they dead? If not, were they ignoring calls because they were, indeed, guilty of the mutilations and murders?

She didn't want to think about either. But they had to know.

"So what are we looking for?" she asked Quinn as he sat and began typing in a web address. His home page had wallpaper depicting a big question mark in the center of it.

Interesting. Was that because he was a private investigator by background, used to answering questions?

"Okay, first I'm putting on my P.I. hat," Quinn said, not surprising her. "I've already checked to see when my bro or his bride last got into their bank accounts or used their credit cards. I found nothing useful, but I'll do it again before we decide what's next."

He had typed in the web address of a major credit-card company and now inserted a number and password. Had he already known Simon's account information, or had he used his investigation resources to learn it? He next did the same with Grace's account—and he was less likely to have been given her info than his brother's.

He checked not only on this site but a couple of others, apparently knowing data on multiple accounts, including a bank where he said Simon maintained checking and savings accounts. "Grace and he have already opened a joint account here," Quinn told Kristine. But after scanning the latest page of each, he shook his head. "There's a charge for a bed-and-breakfast in Bar Harbor and some meals, ending a couple of days ago. Then nothing. Not even a visit to an ATM for cash."

"Oh," Kristine said sadly. That gave no further answers. But it did suggest that something awful had happened to the newlyweds.

If the suspicions expressed at the earlier meetings were true, that they'd planned this attack to undermine Alpha Force somehow, they could have started new accounts under assumed names.

But at least they could still be alive.

No. She wanted to believe they were okay, and she knew they wouldn't—couldn't—be responsible for the attacks.

"I'll check some news sites next," Quinn said, "looking for more current detail about that damned fatal assault in Acadia."

Where two people had apparently been mauled by wild animals and died. Not something Kristine would usually want to learn the gory details about, but this was different. Maybe somehow those details could lead to more information about Grace and Simon.

"Good idea," she said and watched as his long, thick fingers sailed over the keys. She had a passing wonderment about how those fingers would feel playing over her... Ridiculous!

She settled down to watch the screen over his shoulder. There wasn't a lot of data in most of the news stories Quinn brought up at first, but enough to make Kristine wonder.

Even so, she still wasn't willing to accept Simon and Grace's involvement.

Quinn turned on the sound as he went into a video news clip from a local Bar Harbor television station.

That one was so horrible that parts of the pictures were blurred.

Enough was shown to display how mutilated the bodies were—gashed and bloodied, as if ripped by teeth and claws.

"The authorities are still investigating," the announcer intoned as the camera panned around what appeared to be a clearing in a forest, described as part of Acadia National Park. "So far, they appear to believe this was an attack by some kind of wild animal that has not yet been identified. This is the worst event in the park since a man walking his dog apparently fell to his death and, before that, a young tourist was killed by a rogue wave along the shore several years ago. Back to you, John." The picture returned to an announcer in a studio somewhere before phasing out.

"Some kind of wild animal," Kristine mused aloud.

"A wolf?" said Quinn. "Two wolves?"

"They're not speculating on that—or at least this reporter didn't," Kristine responded.

"Yeah, but—" Quinn clicked on another site, one for which he had to enter a password. Kristine couldn't be sure, but it appeared to be some kind of official law enforcement website, although Quinn got off the main page immediately to do a search for Acadia.

What showed on the screen was a detailed list of crimes in the Bar Harbor area. Next, he clicked on something that brought up this specific crime.

Kristine watched his face as Quinn squinted at the small print that came up. "Couple of agencies are involved in this investigation," he said. "There's some speculation about what kinds of animals could be involved. Species that still have habitats around there include foxes, coyotes, bobcats and black bears. Used to be mountain lions, too—and gray wolves."

Wolves. The word hung in the air this time.

"Not Grace and Simon," Kristine whispered, hoping it was true. She put her hand on Quinn's shoulder—whether to reassure him or convince him, she wasn't sure.

The touch was like a bolt of lightning, making her even more cognizant of his hot and alluring presence. But she wasn't a wimp. She had courage—of all kinds. She let her hand rest there...for now.

Even when he turned his head a little and looked at her with those golden eyes.

"So what do you think?" she asked him.

"What do *you* think?" he countered. "You willing to go there to help me investigate—in any form I need to be? Your commanding officers—*our* commanding officers—apparently have to act dead set against our being there."

He'd used the word *dead*. Like the two mutilated tourists.

Like Alpha Force would be, if the perpetrators really were Grace and Simon, and that got out to the world.

Kristine understood why the muckety-mucks like General Yarrow and that guy Olivante from the Department of Defense's Defense Special Projects Agency were so concerned.

Not everyone, even in the military, knew about Alpha Force. But if it were ever shown that the killings were done by shapeshifters, and that those shapeshifters were not just part of some grotesque horror story but members of a very covert and elite U.S. military force, the repercussions could be terrible.

Terrible to the U.S. Armed Forces.

And potentially devastating—fatal—to the existence of Alpha Force.

What would happen to its members then—especially its shapeshifter members?

They'd be humiliated at the least. Outed. Paraded as absurd freaks through the media.

They would never be able to use their very special, unique and amazing abilities to help with national security ever again.

The people like General Yarrow and Team Leader Olivante would be out to do the best damage control they could.

If that meant dealing with Grace and Simon in some terrible way, they'd do it—even the general, who clearly loved Alpha Force. If they needed scapegoats—scape*wolves*—they'd do what they had to.

But both Quinn and she would have different agendas. His might be different from hers, as well.

She wanted to learn the truth. Protect Grace and Simon if they were innocent, which she prayed they were.

But she would protect Alpha Force, too.

Quinn? Well, his main agenda might be to help his brother and sister-in-law, no matter what.

She would work with him, at least until their agendas diverged. Then, she would see.

"Let's do it," she said.

"Good." He paused, then stood. She couldn't read the expression on his face, but it seemed challenging. With a touch of humor added? "Here's what we'll do, then. We'll go to Bar Harbor tomorrow, undercover. And know what our cover IDs will be?"

"No," she said, sure she wouldn't like the response.

"To get the most information about our missing honeymoon couple—" he paused dramatically, then grinned "—you and I will be there on our honeymoon, too."

"What?" Kristine froze. What was he talking about?

And why did the words send the tiniest shiver of anticipation through her?

She shrugged it off. She knew what he meant. But—

"With assumed identities, of course," he said curtly. "Like I said, undercover." Although when she dared to look at him she saw not only humor, but also challenge, in his expression. "That'll help us get the most information possible as we investigate."

"Of course. Great idea." She attempted to sound nonchalant. "We'll try to follow Grace and Simon's trail as much as possible. We'll find and clear them. You'll see."

Chapter 4

The hotel was charming, a converted Victorian mansion right in the heart of Bar Harbor. From what Kristine had seen of it so far, the downtown area was a small, charismatic collection of stores and restaurants, inns and parks and churches, mostly near the water, since the town was located on Mount Desert Island.

A wonderful place for a honeymoon, she thought—if the lovers stayed in their rooms and out of trouble.

But these new, false honeymooners—Quinn and her? They would soon be out and about and looking for trouble…looking for what had happened to their real newlywed counterparts.

"You ready for this?" Quinn sat in the driver's seat of the sedan they had rented after flying into Bangor, about fifty miles away. This was the first time she had seen him out of his uniform since the wedding...unless she counted when she had seen him in nothing at all.

The thought shot a plume of fire through her insides—from anxiety, she told herself. That was all. Before they had left Ft. Lukman, they had talked their plans over with Drew Connell. Since they were here very unofficially, he had agreed that it was better for them to really go undercover, take on alternate identities. Act as if they had nothing to do with the military. Or Alpha Force.

Honeymooners? He'd raised his eyebrows at that but hadn't objected. In fact, he seemed to support the idea.

And despite Kristine's deep misgivings, the pretense actually did make sense. They might get the same kinds of responses to their questions that the missing couple had been given. Be treated similarly by people they ran into here.

Learn something faster than if they pretended just to be acquaintances vacationing together.

They would therefore sleep in the same room. They would pretend, outside that room, to be lovey-dovey. Sexually attracted to one another.

One major problem, Kristine thought, was that it would be too easy for her to feign the latter…

"Sure. Let's go in." She responded to Quinn's question with an assumed bravado.

She jumped out of the car, opened the door to the backseat and pulled out her backpack, which contained mostly clothes. It would have been hard to hide the Alpha Force elixir and light in carry-on baggage, so she had packed them in a suitcase and checked it. Even so, they had identified themselves as military to the Transportation Security Administration folks at the airport. These days, checked luggage screening looked for anything that could be turned into a terrorist bomb. An intense light might not get anyone's attention, but the quantity of elixir might. So might the weapons they had packed.

They had given no explanation of their travel plans to the TSA people who had checked them out. Fortunately, no one had questioned them too closely. Not that they'd admit what they were up to—or that one of the tools they would take advantage of here, as soon as possible, was Quinn's shapeshifting ability.

"I'll take that, honey."

Quinn's deep voice behind her made her jump. *Honey?* The word shouldn't give her shivers—at least not of pleasure. No, it was the harbinger of the night before them.

"No, thank you, dear." She turned and gave him a couple of bats of her eyelashes, concurrently lifting her chin as if challenging him. "I can handle this, as long as you get our large bags out of the trunk and take care of them."

"They're on wheels." His voice was no longer syrupy sweet. He evidently didn't like her contradicting him. "You can pull yours."

Too bad.

"I appreciate the offer, sweetheart, but as you know, I'm used to carrying my own backpack." She reached over, patted his cheek that suggested the initial coarseness from the black shadow of a beard, then maneuvered the pack onto her shoulders. She started toward the door of the hotel without making sure he was dealing with the bags. She knew he would do just fine.

He caught up with her as she reached the registration desk. Amazingly, in only the short amount of time they'd had after making their decision and heading here, Quinn had already obtained fake IDs for them, including driver's licenses and credit cards.

He had obviously maintained his contacts as a private investigator despite enlisting in the military—and not just his online skills and passwords. Maybe he intended his enlistment to be temporary. Very temporary.

She just hoped that would be the right thing for Alpha Force.

She, on the other hand, considered herself all military despite the civilian roles they played now.

"Hi," she said to the woman behind the desk, who was clad in a brown suit and weary smile. "We're the Scotts." The first names on their ID cards matched their real ones, for ease of remembering them, but they'd taken on a false surname for their investigation. "Kristine and Quinn. Do you have our reservation?"

The woman, with a pin on her lapel that said she was Betty from Newport, began typing on a computer on the desk in front of her, and then her grin widened. "Yes, we do." She ran through the formalities of taking a credit card—with their newly acquired IDs—and putting together key cards for their room. "Enjoy your stay," she said.

"I'm sure we will." Kristine made herself gush, even though she wasn't a gushy person. Then she leaned toward Betty conspiratorially. "Do many other people come here on their honeymoon?"

"Why, yes." By then Betty was beaming. "Another newlywed couple even checked in a few days ago. They're gone now, though."

"Did they have a good time?" Quinn asked from beside Kristine.

"I'll bet they did, although I didn't see them again. Anyway, I hope you enjoy your stay."

On their way to the elevator, Kristine said, "Your seeing their credit card charge doesn't mean anything. The way checking out is handled now at most hotels, with bills just slipped under the door during the last night of a reservation, there wasn't anything suspicious about how Simon and Grace disappeared, except—"

"Except that word might have gotten around to the staff if they'd failed to take their belongings."

"Right. So they apparently took their stuff. If so—"

"Where are they?" he finished.

Quinn had pretended not to notice Kristine's dismay when they reached their quaint room with antique furnishings that suited the character of the converted mansion—and found only one queen-size bed in it. She hadn't said anything except to thank him for hefting her suitcase onto one of the folding luggage stands.

They had already decided to unpack quickly, then leave right away to grab dinner at whatever spot the concierge at the inn said was the place he recommended most often to guests.

That meant it could be the place where he'd sent Simon and Grace.

Quinn and Kristine were there now, sitting at a table with a red checked tablecloth in the center of the main room. The BarHar Bistro was crowded, including the anterooms off to the sides. Apparently their concierge wasn't the only one to recommend it—or locals already knew about, and frequented, the place. There wasn't much space for the waitstaff to maneuver between tables, and the elbow room for diners was limited, as well.

Quinn hoped that the overcrowding was a sign that the food was good, not just that it was an in place where people dined simply because it was popular.

The place smelled tantalizing to Quinn's enhanced senses. The acoustics weren't great, though—probably not even for a regular human with lesser hearing. The undercurrent of voices was a loud, unpleasant hum.

Kristine had been pretending to study the menu, but he saw her eyes darting sideways often.

"What looks good to you, dear?" he asked aloud, then leaned slightly across the table toward her. "I suspect," he added more softly, "that strangers here wouldn't be noticed much."

She nodded glumly. "My thoughts, too."

A perky blonde in black pants and white shirt sidled around one of the tables nearby and approached them. "Welcome to BarHar. My name is Steph, and

I'll be your server this evening. Can I start you with something to drink?"

Showtime, Quinn thought. "You sure can. Champagne. We're celebrating."

"Really?" Steph asked, as Kristine forced a sunny smile onto her face. "What are you celebrating?"

"We just got married," Kristine chimed in. "Do you recommend any particular champagne to other newlyweds who come in here?"

"That's assuming we're not the first," Quinn added with a laugh.

Steph responded as they'd attempted to program her. "Oh, you're definitely not the first."

"But we're the most recent," Kristine said. "Aren't we?"

"Well, yes. At least I don't know of any others here tonight. But there was at least one other couple here last week."

"Really? I'll bet they weren't as good-looking as us." Quinn knew he was laying it on too thick. In fact, this might not be a good idea. He was well aware that Simon and he resembled one another— and it might be a bad thing to have anyone associate the two of them, especially if Simon was suspected of committing a crime.

But if Bar Harbor authorities suspected Simon and Grace, that, thankfully, didn't seem to have gotten out even to the local media, nor had it otherwise been made public.

Yet.

"Maybe not," Steph said. "But they were good tippers." She winked at them. "Here's the champagne I recommended to them." She pointed to a fairly expensive one on the wine list Quinn had been pretending to study.

"Looks good to me. Did you recommend any entrées to them, too?"

"I did, but I think they both ordered steaks."

Ah. That was a good indication that the couple were his brother and new sister-in-law. Shifters, at least those who changed into werewolves, ate a lot of red meat to satisfy their feral needs.

He glanced up at Kristine, who nodded slightly. She'd gotten it, too.

"Well, please bring us the same champagne, and we'll figure out what else to order." The steak sounded good to Quinn, but Kristine might not yet have decided.

When the server left, Kristine was the one to lean toward Quinn. "Looks like we're on the right track. But just following…them…won't necessarily get us the information we need." He liked how she was being discreet. Not that it was likely for anyone to be eavesdropping on them, but even if someone at a neighboring table was listening in, they wouldn't be able to follow the underlying meaning of their conversation.

"No, but it's a start. We'll be more proactive soon. Although—" Quinn had started doing his own eavesdropping—much more easily, with his abilities, than anyone else in this room was likely to be able to do. He now focused in on who had uttered the words he had been listening for: *Acadia* and *body*.

Fortunately, the speakers were at a nearby table, one just behind him. He slid his chair back slightly and said to Kristine, "Excuse me for a minute, dear." But instead of rising and heading for the restroom, he turned toward the speaker. "Sorry to interrupt, but I couldn't help hearing you mention those awful deaths that occurred a few nights ago. My wife—" He stopped and grinned at that, as if he was enjoying using the word for nearly the first time. "We just got married and we're here on our honeymoon, but we almost changed our plans, hearing about such a terrible thing. Wild animals killed some tourists in the park, right?"

There were four young, brawny guys around the table. "That's right," said a tall basketball-player sort with spiky hair. "We came here planning to hike through the park but we've got second thoughts, too."

"I live here," said a young woman at the next table over. "All of us in town are also concerned.

But you tourists—well, as long as you're careful, you should be fine."

"Spoken like a good local promoter," Steph, the server, said, joining them. She had their champagne, plus two empty flutes, on a tray. She put them on the table and poured a little into each glass. As Quinn and Kristine both took preliminary sips, she moved around again and continued, "But…well, I enjoy hiking in my spare time, too. I haven't heard what's going on with the investigation, except that the thought is like you said, some kind of wild animal got those tourists. No one's sure, though."

"Are there many wild animals in Acadia?" Quinn asked. "I mean, I'm sure there are squirrels and rats and such, but what kind might be dangerous enough to kill people?"

He noticed that Kristine had maneuvered her chair around the table to sit beside him, notwithstanding the crush of other nearby patrons. She was listening attentively. He liked the seriousness of her expression beneath her sexy and short hair, as dark as a moonless night sky. She was one attractive soldier, and she was doing a hell of a job as his undercover wife.

"There are coyotes," the local woman said. "Bears, too, and even bobcats. But they don't usually attack people. I heard in the news that the people killed were two sisters from St. Louis who were active members of a national wildlife preservation organization. Maybe they got too up close and personal with some creature."

"Can happen anywhere that there are wild animals like that," said one of the guys at the table who hadn't spoken before. "Too bad we can't shoot 'em."

"No hunting and trapping in Acadia," the woman chimed in, looking angry that killing wild animals had even been mentioned. Quinn liked that attitude.

"But park rangers can probably kill vicious animals that hurt people," said Basketball Player, and his comrades nodded.

"Whatever happened," said Steph, "I'm sure everyone visiting the park will be on guard to make sure it can't happen again. Now—" She faced Quinn and Kristine. "May I take your order?"

"At least we have a general idea of the position of townspeople and tourists," Kristine said later as they walked along the sidewalk, past souvenir, clothing and other shops still open for visitors' pleasure. It was dark outside, but the narrow street was lined with lights.

"Yeah, and fortunately no one we spoke with has claimed that the killings could have been done by shapeshifters," Quinn responded. He reached over and took her hand. At her glance, he prepared to remind her of their cover.

But she didn't pull away. In fact, she grasped his hand even harder.

Which almost made him smile. At least until her next words.

"Even if there are any suspicions like that," she said, "no one's about to admit them aloud without any evidence. Not unless they want other people to doubt their sanity."

He stopped and looked at her. "Right. Sane people don't believe in shapeshifters, do they?"

"Looks like there's a lot of insanity going around," she said, and smiled. She raised her chin a little. He'd already begun to appreciate that as a characteristic gesture, a statement of challenge and determination. "But we still haven't gotten any clue about where Simon and Grace might be," Kristine continued. "You're the investigator."

"Yeah, I'm the professional investigator," he agreed, "but I heard from Grace how much she relied on your ideas to help in Alpha Force assignments."

Kristine's grin looked proud but she shrugged her shoulders modestly. He liked her unassuming nature despite her obvious drive and intelligence.

"We'll work on it more tomorrow," he said. "Take

the same tour they did, for starters. I'm also working on some other ideas."

"Sounds good."

They walked on for a while in silence. Kristine halted outside one small shop that sold pet supplies. "I'll bet that Grace stopped in here. She'd have wanted to bring something back for Tilly." That was Grace's cover dog. All of the shifters had one that resembled them in shifted form.

Quinn hadn't gotten one yet, and neither had Simon. They were too new to Alpha Force. But he had seen how Kristine had lovingly said goodbye to her own assigned dog, Bailey, who had traveled with her on her last assignment along with Grace and Tilly.

Another admirable trait. The woman liked dogs. Real dogs. And apparently she also cared for shifters.

He was going to have to watch himself around Staff Sgt. Kristine Norwood. He was coming to like her too much.

And that could be a mistake.

"So what's your next idea?" Kristine finally asked, breaking the growing silence between them. Not that Quinn had found it uncomfortable—but he had been using it to think. And to plan.

"The night's still young," he said. "Why waste it? I'm ready to prowl."

* * *

He knew, of course, that Acadia was a national park with established entrances. At least this first time, before they had oriented themselves about locations, he didn't want to be seen driving in so late in the evening. Not many tourists were likely to be around, even though the park was open—or at least the campgrounds were.

As a result, he drove them both in the rental car along one road at the park's outer perimeter, and then another, until he spotted a turnout surrounded by lots of vegetation, right beside a sheer cliff.

Insurmountable for mere humans. Not for a shapeshifter.

"Let's do it," he said.

"Here?" Kristine looked both puzzled and skeptical. He enjoyed watching the expressions play across her unconventionally pretty face.

"Here," he confirmed. He parked at the end of the turnout closest to the thickest shrubbery. "It's fairly isolated and I doubt we'll see many cars at this hour."

"Okay." She opened her door. He popped the trunk open and she extracted her ubiquitous backpack—once more filled with the equipment he needed.

In only a few minutes, he had drunk a dose of the elixir and stripped—enjoying Kristine's attempt to appear nonchalant and disinterested while sneaking peeks at his bare body. Which only made said body react the way he knew it would. But only for a minute—until the light she trained on him began its job.

He felt the usual tugging and pulling…and then his shift continued.

This was as much bliss as a shapeshifter could experience. No full moon. Complete mental sharpness.

If only his leap onto the mountainside five minutes ago, and his initial stalking into the park, could yield useful information.

Unlikely, though. It was a distance from where he thought he'd heard the mauling of the tourists had occurred.

He inhaled the complicated and intriguing scents of other wildlife—the coyotes and bobcats he had anticipated, as well as smaller, unimportant creatures.

This was merely an initial foray, a more-than-pleasant test. He would accomplish more with future shifts around here, but at least he had gotten his first wild taste of Acadia.

For now, he would simply revel in the freedom and ability to enjoy it. Not to mention his current, undoubtedly brief independence from the military, its structure, its orders.

He had wondered long before enlisting if the elixir Simon had told him about would be enticing enough for him to give up his life, his freedom, his sanity.

If all had gone well, perhaps it would have been more than enough to experience this amazing kind of shift as often as possible.

But all was not going well, with his brother, and now with him—while he was, in some respects, AWOL from his official assignment.

What would happen if he found Simon and Grace?

What would happen if he didn't?

He had to find them, of course. Alive and well, and with a full, logical explanation of where they had been, and how they had not been involved in the park killings.

And then he would not have to wonder whether he could continue to immerse himself in a life that required him to follow the orders of strangers, some of whom he despised.

But a life that included this marvelous elixir.

And an aide like Kristine. For now.

Kristine, the dedicated and permanent soldier. Attractive, smart and sexy...but a nonshifter.

A scent blew toward him—a coyote. Drawing closer. It must have smelled him, too.

He paced farther into the forest. Not even a hint of the aromas of Simon or Grace, shifted or not.

His frustrations mounted.

No answers tonight.

Chapter 5

Kristine sat alone in the locked, dark car. Waiting.

She hated waiting for anything.

But she had taught herself patience while staying behind as her shapeshifting charge Grace dashed about the countryside in wolf form after Kristine helped her shift.

She had worked a lot with Grace. Learned her habits. Helped her not only as a shifting soldier, but also in the solution of a problem that could have put the entire world at risk of unleashed biohazards.

Kristine had gotten shot in the process. But she was fine now, physically.

Mentally, too, she reminded herself—although

she was damned worried about her charge, her friend, Grace.

One step at a time. Quinn and she would find Grace and Simon. They had to.

For now, she watched through the windshield and the car's side windows, scouring the mountainside in the scant light of the bright stars overhead for any movement that would indicate the return of the wolf that was Quinn.

Since this wasn't a night of a full moon, and turning on any kind of light was a bad idea in this area, where she wanted no one to spot her, she merely slumped behind the steering wheel of the rental car.

Too bad she didn't have the senses that her charges did while shifted, or even some of their enhanced senses in human form. Grace had described them to her, at least somewhat.

If Kristine had better hearing, maybe she could at least hear when—

There. Right in front of her. A movement within her line of vision.

Something had leaped off the hillside. In the little that she could see in the almost complete darkness, the shrubbery clinging to the side of the mountain remained in motion.

A figure moved in front of her on the roadside turnout. A wolf?

Just in case it wasn't what she anticipated, she

clutched the service weapon she had brought along, preparing to use it if necessary.

As quietly as she could, she opened the car door.

That created a haze of light—light in which she could see that something writhed in the bushes in front of her.

A shifter regaining its human shape?

The hell with being seen. Holding the gun in one hand, she grabbed a flashlight, too, turned it on and aimed them both at the moving figure.

In time to see the last of Quinn's transformation back into human form.

He was back in the car, back in his jeans and T-shirt. Exhausted partly from the shift and partly from his ongoing frustration.

"Did you see anything useful?" Kristine asked, as she drove the car from the turnoff onto the twisting mountain road.

"No. I didn't see, smell or hear anything at all that could help us. But at least I've oriented myself a bit more to this area and shifting around here."

Beside him, Kristine said nothing for a minute. And then, "Are you all right?"

"Yeah," he said. "Fine." And he actually was. As he breathed deeply, he felt his strength—and his determination—increasing. He was here. Simon and Grace had to be somewhere around this area, too.

Of course he would find them.

They would find them. Kristine, with all her military training and dedication, would continue to be an asset.

As she had already been, tonight.

"Thanks for watching my back," he said gruffly, only to see her turn her head to glance at him.

"It's what I'm here for," she retorted in an equally gruff tone that made him smile.

The time Kristine had been dreading had arrived.

Okay, it wasn't that big a deal. They were here undercover. They were both adults, rational people, soldiers.

At least she was a soldier, and he had enlisted as one. But that shouldn't matter here anyway.

The point was that they were here under assumed identities. False ones.

And now, after dinner, a preliminary assessment of the town, plus the first of Quinn's shifts in this area—and she anticipated many more—they had to get some sleep to be rested enough to dive right into their roles tomorrow.

Find answers.

Learn where Grace and Simon were, and rescue them, if necessary.

Assuming they were still alive.

That was what was important.

Who was sleeping where, in this small, quaint room with only one bed, was not a big deal. No bigger a deal than her acting as Quinn's aide for shifting.

He had just crossed the room and closed the drapes. The room didn't get any darker, since the lights were on.

"Would you like to use the bathroom first?" Kristine asked neutrally.

"After you, sweetheart." His tone was ironic. Not serious at all.

A good thing.

"Fine," she said briskly. "Then, when you're changing, I can take the duvet and make myself a bed on the floor. I think you'll be okay with the sheets already on the bed, and—"

"And you don't think the maid would notice tomorrow?" His brows were raised, emphasizing that irony he had already projected.

"We can remake the bed in the morning to look as if we used it like the honeymooners we're pretending to be."

She looked him straight in the eye, challenging him to object. He certainly didn't think they were going to have sex as part of their cover…did he?

And why did the idea twist her insides with molten lava?

She liked how they were getting along so far—

on a friendly and professional basis. That was all. But she had convinced herself that any sexual attraction she felt for him was absurd. Unmilitary. Something she would laugh off. Ignore.

Wouldn't she?

"No need for you or me to sleep on the floor." His tone was sharp now, as if he was responding to an insult. "We can both act professionally. Share the bed without…sharing anything else. Okay?" Now he was the one challenging her.

"Okay," she responded as coldly as she could manage.

But as their eyes met, the challenge felt clear. Hell, she could handle it. She could handle *him*.

Almost as if she was daring him, she took a step closer. Or did he move first? Suddenly, she was in his arms. His lips were hot, tasting as human as any man's she had sampled before. But not the same. Better. They were sexier. More searching. Magnetic and alluring.

Challenging.

His body against hers—it was as hard as she had imagined. Especially there, below. Where the thick, sexy organ she had viewed before was now touching her, taunting her. Sure, there were clothes between them, but she felt him now. Hard. Erotic. Causing her insides to react with a need she didn't want.

Didn't want.

She pulled away fast, before she could change her mind. "Very interesting," she said, trying not to sound out of breath at all. "All the more reason I should sleep on the floor. But I won't." This time, it definitely was a challenge.

"Fine."

A while later, when they both had settled onto the bed, backs toward one another, Kristine was even more aware of Quinn Parran's large, warm—highly sexy—presence behind her.

He's a shapeshifter, she reminded herself yet again. She might like them, but sleeping with one? Plus, he was a new soldier. A renegade, not a dedicated member of the military the way she was. An investigator she needed to work with for Grace's and Simon's sake. That was all.

But she lay there, eyes open, long into the night, listening to Quinn Parran's deep breathing, and not moving at all.

Otherwise, she just might touch him once more.

Most mornings, Kristine enjoyed her first cup of coffee but figured she could survive without it.

Not now. There was a lot she had to accomplish today, and since she'd hardly gotten any sleep last night, a strong dose of caffeine was first on her morning agenda.

She only wished it contained ingredients to rein in her libido.

At the moment, she sat across from Quinn at a table in a coffee shop along Main Street, the primary tourist avenue in Bar Harbor, just a couple of blocks from their hotel. The only good result of her restless night—fully aware of his presence luring her—was that he, too, looked tired. There was a slight dullness behind his golden eyes, and he also held on to the coffee mug in front of him as if it were a lifeline.

Had he remained aware of her, too—and had that also made him lose sleep? Perversely, she hoped so. If she had to suffer that way, then why shouldn't he?

Maybe, for the sake of the mission they'd taken on, they could prevent another morning like this by indulging in sex tonight....

The thought disseminated electric tingles everywhere within her, even as she rejected it. It would only be a diversion. They had to find Grace and Simon—and ensure that they hadn't been involved with the deaths in Acadia. That was paramount to anything else.

No matter how tempting.

She took another sip of coffee, glad that the server had left an entire pot. They were still waiting for their breakfasts to be served.

"So what do you think?" Quinn asked, breaking the silence at their table, although the restaurant was crowded and they were surrounded by low conversations. Like her, he had on jeans today. With hers, she wore a pale green buttoned blouse that she hadn't tucked in. She couldn't help noticing how Quinn's black T-shirt hugged the muscles of his chest and upper arms. At the moment, the table blocked her view of below—a good thing. "Are you up for a bus tour?"

Anyone eavesdropping would think they were tourists attempting to decide what to do today. But they already knew.

There was a rack containing tourist information near the front desk at their hotel. Prominently featured were brochures for one of the island's tour-bus lines. That line was also the one recommended by the concierge on duty that morning. He'd said that all guests to whom they recommended that outfit came back pleased, so it was the tour company they suggested most often.

When he continued to extol their services, Kristine wondered if the concierge received kickbacks. Fine. Quinn and she needed to learn all they could about the Bar Harbor area as fast as possible. And if they could learn it from the most likely company to have shown last week's newlyweds around, all the better for collecting information.

"A bus tour sounds great, honey." Kristine

beamed as the server brought her breakfast of scrambled eggs and toast.

"Good thing, since I already made reservations for the one recommended at the hotel. We leave in forty-five minutes." Why did the way he quirked one edge of his mouth look so sexy? She knew that what he said was intended to be yet another kind of challenge. She had made it clear that she wanted to be involved in all decisions despite the fact he out-ranked her in the military.

But what they were doing here was independent of Alpha Force—at least somewhat.

So, Kristine didn't bite at his goading. She didn't even start to chew him out.

She suddenly realized that even after work-ing as an aide to a shifter for as long as she had, her thought processes hadn't completely adapted. Thinking about biting and chewing in the presence of a werewolf… She smiled at the idea.

Quinn raised his dark brows slightly, then smiled back. He had ordered an egg dish, too—a combo that included a small steak.

"We'd better finish our breakfasts as soon as we can," Kristine said. "I'd like to stop in at the local tourist center to see what other information we can pick up." Shorthand for saying they'd also ask about any recent visitors who'd admitted to being honey-mooners.

But as it turned out, they learned half an hour later, no one at the town's main tourist information center remembered seeing anyone like Grace and Simon—even though Quinn gave detailed descriptions. His skill wasn't surprising, Kristine thought, with Quinn's private investigator background. He might have tracked other people before—in both of his forms. Knowing how to ask the right questions in the right way had to be part of his former career.

They hurried to the parking lot for the bus tour Quinn had scheduled. Quinn grabbed her hand to help quicken her pace. Kristine continued to play along with their honeymooner cover while much too aware again of the innocent contact.

As they sprinted along the narrow Bar Harbor sidewalks, past stores and tourists, Kristine kept reminding herself that the man whose sleek, muscular form raced by her side was someone she could only pretend to want to touch all over.

Doing it while they spent at least another few nights together remained off-limits.

Quinn muscled them into the bus before any of the other tourists. Now they sat on the right side, across from the tour guide, who was positioned behind the driver.

Quinn had the aisle seat, and Kristine sat by the window. Stragglers still entered the bus, which was already warm and crowded even with most windows open.

That prevented Quinn from getting too friendly with the guide. The questions that formed much of the reason for this tour had to wait.

The vehicle was configured like a school bus. Maybe it actually had transported students in its youth, since the seats weren't particularly wide.

Which meant Quinn's hips were snug against Kristine's, reminding him of his uncomfortable night of knowing she was in the room with him. Hearing her breathe—and not the deep respiration of sleep most of the time.

Kissing her. Feeling her against him, however briefly, as he'd taunted her. And then sensing her warm, sexy presence right beside him in that bed that might as well have been a mile wide, considering how far they stayed from each other.

Yeah, they might be undercover, but they weren't *under covers*—not together. He had to keep reminding himself that they weren't really even coworkers. He was her temporary superior officer, and she was his aide.

Another good reason for him not to have joined the military: all the protocol and rules about fraternization and other similar nonsense.

But he remained resolved never to push Kristine to have sex with him, no matter how badly he ached to touch her all over, to bury himself in her. His feral instincts hadn't taken over completely. He wouldn't let them, no matter which form he was in.

And no matter that Kristine had seen him naked, both before and after his shifts so far with the Alpha Force elixir.

For the sake of learning what was going on with his brother and sister-in-law, he'd follow the rules, at least all he could. He'd act like a good little soldier despite being on an unofficial mission. He'd follow Kristine's lead wherever it made sense, since she was more experienced.

At the moment, she was thumbing through a Bar Harbor magazine, though her speed suggested she wasn't paying much attention to the articles and ads. He turned back toward her. "Is that worth looking at?"

"We won't find what we're looking for in it," she said with a sigh, her chin raised in its normal challenge to the world. He resisted an urge to touch it.

"But we might get some ideas of where else to look," he reminded her. "Like...well, other than Acadia Park itself, are there any wildlife sanctuaries? You know I'm particularly interested in seeing local animals."

And trying to learn if there were any kinds that could have attacked those tourists. Especially if those victims had brought it on themselves by purposely getting too close to dangerous wildlife.

"There is a private conservation easement on some property bordering Acadia." Kristine turned a few pages and pointed to a description of a local sanctuary. "I'm not sure if anyone can visit, but it's seeking donations."

"Not necessarily helpful, but—"

"Okay, ladies and gentlemen," interrupted a gruff male voice over the bus's loudspeaker. "We're finally ready to get on our way."

Quinn turned back toward the tour guide. He appeared to be in his fifties, with a scruffy salt-and-pepper beard and a green Acadia cap preventing anyone from seeing whether the rest of his hair matched. He wore a gray long-sleeved shirt and coordinated pants that looked vaguely like a uniform, and he wedged a small microphone near his narrow lips.

"I'm Wendell, your guide today." He gave a spiel reciting rules and suggestions, then told the bus driver he was ready and they took off.

The narration was loud and would have been really interesting had Quinn actually been a tourist. In fact, he did look through the windshield toward the sights the guide pointed out—churches and parks and museums, including one specializing in local Native American culture and another focusing on natural history. Some architectural features on buildings were also worth noting. Because this was an island, the coastline appeared now and then; the Atlantic Ocean was brilliant blue beneath a clear sky, and calm that day.

Finally, they headed toward Acadia National Park. Despite his previous evening visits, that remained the place of most interest to Quinn. Plus, the tour leader got quiet while the driver headed in that direction.

Quinn felt a light squeeze on his arm. He looked over and saw Kristine's eyes wide, her full lips pursed slightly, as if she sent him a silent message: it was time.

He smiled, covered her hand with his—a feigned newlywed gesture—and nodded. He didn't release her hand, though. He liked the feel of it as he gripped it.

His body, unsurprisingly, also reacted as if she was doing more than touching his arm.

Squelching a sigh, he turned back toward the guide.

But Kristine acted first, squeezing his arm harder as if to communicate something—like, *let me*—then called to the man across the aisle.

"Wendell, my new husband and I have planned to come here for our honeymoon for ages—but now we're a bit worried. We heard about those poor tourists' deaths in Acadia National Park. They were mauled, weren't they? Do the authorities know what kind of animal did it?"

The man looked stricken, hazel eyes huge beneath his scruffy gray brows. He pulled the microphone away from his mouth, clearly not wanting the crowd on the filled bus to hear. His voice was hardly audible over the bus's growling engine. "No, ma'am, 'fraid they don't have any answers yet— at least none they're talking about, though they're looking. I assure you that we'll keep all of you close on this tour. No one'll be hurt."

"Thank you so much, Wendell." Kristine sounded relieved and even a bit flirtatious.

Maybe she was the better one to take the lead on this. What man wouldn't try to soothe the concerns of a woman as pretty as her—especially when she turned on her vast charm? She hadn't done that with him, though. Probably a good thing.

"But," she continued, "I read that it could be wolves. Are there wolves in Acadia? I researched the park on the internet and thought that there weren't any wolves around here now."

"That's right." Wendell nodded. "Used to be in the past, I've heard, but not at present. Could be coyotes or even wild dogs, I suppose, though I've never heard of any attacking people before. I'm sure the authorities will figure it out soon. Meantime, we'll just be extra careful. Ah, here we are."

The bus pulled in through a gate, and Wendell talked to the park rangers standing in the booth.

In a short while, the bus was moving again. The park was an amazing conglomeration of mountains overlooking the ocean, as well as numerous lakes. The vistas were wide. The forests were vast—and could hide any number of wild animals such as those Quinn had sensed last night.

But most wild animals stayed far from humans, even those that presented possible danger. If they attacked, there had to be a reason like hunger, or fear.

Considering how lush this area appeared, it probably hid a lot of possible prey, so hunger was unlikely.

Fear? Maybe. Those tourists could have come across some creature in the wild and baited it in some way—even just out of wildlife-loving curiosity—until it attacked.

But the most likely scenario, in Quinn's opinion, was that someone—who? and how?—knew of Simon and Grace, their belonging to Alpha Force, and what Alpha Force was. The attack did, after all, occur on the night of a full moon.

The clues so far were few. But to save Simon and Grace—and maybe even Alpha Force—Kristine and he would nevertheless locate those newlyweds. Fast. They had to.

And they would also uncover who was trying to frame them, and how…and why.

Chapter 6

The bus bumped and climbed slowly along a narrow uphill road. Kristine watched from her sideways angle as the Asian-American driver concentrated on what he was doing. His hands were clasped tightly on the wheel and he frowned while staring straight ahead.

Glancing out the window beside her, Kristine looked out onto a cliff composed of magnificent rock formations that plunged down to the water below.

And smiled as she took in the gorgeous sight.

"It's beautiful," she said.

"Yeah."

At his uncharacteristically soft tone, Kristine glanced toward Quinn. He was looking at her.

She swallowed in confusion. Well, gee. They were supposed to be acting like honeymooners. He was just doing a good job.

Even so, she quickly turned away from both Quinn and the window.

Wendell now leaned back in his seat, apparently assuming he'd answered everything Kristine intended to ask. Not so.

Why wasn't Quinn jumping in with questions, too? He was the former investigator, not her. So far, Kristine had kept things general and vague. She hadn't figured out a graceful way to segue into what they really needed to know: Had Grace and Simon been on this tour? That could be hard to ask since the guide hadn't sought the names of his current passengers, nor even where they were from. He probably didn't get to know any tourists well enough to identify them by name.

But there was one thing he could do: now that they were in the park, he could surely point out where the mauled tourists' bodies had been found.

Why didn't Quinn extract that from him?

Twisting slightly to make sure Quinn was looking at her, Kristine shot him a look she intended to be both quizzical and to show irritation.

His broad shoulder nearest her lifted in the merest shrug, rubbing against her arm in this cramped seat, reminding her—as if she had forgotten—that their bodies remained in physical contact. Then he shot her a smile and squeezed her hand as if encouraging her.

Did that mean this former P.I. thought she was handling things okay?

Why did that assumption of his approval shoot a twinge of pleasure through her? She didn't need his endorsement. She needed his expertise.

Well, since he hadn't jumped in to help, she'd just wing it, try to get answers without coming on like some kind of official investigator—which she wasn't.

"This is such an incredible ride," she gushed over the aisle loudly enough to be heard across the bus's straining engine.

Wendell glanced at her in surprise, as if he didn't expect passengers to talk to him while the view was so incredible.

That gave Kristine the opening she wanted. "I'll bet everyone who takes this tour tells you how wonderful this part is, right? How many tours do you guide every day? Are they always full?"

Wendell's scruffy face crinkled as if in pain that she had interrupted the break in his narration. But the expression turned into a smile. "You're really interested in all this, aren't you? You're the kind of tourist who makes this job fun."

He got back on the microphone. "One of our passengers has been asking some good questions," he said, "and the rest of you may be interested in the answers, too." He began to describe a typical day and week of a tour guide like him. "Our company has four buses. They all run on propane, since that's better for the environment. This time of year, in early summer, all four are sent out daily about two hours apart, and usually they're all filled."

He continued talking in generalities, making Kristine sigh in frustration. She looked up at Quinn's amused expression. "Interesting, but not exactly what you were looking for," he said softly. "Right?"

"I suppose you can do better," she fumed. "In fact, you should be able to—so why aren't you?"

"Because I enjoyed watching and listening to you."

She opened her mouth to say something sarcastic—then stopped. His brows had risen into an expression that suggested bemusement, as if he only now realized that what he'd said was true.

Almost unwillingly, he continued, "You were doing a damned good job, Kristine. I couldn't have handled it any better. But there are still things we need to find out—more specific stuff about passengers, and what our guide knows about what occurred here last week. Want the pro to show you how?" His words sounded as egotistical as she'd expected, yet the ironic expression on his face looked almost self-deprecating.

That made Kristine mad. Between the two of them, she wanted to be the one critical of him, not vice versa.

"Yeah," she said softly. "I'd love a lesson from an expert like you. I suspect you could teach me a lot about all kinds of *stuff* we've been thrown together to deal with. And while you're at it, maybe you could teach me how to be a good investigator, too." She looked up into his eyes. Their golden color almost glowed with sensuality as he stared back. He clearly heard the sarcasm—and the hidden meanings—in what she'd said.

They'd been thrown together mostly to deal with his shifting. And, oh yeah, he went into and out of it nude. As if that recollection was ever far from Kristine's thoughts.

"Okay," Quinn said smoothly. "I'll start with some of the hardest. The rest of what I can teach is easy."

Judging by his words and smug grin, the chip was back on his shoulder—as if it had ever fallen off. Too bad it didn't pound away the seductive air about him that was nearly irresistible.

Good thing he wasn't just Kristine's military comrade. He was essentially her superior. Plus, he was a werewolf in soldier's clothing. Those, she could continue to resist.

She hoped.

"Wendell," Quinn called, "here's something I'll bet every tourist on this bus is curious about. You said we'd be safe with you on this tour, but…well, are we going anywhere near where those tourists were attacked the other day? I think we should all be told where it was. That way, if we come back on our own, we can stay far away."

The guide's expression was clearly uncomfortable. "Well…the thing is, that happened in the middle of some of the most interesting stuff around the park. So, yes, we'll be near there. The authorities have it under control. You have nothing to worry about now, but—"

"But you'll tell us, won't you?" Quinn stood up despite the shakiness of the bus and turned toward the other passengers. "You all want to know where to avoid, right?" he called. "Wendell says we'll be getting near where that attack happened. Everyone think he should point it out?"

"Yeah." "Right." "Definitely." "Yes!"

The chorus of responses once more made Wendell seem to cringe, but he nodded. "Okay. We're actually coming up on it real soon. I'll let you know."

* * *

About twenty minutes later, Quinn's questions finally paid off—at least some of them.

The bus had parked beside a sheer but not very high cliff along a road. Lots of other vehicles were there, too, and Quinn could see why. A rustic visitor center was located on one side of a small, filled parking area.

"We'll stop here for about half an hour," Wendell said into the microphone as he stood at the front of the bus. "There's a great view of the water over there." He pointed across the narrow street toward where a lot of tourists scrambled over some rocks. "You can use the restrooms, if you'd like, and there's also a ranger station and souvenir shop inside. And—" He seemed to hesitate.

"And?" Quinn prompted, although he had a good idea of what Wendell was reluctant to say.

"Well, there's a stream that runs to one side of the center, with paths around it. Usually, I encourage our visitors to come back and start their park hikes from around here. But...well, those poor tourists were found not too far from this center, off a trail in the hills just behind it. That's the place to avoid now—not that you could go hiking there anyway. Far as I know, the place is still blocked off by the authorities who're investigating what happened."

"Thanks for letting us know." Kristine smiled at

their guide in a way that suggested her understanding and sympathy.

Damned if the old fellow didn't blush. Interesting, Quinn thought, that a woman who was all soldier while in uniform was clearly all woman when not in her camos—when she wanted to be.

With him, she'd tried to keep it all business. Of course, it was better that way—as much as he regretted it.

"Let's check out the visitor center, dear." She stood, smiling in the sweet way she had taken on as part of their cover.

"Absolutely, honey," he agreed.

They didn't spend a lot of time in the building. The kinds of souvenirs they were interested in weren't to be found there.

Instead, they wandered the paths alongside the visitor center until the bus was ready to leave.

The air was warm and slightly breezy. The area smelled of the multiple kinds of vegetation growing after spring's first spurt of rebirth, and the slightly stagnant waters nearby.

Quinn was amused and impressed by the way Kristine oohed and aahed about the trees and plants, the birds that flew around them and all the stuff real tourists might be interested in. But as they walked, she also seemed to study the way the paths led away from the area and into the hills.

At one point, she pulled on his arm, and he lowered his head so she could whisper into his ear.

"Can you...sense just where Wendell was referring to?" she asked.

He understood her meaning. But just then, his enhanced human senses picked up neither scents nor sounds that told him where the murders had occurred or the investigation was being conducted.

"No," he responded quietly. "But I understand the park is open twenty-four hours. I'd love to come back to this area and hike a bit at twilight—again—wouldn't you, dear?"

Kristine drove their rented sedan when they returned to Acadia a short while after their bus tour ended. It was still daylight—barely—and she'd turned on all the friendliness she could muster when she paid their admission to a park ranger at an entrance.

Inside, as she drove back toward the visitor center, she'd felt nervous.

This wouldn't be the first crime scene she'd visited since joining Alpha Force. She'd even been involved not long ago in something really big, potentially preventing a major bioterrorism event.

But then she'd felt more in her element. She'd even been able to utilize her nursing skills on that mission. Sure, she'd gotten shot then, but she'd been wearing a protective vest and hadn't been badly injured.

And being aide to another shifter—Grace—had been a piece of cake compared to what she anticipated once again with Quinn.

"Take the next turn to the right," Quinn said from the passenger seat. She glanced over. He was simultaneously studying a map of the park and a handheld GPS reader. "The road will take us up the mountain above the center—most likely above where the victims were found. There's bound to be someplace there secluded enough for you to conceal the car this time—and for me to shift again."

Kristine obeyed without comment. The already narrow road constricted even more as it wove around rocky crags and climbed higher. She had to pay close attention to her driving but glanced toward Quinn now and then. His head turned frequently toward the passenger window, so she figured he was trying to keep track of where the visitor center was, now below them, as well as the area above where the killing had occurred.

"Are we high enough yet?" she asked after a while.

"Yes, but I'm not sure—here we are. Take this road to the right. Let's go about a quarter of a mile, and there's supposed to be a turnoff soon. You should be able to park there."

She quickly came to the turnoff. It was just off the road, not the most secluded place to park. On the other hand, they hadn't seen any other vehicles for a while, so this wasn't a bad place to start the night's activities—particularly since there were plenty of lush bushes beneath thick, leafy trees.

There surely would be a place outside the realm of any prying eyes for them to do as they planned.

Kristine maneuvered the car as close to the cover of the plant growth as she could and pressed down on the parking brake with her foot.

"Are you ready?" she asked Quinn, pasting a confident smile on her face despite her unease of anticipation.

Whatever the rest of this night brought, she felt certain of only one thing: she was about to see Quinn Parran naked yet again.

Quinn had figured out approximate coordinates from the information Wendell had provided, and he had programmed a target area into his GPS.

Now, he walked beside Kristine, deep into the forest above the area where he believed the tourists' bodies had been found. Their footsteps crackled on the dry undergrowth, and only the slightest illumination sprinkled onto them from the area above the trees.

That would disappear soon, since it was nearly

sundown—once more the perfect time for him to change.

He didn't intend to get too close to the crime scene. That would be stupid, especially since the authorities claimed to be looking for wild animals, maybe wolves, to blame the killings on, and the officials might have a continued presence here, even at night.

They wouldn't find any actual native wolves in the park. But had his brother and sister-in-law been involved—or were they, as Quinn believed, being framed?

To find them—and the truth—he had to rely on his true character.

And at the moment, that also involved relying on the woman beside him on the narrow forest path.

Once again, he inquired, "You sure I can't carry that backpack for you?" She had removed other contents at the hotel and slipped what was essential tonight into it.

"What part of 'I can do it myself' don't you understand?" She glared up at him with those stern blue eyes flashing with irritation, her chin raised.

He grinned. "Well, you know, we werewolves don't always understand the English spoken by regular people."

She blinked, then managed a small return smile. "I learned that from my prior superior officer. She always enjoyed pretending not to get it when I said something she didn't want to hear." They'd still been walking, but Kristine suddenly stopped. The expression on her face looked horrified. "I just spoke about Grace in the past tense, damn it. She's fine. She has to be."

"She is, and so's Simon," Quinn assured her, hoping it was true. "We'll find them and straighten out this whole mess."

"We will," Kristine agreed with obvious determination.

He couldn't help it. He bent down and kissed her gently on the mouth.

To his surprise and pleasure, she reciprocated.

In moments, they stood still on that narrow, confined path, outside the view of any other human or shifter, and kissed once more.

Her lips were moist and pliant as he opened them with his tongue, thrusting inside and tasting her with the senses of a more-than-human. Hell, he didn't just want to share kisses with her. He wanted to touch her everywhere. Thrust inside her. Slowly. Then faster, until they both exploded…

That wasn't going to happen now. Probably wouldn't happen ever. It *shouldn't* happen.

Reluctantly, he pulled back. "Guess that was for luck," he said, making a joke of it.

"Yours or mine?" she quipped back, although

she looked almost stunned. She apparently hadn't intended to kiss him—and that was mutual.

"Both." He looked around. They were some distance from the car, surrounded by forest. "This looks like as good a place as any. You ready?"

"I will be in a second."

He helped her pull the backpack off. From it, she extracted a vial of shifting potion.

He considered catering to her obvious discomfort at his nudity, then shrugged it off. She'd seen it all before, would see it all again later.

He took the container of liquid from her and downed it. It tasted slightly minty, mostly unappetizing—but damned good, considering what it accomplished.

Then, looking straight into Kristine's unwavering, if uneasy, eyes, he began to strip.

Chapter 7

She'd seen it before. Several times. Watching Quinn strip off his clothes in the barest light of the waning day should have felt like *been there, done that,* nothing new to this well-trained nurse, this experienced aide to shapeshifters.

It was far from that easy. Kristine couldn't remain that blasé, no matter how hard she tried.

It didn't help at all that, despite the serious work he had to do here, Quinn had turned it into a game this time, even more than before. A quick one, to be sure, but he was still playing with her.

He pulled off his shirt first, wadded it into a bundle and flipped it nonchalantly over his shoulder as if it was a basketball made of rags.

All the while, he continued to look into her eyes and smile. And, oh, his smoking-hot expression, as if he knew exactly what she was thinking.

As if he undressed her this time, just as realistically, but only with his lustful gaze.

He undid the fastening on his jeans, pulled down the zipper and hooked his thumbs into the sides. In one swift maneuver, he removed both his pants and the boxers below.

He stood straight, stretched, turned sideways and back from the waist while flexing his muscles. All of them—all of *him*.

His maleness nearly made her lose her breath from wanting him. How wrong that was.

Especially now.

Now. Of course. She reminded herself of the obligation she had to fulfill for Alpha Force. Even if she wasn't under orders, she had a job to do: to find Simon and Grace, while protecting the unit that was so important to her.

She bent down, sliding to her knees while at the same time turning—and drew the very special light needed to make the shifting potion work from her backpack. It wasn't very large, but the illumination it gave off always matched the intensity of the full moon.

She glanced around to make doubly sure that their location was secluded enough, hidden well within the forest, so authorities below were unlikely to see the light.

Then she turned it on. "Are you ready?" she asked Quinn, knowing full well from past experience that once Quinn had downed the elixir, all he needed to do to prepare for his shift was to take off his clothes—which he'd definitely done.

"I sure am." He drew himself up to his full height, in all his bare glory, clearly showing off everything he had—and getting the lustful reaction he undoubtedly sought from her.

Not that she'd admit it. "Good. Here goes."

She turned on the light, illuminating even more that gorgeous, all masculine body that she refused to allow to tempt her—too much.

She watched while he began to writhe under the brilliant glow as his limbs changed, his perfect body changed shape and grew fur all over. That should have turned her off completely.

It wasn't exactly seductive.

But it also didn't erase the memory of moments earlier, of what she'd seen and lusted after.

"Be careful," she said softly, as his form morphed even further, into the low, feral appearance of a wolf.

She wasn't sure whether she was talking to him or herself.

He stood still for a minute after his change was complete, allowing the discomfort of the shift to dissipate.

The forest floor was soft and moist around here, with decaying leaves beneath his paws. The greenery around him smelled vibrant and heavy, and among the scents he inhaled were those of creatures—rodents, birds, others, some active at this hour, others settled in to wait for daylight to return.

The woman who had helped him with his shift once more stood before him, watching, the light that assisted him now turned off.

He would return here soon. To where she waited. As he had each previous time.

With a slight nod acknowledging her, he loped off in the direction of where he needed to observe and investigate this time while in wolfen form.

As with the prior occasions when he had shifted with the aid of the elixir made available by his new employer Alpha Force, he reveled in the fact that his humanity remained strong beneath his canine appearance.

This time, he also remained fully aware of the mission he had to perform in exchange. Wanted to perform.

He had to help his brother and sister-in-law.

He was fully aware of the potential danger of being in shifted form now, when those officially investigating the killings that he, too, needed to solve, would be watching for a wolf to blame, and he was in the area where those killings had occurred.

That meant caution was particularly essential to what he attempted to accomplish this night. He thrust his long muzzle into the air and again inhaled the scents around him. Still nothing menacing...at least not now.

He slowly stalked through the darkened forest, toward paths leading below to the site of the killings.

As he got closer, his acute hearing picked up the sounds of voices. The area of his destination was dark, yet he made out the glow of flashlights.

As he had assumed, the investigation into the deaths must be ongoing. That increased his need for caution.

Instead of getting closer, he began walking in a large circle around the site, allowing his senses freedom to discern anything outside normal forest scents and sounds.

The first loop was slow by design. The soft voices from its center were distinct—a man and a woman—but he did not know to whom they belonged, nor did he make out what they were saying.

He made his next ring closer. The two sounded at ease with one another as they whispered about blood and local wildlife and death, and speculated whether traps they had laid would capture whatever creatures had dared to kill humans.

Danger! Would he sense those traps?

Yes, he had to perform his mission, but getting

caught would be disastrous. Yet if he slowed more, he might risk changing back before he'd planned to. The amount of elixir he had ingested would likely permit him to remain wolfen for perhaps two hours, no longer. That had been the plan this time.

He proceeded even more slowly. He kept his nose near the ground to try to catch the scent of any recent human presence in this remote area, as well as any metallic or other foreign smells that could warn him of a trap.

His next circuit would not be entirely around the subject site. It would be too risky.

But he did draw closer, very carefully. Saw, through the trees, the clearing where the humans waited, their flashlights on as they continued to talk. Viewed where they had parked a moderate-size SUV.

They surely were not attempting to hide from any wild creature. Not with their lights, their voices.

Whatever their intent, he remained distant, though he drew close enough to inhale scents that would allow him to identify them in the future.

Still careful, he approached the area containing the vehicle, a small parking lot off one of the mountain roads. Nose toward the ground, he carefully stepped forward—and stopped.

It was not danger he smelled but a combination

of scents that he recognized—light and barely discernible now, as if nearly dissipated with time.

Simon and Grace had apparently been here sometime in the recent past...shifted. Both of them.

Did that mean they had in fact been involved in killing the two humans?

Or had they been here for another reason?

The voices suddenly grew louder. "I've had enough of our surveillance for tonight," said the woman.

"Me, too," said the man. "A beer sounds a whole lot better than hanging out here. We can check the traps tomorrow, but I have a feeling we're not going to catch anything tonight."

"Or possibly ever," the woman replied. "I'm ready for that beer."

They stood, approaching not far from where Quinn lurked near their vehicle. He crouched down and froze, in case they moved in his direction or shone their lights this way.

They didn't. Instead, they got into the vehicle and drove away.

Who were they? What had they really been after? And if they'd been so sure they would be unsuccessful, why had they bothered at all?

Kristine was waiting exactly where he had left her. He'd had no doubt she would be there.

Even so, when Quinn had returned, he had observed her presence yet stayed a short distance away. Now that he was finished shifting once more to human form, he was glad she was nearby, so close he could see her through the intervening trees.

For now, though, he let himself rest on the damp, chilly ground, naked, sore and exhausted.

One thing the Alpha Force elixir didn't do, any more than his brother Simon's pills did, was to make the change easier or more comfortable. No severe pain—he was used to shifting during the full moon, at least, and this didn't feel much different—but his muscles ached.

"Welcome back," said the soft female voice that was growing familiar to him. Was that a good thing?

Sure it was, at least for now.

Quinn had closed his eyes for a few seconds, and when he opened them again Kristine was leaning over him. Obviously his shift had not been silent. She'd known he was there.

Now, she covered him with his clothing, and he noticed that the T-shirt he had wadded up after removing it had been smoothed out nicely.

"Thanks," he said. "Let me get dressed and we'll talk."

"Good idea." He wasn't sure whether she referred to his getting dressed or their talking or both, but as he stood he saw her walk back to the clearing and lean over her backpack, busily relocating the stuff inside.

A good way to avoid continuing to look at him, he supposed. Despite the fact they'd done this before and she was an experienced Alpha Force shape-shifter's aide, she clearly remained uncomfortable with his nudity.

Which made this all the more fun for him—a good thing. He needed a bit of levity. Despite, or maybe because of, the talk about unfilled traps, he was even more worried about his brother and sister-in-law now than he'd been before.

He had taken his time returning here, to his rendezvous point with Kristine, after the humans had left the crime scene area. He had waited for a while to make sure they didn't return and that he didn't sense any other human intrusion.

Then he had wandered around inside the yellow crime scene tape, scenting the ground and the air and the foliage. Prowling even more than he had that first night in Acadia, when his shift had simply been an experiment and exercise, just to test how it could be done here.

This time, he became certain that Simon and Grace had been there, probably on the night of the full moon. Despite the passage of days, Quinn was able to determine even more of their trail via their faint shifted scents. They had most likely arrived at that parking area in human form, although he picked up no odor except their wolfen ones, and they had apparently maneuvered around the same vicinity.

At the same time as the killings? That he couldn't tell, but he did discern two separate scents of blood.

"What did you find?" Kristine asked him. "You... you look like you're pondering things. Was there anything helpful?"

"Let's head back to the hotel. I'll tell you on the way."

Once more, she drove. After a shift like that, his human senses had again taken on even more of the acuity of his wolfen ones, at least for a short while. He couldn't help it. He inhaled her scent and analyzed it, too. The slightly spicy, definitely hot aroma of whatever perfume she wore had all but disappeared. Now, her smell was still sexy-soft and slightly tangy, as if she had been worried enough to perspire at least a little in his absence.

From concern about him, or about their mission?

They were interrelated, he reminded himself. Even if he found her scent damned sexy, that didn't mean she reciprocated. It was better that way. Fewer potential complications.

"Here's what I saw." He told her about the people he'd heard and glimpsed. "Their presence seemed off to me somehow. It was like they were waiting for some animals to attack them, like what happened to the tourists, but they didn't really believe it would happen."

"Because the animals had moved on?"

"Maybe. Or they knew something about what happened that didn't involve wild animals still lurking around there. They mentioned setting traps, but I didn't find any."

"Do they know about Alpha Force—and Grace and Simon?" Kristine's breathing had become slightly irregular, and Quinn heard her distress.

"That's one possibility," he said. "Or it was all a setup from the get-go, and these people are aware of it. Or both—somehow, those folks or others know about Grace and Simon and therefore Alpha Force."

"We'd better figure out who they are," Kristine said. "Any chance they're part of the official DSPA investigation?"

He looked at her, impressed with her intuition. That was what he'd begun speculating, too.

Which would make this investigation a lot more complicated for two people on their own to figure things out.

"Guess you're as much of a cynic as I am," he said. "That's now on our agenda to find out."

Chapter 8

He was tired, the way he always got after a shift, but he knew he'd get his second wind.

Right now, they needed to learn who those clowns were who'd set up their pathetic surveillance at the crime scene.

Once they did that, they could figure out why.

"Drive slowly, please," Quinn told Kristine. "And keep on the lookout for a small, beige SUV—a Honda with no license plate."

The two who'd been there had made it clear they wanted a drink instead of hanging out to watch for dangerous animals. That had worked out well for Quinn to do as he'd needed and conduct his own investigation of the area, but it also gave them time to drink and run.

For now, Kristine did as he asked, driving their rented car along the streets of Bar Harbor, zeroing in on the restaurants and bars where the group may have headed.

Quinn liked her concentration, the way she maneuvered out of the way of other vehicles that clearly wanted to get from Point A to Point B without catering to the slower-moving cars in front of them. No one else gave a damn about what Kristine and he were up to, and that was how it should be.

He also liked how Kristine drove even more slowly as they came to open-air parking lots, including those without a bar nearby. How she looped through them so they could surveil all the cars within them, use process of elimination and move on.

Fact was, Quinn liked *her,* and her dedication to their fortunately unofficial mission. And if he added in her sexiness, her cute seriousness in trying to ignore how part of their mission involved her taking care of him before and after shifts—and while naked—he *really* liked her.

Not to mention how much he wanted her. In bed. Especially if he could remove the imaginary barrier between them in their hotel room this night or one—and preferably more—of the ensuing ones while they were still here.

Down Main Street they went, nearer the water on West Street, and along some of the other avenues containing eateries and hotels and bars.

But in less than an hour, they'd seen it all. Bar Harbor wasn't a large town.

Wherever their prey had gone, it could have been out of this area, even off Mount Desert Island.

At a stop sign, Kristine turned toward him. Her face was solemn in the pale illumination from a street light outside the car, and he wanted to reach over and stroke it comfortingly. "I'm not sure where to try next," she said.

"I think it's time to give up for now," he replied. "We'll find them—but not tonight."

They were back in their hotel room.

It was far from the only thing Kristine had thought about that day—what their second night there would be like. But she admitted to herself that the anticipation had formed an undercurrent within her brain…and the rest of her body.

Not that she anticipated doing anything different from the night before. They had set a precedent. One she could live with. She hoped.

But she had seen Quinn naked yet again that day. Twice. That didn't help her keep her mind off the inevitable reaction her body would have when she got into bed with him, no matter how innocent her intentions.

Better that she recall why he'd been nude. His shifting. That wasn't sexy...was it?

Somehow, it didn't turn her off. Not the way she hoped it would. In fact, she had become rather intrigued by the whole idea of shapeshifting. That was a reason she liked being part of Alpha Force, though she'd never even considered the possibility before she'd been recruited from a regular military unit— except in books and on movie screens, all fiction.

And not particularly sensuous. Not like the reality.

And now, the moment she had walked into the room and laid her backpack on the floor, her gaze roamed inevitably toward its center—and that damned solo bed.

"Mind if I shower first?" Quinn asked. He'd come in right behind her. A faint, not unpleasant scent of the forest emanated from him, and she figured that it must seem a lot stronger to him. Grace had told her that even in human form, werewolf shifters' canine senses remained keener than most humans'.

"Fine," Kristine said neutrally, trying hard not to imagine what he would look like bare beneath the pulsing water, gyrating to get clean.

She didn't exactly succeed in controlling her imagination, but it didn't matter. She would use the opportunity to put on her robe, then duck into the bathroom later, when it was empty.

While he showered, and as a distraction, she changed clothes, then got out her laptop and into the files she had started since she began working with Quinn, including her initial interview with him after he had first shifted using the Alpha Force elixir— and had clearly enjoyed it.

Now, she made notes about what they had done that day—and how little they'd accomplished. She jotted down the route they had taken in town while trying to locate the vehicle of the people they sought, the one they'd driven away in after leaving the crime scene. Quinn would have more to describe since he had seen them, though not exactly up close and personal while he hung out at a distance, shifted. But he'd seen enough, and heard enough, to tell her they may have been sent there to wait for feral coyotes or whatever had killed those tourists. Even trap them.

But whatever their assignment, they had laughed about it. As if they weren't taking it seriously.

No wonder Quinn didn't trust them. Neither did Kristine.

They'd call Major Connell tomorrow to report in and see if he could get any information about the investigators officially attempting to tie the crime to the military, and therefore to Simon and Grace. Kristine wouldn't be surprised if the people Quinn had seen were the feds assigned to the case.

Even so, how much, if anything, did they know about Alpha Force? And were they attempting to harm it?

Quinn and she needed an explanation for the nonchalant surveillance, and casual attitude, at the crime scene that evening. Was it because the people who'd been there knew what had really happened to those tourists and were only going through the motions of a pseudo-investigation?

She'd let her mind wander enough that she was startled when the bathroom door opened. "Next!" Quinn said.

She quickly dashed past him, barely glancing up to see that he was grinning at her.

If only she could force herself to hate that sexy, knowing little smile he kept aiming at her—as if he knew she wanted his body.

But she didn't hate it. In fact, it somehow seemed part of his charm. His sensual appeal.

Damn him.

She took her time in the shower, hoping—but not expecting—that he would be asleep when she returned to the room.

She could see him in the faint light from the bathroom behind her, with the door mostly shut, when she peeked in later. He was just lying there, very still, breathing deeply. Was it possible?

Quietly, she removed her robe to reveal her unsexy pajamas, sneaked around to shut off the light, then slowly returned to her side of the bed, careful not to trip on anything—or to run into him in case he was dangling an arm or leg.

She eased back the covers and slid under them onto the firm mattress.

And gasped as he moved quickly, rearing up onto his legs and leaning over her.

He lowered himself quickly until his mouth was on hers. He kissed her—gently, nibbling, searching, teasing with his tongue until she nearly blazed into a spontaneous combustion of need for him, reacting to his kiss by meeting it with her own.

She stretched upward, wanting to feel all that hardness of his body against her once more, all over. She succeeded…somewhat. For just an instant, she felt the teasing touch of his erection through their clothing, as it barely skimmed the most inflamed and needy area of her straining body.

But before she could press even closer—better yet, start searching his body with her hands—he was gone, flopping back onto his side of the bed.

"Good night, Kristine," he said. "Sleep well. We've got a big day tomorrow."

* * *

Sleep well? Easy enough for him to say. But Quinn got out of bed the next morning as tired as if he'd stayed up all night to plan that day's strategy.

In a way he had. That was how he'd tried to keep his mind—and hands—off the hot woman who lay beside him.

He figured that six o'clock was a respectable enough time to leap out of bed as if invigorated by his own, nonexistent, good night's sleep, then shower, shave—and remove himself from Kristine's presence for at least a few minutes to get his body back under control.

When he came out of the bathroom, a towel wrapped around his middle, he found Kristine up and in a terry cloth hotel robe, rooting through her suitcase on its stand. Did she still have those blah, unisex pajamas on underneath—or had she stripped them off first? Too bad he hadn't been there to find out.

"Good morning," Kristine said, turning around. She kept her eyes on his, and her obvious discomfiture at his near nakedness almost made his own unease bearable.

Almost.

She had no makeup on yet, not surprisingly, but her face was as lovely as he'd ever seen it—youthful and vulnerable, a woman's visage and not a soldier's. For now. Although she did raise her chin as he continued to stare at her.

"Good morning," he repeated. "Soon as we're ready, I want to call Drew Connell, bring the major up to date. See if he has any information for us. Maybe he'll be able to get an official ID on those yo-yos I saw yesterday."

"Good idea." She grabbed some clothes and her cosmetic bag and raced past him into the bathroom. Making him smile.

When she emerged ten minutes later, he was dressed in jeans and a gray T-shirt that commemorated a trip he'd once taken to Yellowstone. Wolf country. Real wolves—although their protected status under endangered-species laws kept changing.

Werewolves were presumably fair game anytime. Especially if they were accused of killing a couple of normal people, as the claim might be around here among those with awareness of Simon and Grace, and Alpha Force.

Members of Quinn's family had been killed when Simon and he were kids. Their murderers had claimed also to be werewolves—and had slaughtered their aunt and cousin when they had admitted to being shifters, too.

Their uncle had executed those nonshifting killers in turn—but the whole family still remained wary about revealing their true nature.

Of course, Quinn trusted Simon, who'd disclosed the truth and joined Alpha Force.

Now Quinn wondered if their enlistment in the unit had been a mistake.

"You ready?" Quinn asked more gruffly than he should have. His patience was growing fragile. He needed to find his brother and sister-in-law, learn what happened for real in Acadia Park. No more delays.

"Sure." Kristine looked at him quizzically. She'd donned jeans, too—and a plain navy sleeveless shirt that made her blue eyes seem even brighter. Not to mention the way it hugged her in all the right places. Her feet were still bare. She looked too damn distractingly good. "Are you okay?"

"Yeah," he lied. "But my P.I. juices are flowing today. I want answers, and I want them now."

"I'm with you," she said. "But we need to do this right. Let's call Major Connell."

"Fine."

She grabbed the secure satellite phone from her purse and sat at the edge of the bed. Not a good choice of location, but he joined her despite how his recollection of his sleepless night scratched at his brain.

"Hello, Kristine." Drew's voice soon emanated from the phone's speaker. "Quinn with you?"

"Yes, sir." He didn't mind acting all military when he needed the commanding officer's input.

"What's going on?"

Quinn gave a recap of their tour yesterday, and what he'd seen and heard after nightfall. He wasn't specific about what form he'd been in. The major would know that by inference.

"No idea who those folks were that I viewed at the crime scene," Quinn finished. "They weren't exactly hiding their presence, so they were most likely part of the investigation, but whoever they were, their attitudes seemed way off. I don't know if they were local or feds. Any thoughts on that, sir?"

"No, but I've an idea how to find out. I got a little intel on the official investigators that clown—er, our revered team leader for the Defense Special Projects Agency, Darren Olivante—had sent there. There's a U.S. Coast Guard facility not far from Bar Harbor, in Southwest Harbor, another part of Mount Desert Island. They may be using some of their boats or additional facilities. Other than the national park, there aren't many federal facilities in the area."

"Should the honeymooning couple take a tour of the island and just happen to wind up over there?" Kristine asked.

"I'd suggest that you set things up first, maybe talk to the local authorities who're investigating the murders, let them tell you about the feds' involvement," Drew said. "That way, your interest in the DSPA guys won't be so obvious."

Exactly Quinn's thoughts—for now, at least. Besides, it would be a good idea to meet the local cops—before they arguably had an official reason to be interested in Kristine and him for being too nosy and possibly messing up their case.

"Got it." Quinn looked at Kristine to see if she agreed—or whether he'd have to somehow convince her.

"Sounds good, sir," Kristine said, aiming those irresistible blue eyes at Quinn.

"We'll get on it right away," added Quinn.

"By the way," Drew said. "Initial coroners' reports on the dead tourists indicate that there was saliva on their bodies. Canine saliva."

After grabbing a quick fast-food breakfast, Kristine and Quinn walked to the police station hand in hand, in the cool springtime air. Kristine wished they'd chosen some other kind of cover for their scheme rather than acting as newlyweds. It was damned hard being this up close and personal with Quinn after spending another night pretending to sleep, to shrug off that kiss he had given her as they lay down, to not notice his hard, hot body so near.

"It looks like another lovely day," she said, feigning the cheerfulness that went with their pretext.

She gazed up at the sky over the low, picturesque buildings of Bar Harbor. The few clouds were fluffy white and nonthreatening.

"Right." Quinn didn't sound nearly as much in character as he should be. She shot a scowl his way and got a shrug of one broad shoulder in return. "Lovely," he repeated and added, "What a wonderful time to be touring Bar Harbor, isn't it, dear?"

Okay, he was going overboard now, even though the few other people strolling along the sidewalks nearby might be able to catch only a word or two they shared. She didn't answer, and she was glad when they reached the police station—in as picturesque a building as the rest of them in Bar Harbor, she supposed.

Inside, a uniformed officer behind a desk greeted them, his youthful face radiating helpfulness. The name tag over his shirt pocket said Canfield. "Can I help you?"

"We're just visiting," Quinn said.

"On our honeymoon," Kristine added with a simper that was about as characteristic to her as turning cartwheels in the middle of a busy intersection.

"On our tour yesterday, we were shown the general area where those two poor tourists were killed, and—"

"We're just concerned about our safety. The local newspaper has some stuff in general about the investigation, but we want to know what's really going on and how to stay safe. Could we talk to one of the investigators?" Kristine finished up their tag-team approach that she hoped would seem the exemplar picture of innocence.

The smile on the cop's face fell. "I'm sorry, but ongoing investigations can't be discussed." Especially with snoopy tourists, Kristine figured, though the guy didn't add that.

"But we need to make sure of our safety," she repeated. "Please, can't we see someone in charge and just ask our questions?" She glanced toward Quinn, seeking his backup. The pleased look he shot back suggested he again liked what she was doing. She grinned back, then turned again toward the cop. "Please," she repeated, tilting her head pleadingly as she looked him in the eye.

In a few minutes, they were shown through the station and into a fair-size office.

"These are the two tourists who want to hear about the murder investigation, Chief," said the cop who'd brought them here.

The sign on the desk read Police Chief Al Crane. He was short, a bit portly in his uniform, and the scowl he leveled from beneath shaggy gray brows suggested that the last thing he wanted to do that day was talk with them.

Even so, he waved them into chairs facing him as the other cop left.

"Not much I could tell you even if I wanted to," the chief said. "A lot of the investigation isn't being handled here. Plus, there are aspects that we can't tell anyone."

"But you're getting somewhere with the investigation, aren't you?" Quinn asked. "Haven't you been checking out the crime scene?"

That question made Kristine glance at Quinn. Was this man one of the people he'd seen there while shifted?

No way she could ask now.

"Do you know yet what animal killed those tourists?" Quinn persisted.

What appeared to be anger darkened Crane's face even more. "Yeah, I wish," he said sarcastically.

"Then you don't know? You haven't captured it? All of us tourists are still in danger?" Kristine cut in, wanting to continue to lay it on thick in their quest for answers and cooperation.

"No, course not. We're patrolling more, making sure things are as safe as possible. But you know the killings took place on federal property, so there's not much we can do at the crime scene. It's up to the feds."

"So the feds are hunting the animals?" Quinn asked. "And you're not? Really?" He didn't wait for the chief's answer. Maybe it was just as well. The guy looked really pissed. "Can you tell us which branch of the feds? I really want to talk to them, to hear what kind of beast they're after so we'll know what to stay away from—and where we can go and still stay safe, including in Acadia."

"Yeah, it's the feds. Sure, you can go try talking to them, but good luck. They seem to want to collect information, not share it. I'm not even sure which branch they are, although..."

"Although what?" Quinn demanded.

"Although nothing. I'm not prepared to share rumors with anyone."

"Then you have heard something?" Quinn wasn't giving up.

But the chief merely shrugged.

"Well, we'll try talking to them," Kristine said. "Maybe they'll at least be willing to provide safety information to people like us."

They were soon on their way out of the police station. The formerly empty areas were now populated with other cops—three or four of them.

Until they were alone, Kristine would have to hold her questions that had arisen after their discussion with that police chief, despite how they threatened to erupt from within her. Her curiosity had been stoked by some of Quinn's questions, not to mention his attitude.

Her curiosity became even more relentless when Quinn stopped abruptly.

"What—" Kristine began, but he was no longer at her side.

He approached the nearest of the cops, a slim and pretty female officer who filled out her uniform well.

Kristine shouldn't have felt even a hint of jealousy at his surprising attention to the woman—but she did.

"Hi, Officer...Angsburg." He'd hesitated only an instant after reading her name tag. "And Officer Sidell." He had turned toward the nearest male officer, a squat but large-chested guy with hardly any hair. "I want to tell you how much I'm enjoying Bar Harbor, but I have to admit I'm worried after what happened to those two tourists a few days ago. I'm here partly to ask the police to be sure to watch over us. Okay?"

Both officers rushed to reassure him that the department was on top of the situation. Nothing else bad would happen around here. They'd see to it.

"But I was told that you guys here weren't involved in the investigation or tracking down the renegade animals. Now, you two look like you'd be great at it. I'd trust you to keep things under control if you were in charge. Do you have any information you can share with tourists to make us feel safer?"

Officer Angsburg flushed. "Sorry, we don't. We have to follow department and jurisdictional policies, and we're both just cops, not investigators or even hunters."

Quinn looked expectantly at Officer Sidell, who nodded his agreement. "But everything'll be fine around here from now on. And the...creatures who harmed those tourists? They'll be found and dealt with. No doubt about it."

In a few minutes, when they were outside again, Kristine looked at Quinn. His face had lost the affability he'd shown to the cops and was now a grim mask.

"What was that all about?" she demanded. "I mean the way you acted around those cops, especially the ones you just confronted. They just repeated what that chief said. Did you think they somehow could do a better job than the rest of the department as far as protecting tourists? Or, better yet, giving us information?"

"Unknown," he retorted. "But possible." He glared down at her. "The yo-yos at the *federal* crime scene? They were those two cops."

Chapter 9

What the hell had local cops been doing out of uniform at the crime scene?

Quinn stood with Kristine outside the police station. His private investigator's mind grappled with the problem. Should he really quiz those cops in depth instead of just hinting around? Or would that blow everything?

He was glad he'd used the Alpha Force elixir to shift last night. Those cops might well have noticed another person sneaking around them in the woods. Of course, they were supposed to be watching for wild animals, but they wouldn't have assumed that any wolf prowling the area had human cognition and the ability to observe them while remaining alert and avoiding detection.

He was even more impressed, in that respect, with the improvement over Simon's concoction.

Grasping Kristine's hand almost automatically, he leaned over and quietly rehashed what he had seen and heard. The two people he had just seen again at the police station had not been quiet at the site and had apparently not even wanted to be there, considering how fast they'd taken off—and it had sounded as if they'd planned to go straight to the nearest bar.

Why had they really been there in the first place? And what—

"Mr. and Mrs. Scott?" The voice came from behind them. Quinn almost didn't react. His mind was veering in other directions from the cover Kristine and he had assumed.

But Kristine was alert. She tugged at his hand, even as she turned. "That's us." She feigned a giggle. "I'm still trying to get used to it, though. We just got married."

She was talking to a tall, skinny guy with an almost skeletal face—and watchful hazel eyes that suggested he was analyzing every iota of data around him. His scent was sharp, some kind of shaving product overlaid with an expensive male cologne. If the smell hadn't been washed out somewhat by the brisk breeze wafting from the nearby sea, Quinn might have puked.

"I just spoke briefly with Chief Crane, and he sent me out here," the man said. "He told me that a newlywed couple was just asking about the official investigation into the mauling of those tourists in Acadia. Is that you?"

"Yes," Kristine said.

"Well, I'm an investigator for an agency of the federal government that has jurisdiction. Like he told you, we're involved with the investigation because the deaths occurred in a national park. Let me assure you that we're conducting the inquiry as quickly as possible, and—"

"Which branch?" Quinn inserted quickly. He could guess, though, considering who'd shown up at Ft. Lukman when Simon and Grace had disappeared. And it was very interesting that this guy had come after them when Crane had suggested that the feds weren't being very cooperative.

"That doesn't matter," the man said, his glare apparently intended to cut off all further inquiry.

As a private investigator, Quinn had run into that type before—and enjoyed playing them. "Maybe not," he said cheerfully. "But someone from U.S. Fish and Wildlife might look into this differently from someone from, say, the Department of Defense."

"Could be," the man said. "You sound somewhat knowledgeable, as well as interested. What's your background, Mr. Scott?"

Quinn knew he'd better modify his attitude. Otherwise, this guy, and any colleagues he might have around, might look more closely at Kristine and him, and their flimsy unofficial cover.

Or maybe they already saw through them.

"I'm in retail sales, back in Ohio," Quinn said. "I'm assistant manager at a major discount store. My wife, Kristine, is in retail, too—she works at one of the big houseware chains." They'd discussed this before when putting together their cover. There were a lot of salespeople in this country, probably quite a few with the last name of Scott, even in Ohio. Someone checking them out might not find a Quinn and Kristine, but the jobs sounded realistic.

"That's right," Kristine confirmed. "But…well, I have to say I'm really nervous about being here now. We've thought about leaving, but we planned our honeymoon so carefully. Please tell us, Mr.… er, what did you say your name was?"

"Kelly," he replied, without clarifying whether that was his first or last name.

"Mr. Kelly, are you with Fish and Wildlife?" Kristine asked. "I hate to see poor animals slaughtered, of course, but if they've gotten a taste of killing people it could happen again. Are you one of those people who's dedicated to protecting them no matter what? I heard that the tourists who were killed might have been members of some protective organization. If so, isn't that ironic?"

Usually, those were exactly the kinds of people Quinn liked best. That meant they wouldn't shoot wolves on sight. The whole thing about needing to kill werewolves with silver bullets was a myth. Shifters were as susceptible to death by shooting of any kind of ammunition as their human counterparts.

Like what happened to his family members.

"No, I'm not with Fish and Wildlife. And, yeah, the victims have been identified. This wasn't the first national park they visited to observe wildlife, but it'll be their last."

He still didn't say what branch of the feds he was with. Interesting, Quinn thought, though not unexpected. Most likely, he was an official DSPA investigator given the assignment as mentioned by that team leader, Olivante. But whoever he was, he might have information that could help in their quest to learn what really happened.

Which meant that Quinn needed to get to know the guy better. Carefully, of course.

"Then who are you with?" Kristine insisted before Quinn could stop her. Or maybe she could get away with pushiness. Men often forgave in women what they wouldn't tolerate from other guys.

Especially if the woman was as hot as Kristine.

Although the thought of this creep—whose eyes were, not unexpectedly, continuing to assess Kristine—lusting after her made him want to punch something. Preferably Kelly.

But Quinn was nevertheless interested in the guy's answer.

"The Department of Defense," Kelly said as off-handedly as if talking about the nice spring weather. That didn't fool Quinn. Those icy eyes assessed not only Kristine now, but him, too—undoubtedly to gauge his reaction.

Quinn thought fast about how to play this. He needed to buddy up to Kelly, but he wanted Kristine out of it for her own safety.

"You know, I've got some civilian friends in the DoD," Quinn said. "One does engineering work overseas. A couple of others are in D.C. Hey, honey, why don't you go back to the hotel while I schmooze here a little with Mr. Kelly to see if we have any buddies in common?"

He aimed a look at Kristine that even someone with a fraction of her intelligence would understand. It shouted, *Listen to me. Do what I say. No questions asked.*

She sent a stare right back at him that slapped him with, *No way in hell...honey.*

"But I want to hear all about your friends, sweetheart," she said. "I haven't met them, and now that we're married I want to get to know all your buddies."

He wanted to shake her. But damn, didn't she look sexy in all that obstinacy, with her lower lip extended and her blue eyes flashing.

A short bark of laughter emanated from Kelly. "Tell you what," he said. "I'm about to meet a coworker for coffee. Why don't you both come along? We can all share information on people we may know in common."

His quick glance at Quinn suggested that he planned to ask questions, too—and the people he thought they might know in common weren't necessarily the fictional ones Quinn referred to.

This could be interesting. Quinn still wished he'd been able to get Kristine out of it.

But he recognized that the upcoming session would probably not even occur if it weren't for her.

"Sounds good to me," he finally said.

The coffee shop they headed for wasn't part of a big chain—not in this quaint, tourist-filled town. Even so, it resembled the kinds Kristine was used to, with a large counter along one wall where baristas fixed drinks, and tables everywhere else that were already filled with chatting patrons.

As they stood in line, the aroma of delicious coffee filled the air. Kristine knew that Quinn, with his exaggeratedly canine senses, could enjoy the scents even more than she did. She might even ask him...later.

Right now, she was still irritated at his blatant attempt to get her to bug off. Maybe he'd done it to increase the possibility of male bonding, but that wasn't likely. The chilly DoD guy wasn't about to become so friendly that he'd spill his guts and tell Quinn everything he wanted to know.

Or maybe Quinn considered this fed dangerous and had tried to protect her. If so, that was sweet, but unnecessary. She'd been in the military a lot longer than he had. She could protect herself...and him.

And if this Kelly didn't have the best interests of the military—especially a certain covert unit—in mind, but only some absurd government protocol? Well, all the more reason for Kristine to play him and learn what he was all about.

For now, the three of them stood silently, as if saving up all their questions and deviousness for when they were seated. Was Kelly's cohort here yet? Apparently so. Their skinny companion nodded toward a solitary African-American guy at a round table.

That fellow was dressed in similar nondescript clothing, and although he appeared shorter and thicker than Kelly, his face was equally sharp and expressionless.

Kristine ordered a medium-size mocha. She deserved the chocolate kick. They were no doubt about to engage in a verbal battle exercise.

Both men unsurprisingly ordered plain brewed coffee. Quinn insisted on paying for them all, successful pseudo–retail manager that he was. In a few minutes, they joined Kelly's buddy at the table. It was surrounded by others filled with people either talking or working on laptops or tablets. The place was noisy—a good way to keep somewhat confidential anything they might say.

"This is Don Holt," Kelly said, as they all took seats. "We work together."

"In the Department of Defense." Kristine tried to sound excited, to maintain her cover persona.

"We're within the Defense Special Projects Agency," Kelly said. That didn't explain much—although it resonated with Kristine, since she'd met someone else in that agency recently.

"What kinds of special projects?" she pressed.

"The kinds around here," said Holt. His dark cheeks were puffier than his comrade's, his hairline farther back on his forehead, but the similar expression in his analytical gaze suggested that Special

Projects taught its members to scrutinize deeply as they sought verbal answers.

Quinn laughed jovially. "Okay, guess we're just going to talk in circles, right?" He didn't wait for a reply. "The thing is, no one around here appears ready to assure us that whatever happened to those other tourists won't happen again. How far are you in your investigation? Do you know what kind of animal killed those people? Is it somewhere in your radar so you can prevent it the next time?"

Kelly and Holt glanced at each other, neither responding. Then Kelly took a sip of his coffee. "Let me ask you something, Mr.—Scott, is it?"

Quinn nodded.

"Who are you, really?" Kelly's eyes rolled coldly from Kristine and back to Quinn.

"We're the Scotts," Kristine responded, making herself sound surprised. "We're here on our honeymoon, and my husband is determined to protect me. We heard that there was at least one other pair of honeymooners here last week, but they weren't the ones who were killed. I'd love to talk to them. Maybe they can reassure us about what happened. I don't suppose you know who they are, do you, or where we could contact them?"

"You two are filled with questions, aren't you?" Holt's tone suggested that he hated questions.

"You want answers? Then answer ours first. Who are you?"

Quinn's laugh did not sound humorous. "Are we at some kind of impasse? My wife did answer your question. What'll it take for you to answer at least some of ours?"

"The truth, maybe," Kelly said. "Let me ask something else that'll break what you call an impasse. Either of you know anything about something called Alpha Force?"

With effort, Kristine kept herself from reacting. She shouldn't have been surprised. These guys were from the Department of Defense. DSPA Team Leader Darren Olivante, who'd been at Ft. Lukman just days ago, knew of the existence of Alpha Force, its covert nature—and the special qualities of many of its members.

If these guys were here to conduct the official federal investigation, it wasn't surprising to learn they'd been briefed about Alpha Force. But how much did they know about it?

And did they know that Quinn and she were with the unit?

What, really, was their agenda?

"No, I've never heard of it," Quinn lied. "Are you two members?"

"Nope," Kelly said. "Are you?"

Kristine laughed. "This is getting silly. What are we talking about here? What is Alpha Force?"

"You tell us," Holt countered.

Kristine picked up her purse, which she'd put on the floor at her side. "This all is too squirrelly. I don't know what you're talking about. Do you think this Alpha Force has something to do with what happened here and the killing of the tourists? If so, please explain or we're leaving."

"Hang on," Kelly said. "We're here searching for evidence of what really happened." He actually sounded for the first time as if he was telling the truth. Plus, the icy hardness of his expression had turned into something resembling frustration. "We weren't told much, only that the two honeymooners were part of a unit called Alpha Force and might have something to do with the killings. The tourists were apparently mauled by some wild animals, and that's the story we were assigned to check out. If you have anything you can pass along to help us, let us know. The local cops sure aren't helping. They apparently resent our interference. Some even hang out at the crime scene at night and watch for wild animals, but I gather they've not been especially successful. So..."

He looked at Quinn rather than at his partner, which was probably a good thing for him. Holt was glaring daggers at him. But was that an act?

"You've been asking too many questions to be just honeymooners trying to stay safe," he continued. "What's your real role in this?"

A pause. Kristine considered how best to respond, but Quinn beat her to it. "Okay. You've leveled with us. I'll tell you the truth."

Shocked, Kristine almost stood and grabbed him. He wouldn't—couldn't—reveal their affiliation with Alpha Force, especially to the official investigators.

Would he?

"I'm a private investigator," Quinn continued. "Like you, I'm on an assignment here because those two honeymooners have apparently disappeared. I'm trying to find out if whatever killed the tourists whose bodies were found got them, too. But right now, no one seems to be cooperating in my investigation, either. You want to work together, share information?"

Chapter 10

Quinn wasn't surprised that the response was negative. "We're conducting our own investigation." Kelly's growl suggested how much regard he had for private investigators.

"Figured," Quinn said. "But if you don't cooperate with me, I sure as hell won't share anything I learn with you."

Not that he would have, anyway—not without some pretty heavy editing.

He didn't look at Kristine, still beside him at the table. Even so, he could see the way she clenched her paper coffee cup in her slender fingers. She probably wanted to lace them around his throat and strangle him. He'd do the same thing if their positions were reversed.

He didn't look forward to their upcoming discussion, but he'd done what was necessary, at least for now.

He glanced idly toward Kelly, then Holt. Neither appeared upset by his attitude. They apparently didn't think whatever he might find would be of use to them.

But what Kelly said next made it clear Quinn's assumption had been wrong.

"Fair enough," Kelly said. "Time for us to go. Oh, and incidentally, if you don't want a federal warrant issued against you, you'd better stay out of our way."

Quinn was glad that Kristine remained silent as the two men rose then maneuvered their way among the busy tables to the door.

"What was that all about?" she hissed then. "Why on earth did you blow our cover and tell them you're a P.I.?"

"Just playing the same game they are—for now." He rose quickly. "Come on."

"Where?"

"We're going to reassume our nice, comfy honeymooner cover to the rest of the world and go outside to play tourists. Or that's what I want those two asses to think. They're playing games, and so are we."

She stood and followed him as he, too, exited the coffee shop. "I don't—"

"You don't need to. Just figure what they'll assume if they believe I'm a P.I. They'll expect us to follow them, now that they've left."

"We *are* following them." She sounded utterly exasperated. "Aren't we?"

"Yes, because we want to see where they lead us. It'll be where they want us to go, not where they're really heading. But that'll tell us something, too."

They were outside in the sunlight now. The sidewalk was, as usual, crowded with tourists. He looked down at Kristine. Her gorgeous blue eyes radiated fury, and her chin was raised obstinately.

He wanted to kiss her—to confuse her even more. Not to mention what it would do to him and his body that was already so highly aware of her presence.

Later, he told himself. He'd been acting with admirable restraint around this sexy and frustrating woman. Maybe it was time to ease some of those aches. Soon.

For now, he glanced around—and saw the backs of the two DSPA guys heading down the sidewalk toward the harbor.

He surmised they ultimately intended to break away and head inland. Maybe back into the park.

He grabbed Kristine's hand and maneuvered them both through the crowd of tourists. They'd play these men's game.

For now.

But they had no idea who they were really dealing with. Stalking prey was second nature to him—in either of his forms.

Kristine heard the perverse logic in Quinn's words. She wanted to laugh at the same time she knew she should be snapping at him, giving him orders even though he held the superior military rank.

Neither was acting like a soldier now anyway. That bothered her, but it was how things had to be at the moment, for them to succeed.

But who—the two DSPA guys or them—held more information about the killings and the disappearance of Simon and Grace? Since Quinn and she had so little information, it was probably the others. It made sense, then, to let them think they were prevailing.

Not that Quinn and she would let them.

"Okay," she said. "What do we do now?"

"First, we wait till they discover the tiny tracking device I planted in our buddy Kelly's pocket. They're no doubt aware of it—particularly since I've already located the one they planted on me."

"What!" Kristine shoved her hands into her own jeans pockets. Finding nothing except the usual tissues and card key for their hotel room, she lifted her purse and examined the moderate-size brown leather bag. "Should I dump everything out?"

"Soon," he said. "Meantime, I'll make use of my own secret weapon. My bro Simon isn't the only creative one in our family."

"What do you mean?"

"They aren't shifters." He stopped to let a mother holding the hands of two kids maneuver around them on the sidewalk, then grabbed Kristine's hand again and pulled her forward after the two escaping men. "Neither reacted to what I also attached to them via the coffee cups they held. As a real P.I. before my oh-so-brief military days, I invented a cream that when touched, instills people with a scent that can't be washed off for days—and that also can't be picked up by other people without enhanced senses like shifters."

"Then you can smell where these guys are going?" Despite her sense of repugnance, Kristine was impressed.

"As long as I stay on their trail, I can remain as much as a quarter of a mile behind and still sense them," he acknowledged.

"Even while you're not shifted?"

"I still have better senses than you ordinary humans," he said. She knew he phrased it that way to goad her.

But she just laughed.

* * *

Quinn loved it—the sound of her laugh. The light, carefree expression on her face. It was all he could do not to grab Kristine right there and kiss those full, smiling lips.

But once again, he called up all the restraint he could muster. He had a scent trail to follow, and couldn't let it get too distant. Right now, those guys expected them to follow. Later, it could become more of a challenge.

But by that time, it might be nightfall—when it was easier to conceal a wild animal.

Quinn intended to shift tonight to follow these guys.

He needed more answers—ones that they might have.

It was fascinating, Kristine thought, to hang out with a werewolf in human form. Especially one with a mission.

She'd thought so when she first joined Alpha Force, and the feeling had never waned.

Now, Quinn and she ended up for a while at the Bar Harbor Historical Society Museum, in a charming old redbrick house. That was where the two men they tailed had headed. They knew that thanks to the tracking device Quinn had hidden on Kelly.

Kelly and Holt left without it, though. Kristine

saw them leave from one of the museum's windows, while Quinn retrieved his tiny gadget from one of the displays where Kelly had apparently dumped it. The men must have determined they'd been followed far enough and decided to leave their trackers here.

That wasn't going to happen, though. Holding her hand, as he did so often on this assignment, Quinn led Kristine out of a different exit from the one the men had used. They hung back among the meandering crowds on the nearby sidewalks, in case their quarry spotted them, again indulging in their cover story as a happy sightseeing couple.

All the while, though, Quinn was tracking the men his way. Kristine could tell, from the intense expression on his face, and the way his nose wrinkled periodically, that he was using his special senses to follow the scent trail he had created, which the two men now left behind for him as they continued walking through town.

That way, Quinn and she could hang back and not be so obvious to them.

It should have been a huge turn-off to Kristine, seeing a man act so wolfen and sniff the air that way—although he did act unobtrusive when he glanced up, as if studying their surroundings, toward rooftops or the sky, while capturing scents.

But Quinn's expressions looked strangely alluring. His intensity was even sexy. She couldn't understand her own sexually heightened reactions... yet there they were anyhow.

On Quinn's okay, Kristine had checked her purse for another device. Fortunately, there wasn't one.

After nearly an hour of their cat-and-mouse game—rather, canine-and-prey—Kristine was interested to see that the men ended up at Harbor Heights, one of the most elite older hotels in the town. It was several stories high, painted white, lots of gables and towers.

The valets outside wore formal black uniforms, and the well-dressed people they assisted into cabs seemed to tip generously, judging by the obsequiousness of the staff.

The feds' expense accounts must be generous, too, Kristine thought—no doubt thanks to the taxpayers.

The guys went to the parking lot, though, rather than heading inside. There, they got into a black SUV and drove away.

"Damn," Quinn muttered.

"Let's see if we can find out if this is where they're staying," Kristine said.

He smiled at her. "If so, they'll be back."

They walked inside together as if they were staying there, and Kristine picked up a brochure from a table in the lobby. The hotel's phone number was on it. Outside again, Quinn grabbed his phone from his pocket and called, asking for Mr. Kelly.

"That's his last name?" Kristine questioned.

It was—or at least they had a Mr. Kelly staying there in the same room as a Mr. Holt. Unsurprisingly, neither answered the phone in their room.

Fortunately, the place had a nice restaurant. Quinn led Kristine inside, asking the model-perfect hostess to seat them near the window facing the parking lot.

Kristine hated to waste time here. But she understood Quinn's intentions. So far, they hadn't found any useful clues into what had happened to the mauled tourists, or where Grace and Simon might be.

The feds, with their official assignment, might have more information. They weren't sharing... at least not intentionally. But spending a day tailing them might be a lot more useful than spinning wheels trying to drum up leads in their frustrating investigation.

Quinn and Kristine took their time in the restaurant, which was surprisingly crowded considering how late the afternoon had become. They ate from china plates on a pristine white tablecloth—a roast beef sandwich for Quinn, a salad for Kristine. The servers hovered and offered more coffee, water, condiments and whatever else they might want.

The food was predictably good. The company was even better, despite how uneasy Kristine felt as they gazed into each other's eyes. It was just part of their cover story, she kept reminding herself. He wasn't really interested in her. His gold-tinged gaze wasn't actually intended to tear her clothes off.

Too bad... Or maybe it was a really good thing they were out in public this way.

Eventually, they finished eating. Kristine wondered how much longer they could hang out at the table just sipping drinks. At least there wasn't a line at the restaurant door.

Then, there it was. The same black SUV pulled into the parking lot.

Quinn saw it the same time she did. "Time for us to go."

Quinn had Kristine keep an eye on their quarry as they passed through the lobby. There were plenty of people around, so she'd stay safe. There were also enough nooks and crannies for her to hide and not be spotted.

She came outside a minute later. "They went up in the elevator," she said, stopping beside him in the parking lot that was nearly filled with cars but almost devoid of people.

"Good. I've planted another tracking device on their car now. One that's hard to detect. We'll know next time when they leave and be able to figure out where they go."

"Do you really think they know where Grace and Simon are, and that they'll lead us there?"

"I don't know what they know," he responded grimly, taking her hand again and pulling her swiftly away. He also didn't know where their room was...yet. They might have a window through which they could observe this parking lot.

"Whatever it is, though," he continued, "I suspect it's more than we've got. Maybe this'll be another dead end, but we'll at least have given it a try."

Since the feds didn't seem to be going anywhere just then, Kristine wasn't surprised when Quinn suggested that they return to their original plan. So, once again, they walked back through town, entering tourist information sites, asking questions of both workers there and patrons about what things newlyweds should see—and, oh, by the way, had they met other newlyweds lately who praised one sight or another?

Slow. Stupid. But without any hot leads, at least it was something.

Too bad that the next full moon wouldn't occur for a few weeks. At least then they'd have a better chance of finding Simon and Grace, since no matter what, they'd be shifting.

Assuming they were still here…and also assuming they were still alive.

Kristine and Quinn wandered around for another couple of hours looking lovey-dovey at one another and asking questions. Eventually, it was dusk. They discussed going to a local bar to continue their questioning. And then—

"Hey," Quinn said in a low voice, grabbing his smartphone from his pocket and looking at its screen. "Our guys? They're on the move…and they're heading into the park."

Kristine and he had hurried back to their hotel. She'd grabbed her already filled backpack, and then they'd dashed back down to their rental car.

The feds' car was stopped somewhere within the park, probably close to where the tourists had been killed. Had they found something?

Time to find out.

Quinn drove back into the park via one of the main roads from Bar Harbor, heading toward the parking area where he believed the men had stopped—at the base of Cadillac Mountain.

Unsurprisingly, their car was there. Not many others were, now that it was almost dark.

A good time for him.

He parked. "Got your backpack?" he asked Kristine.

"Yeah, but are you sure this is a good idea?"

"You mean, could it be some kind of trap? With luck, they won't be suspecting a wolf even if it is. Either way, I'll be careful."

She looked skeptical, but they both exited the car. No other people were in the parking lot—not even their prey. Together, Kristine and he walked off the paving and well into the wooded area.

There, he got the vial of shifting tonic from her, then started removing his clothes.

He hadn't wanted to admit it to her, but he did feel a little uneasy this time. He didn't even try to tease her with his naked body.

Soon, he was ready. She regarded him grimly, without her usual discomfort about his nudity. "Be careful," she said, then turned on the light.

On his four strong legs, he walked deeper into the forest, upward along the mountainside, muzzle in the air.

Yes, he smelled the scent he had planted on the men he sought. It was not very strong here, so they must have gone even farther.

The site where the tourists were killed was not far away, although it was on the other side of the same mountain. Perhaps that was their goal. Were they searching it from a different angle, hoping to find more leads about the beasts that had attacked?

If so, they would indeed be hunting at least one beast, which might even have resembled him.

He would be extra cautious.

He moved slowly, slinking in the direction the scent led him, careful not to make any sounds that would reveal his presence.

In this area, there were no trails for humans. The forest was pristine, untouched by people, smelling lush with undergrowth and trees, and the wildlife that actually lived here.

He wished he could explore it more. But not now.

No sounds of voices in the distance this time. The cops must not be there this night, awaiting wild animals that never came. What triggered their presence? Or had they simply stopped coming to the crime scene after their stalking had yielded nothing?

The smell suddenly changed, grew stronger, as if the men were doubling back toward him and their vehicle. Just in case, he dashed behind a tree to watch. He saw them run by, in the direction of the parking lot.

"Their car's there," shouted a voice. "Someone's inside. They followed us, like we figured. Now we'll get them—and the truth!"

Kristine!

Quinn's thin but strong wolf legs tightened as he began to run.

Chapter 11

Chapter 11

Kristine noticed a movement at the edge of the parking lot. Quinn? What was he doing back here so soon?

No—she saw the two feds emerge from the forest.

That worried her. Where was Quinn? Was he all right? Had these two harmed him?

Not much time had passed since Quinn had stalked off in wolf form to look for them. Even so…

Grabbing her backpack again from the rear seat, she quickly exited the car to face them.

The light here was dim, mostly from the gleaming but waning moon that hung above in the sky. Staying beside the front door on the passenger side,

Kristine stood straight, watching as the men approached. She was very aware of the hooting of nearby owls and the skittering on the dried leaves on the forest floor of whatever rodents or other night creatures that might be there. No other noises, besides the men's footsteps, interrupted the nighttime silence.

No wolf howls, or even softer sounds that could be a canine on the prowl.

"Hello, Mrs. Scott." Kelly, dressed all in black from his long-sleeved sweater to his pants and low-topped boots, stopped only a few feet from her. His dark hair even appeared to be part of his nighttime disguise, although his skin was pale and he had used no makeup on his face or hands to enable him to blend fully into the darkness. Even so, of the two men, he was the taller, thinner—and more menacing.

"Hello, Mr. Kelly," she responded coolly. "Mr. Holt. What brings you to this part of Acadia in the middle of the night?"

"The question should be what brings *you* here?" The tone of Holt's voice suggested that his hostility was as vast as the forest looming around them. He wore dark clothes similar to Kelly's and blended into the night even better with the deep tone of his skin.

Kristine, too, had thrown on a charcoal jacket and

dark jeans that she'd kept in the car, just in case. She had tucked her short black hair into an even darker knit cap. But she hadn't anticipated having to hide—unless Quinn needed her to do something to help him avoid these men while in wolf form.

Again, she wondered where he was. Worried about him. How had these men returned without Quinn being right on their tails?

But maybe he really was nearby, in the forest. Watching, in his wolf form, in case she was the one who needed help.

She couldn't count on that.

"I thought I made it clear," she said. "No matter what the rest of you are doing here, I'm just sightseeing. I wanted to see the park at night. But you—are you here as part of your investigation of what happened to those people who got killed in the park?"

"Stop playing games." Holt's voice was sharp. Though he was the shorter and heavier of the two men, he now vied with Kelly for being the more ominous. He took a step toward her.

She immediately grabbed what she needed from her backpack and aimed it at them. A camera.

She started shooting pictures of the men, hopefully making it obvious that what she held wasn't threatening—at least not in a life-threatening sense. She hoped to blind them temporarily with the flash.

Even more, she wanted to make it clear that she now would have evidence of who they were, if they had hurt Quinn. Allies or not, disclosing or not, they all worked for the government and shouldn't harm one another—physically, at least.

"Hey! What the hell are you doing?" Kelly grabbed her arm, nearly making her drop the camera—but she tightened her grip.

"Pretty obvious, isn't it?"

"Look, bitch," Holt said from beside her. He was leaning against the rear of the car. "We don't know who you really are. Your boyfriend, either. No one named Quinn Scott that we found in searches on our usual sites fits his profile. We have our suspicions, though. Is he really a private investigator? If so, who's his client—and what do you have to do with all this?"

"And where the hell is he?" Kelly demanded. "I doubt you'd have come all the way here without him. Is he somewhere in the woods? We think you're with Alpha Force, and we know what some of the claims are about its real nature—although we don't believe them. It's some kind of ruse, right?"

Kristine translated in her mind. They must know—through official channels or not—that Alpha Force was allegedly composed of shapeshifters, at least in part. That was most likely what they didn't believe, which was probably a good thing.

But had someone told them about the unofficial investigation Quinn and she were conducting here? It sounded that way. If so, who?

"I don't know what you're talking about," she lied. She thought fast. She wasn't about to divulge any part of the truth about Quinn and her, even though these men might know it anyway. Was there some way she could pretend to ally herself with them, to get them to divulge whatever they knew so far about the killings—and the disappearance of Grace and Simon? "Look, maybe it's a good thing that Quinn had an upset stomach tonight. He's off in the woods around here somewhere, puking, I think. He doesn't know much yet about what happened to those tourists, but maybe you and I can make a deal. I'll let you in on what he finds out, if you tell me what you've learned, too."

"Why?" Holt demanded. "You claiming to be a P.I., too?"

She laughed. "Not yet. I'm trying to learn from Quinn, that's all. I hope to get a license someday, sure, but if I can outshine him here his bosses at the agency will move me up all the faster." Did this make any sense to them? It didn't entirely to her, but if it happened to work…

"Sounds possible." Kelly's tone was too smooth all of a sudden. Had he bought into what she said, or did he only want her to think so? "So what does he know?"

"Not a lot so far." Kristine tried to made herself sound frustrated. "The people we've talked to seem full of speculations about wild animals and what kinds are around here these days—and some really weird, woo-woo stuff, too."

She threw that out to see if she got any reaction—which she did. Slightly. The men glanced at each other quickly, then turned their attention back on her.

"So you're not part of Alpha Force?" Kelly demanded.

"Me? You're the one who mentioned it, and that those honeymooners who disappeared might be members. But that's all I know."

"What has your boyfriend told you about it?" Holt countered. "Do you think he knows more than you do?"

She tried to send a suggestive look in their direction. "I don't know what he knows," she said. "When we're not out playing newlyweds to see what information we can get from the rest of the world… well, you know."

"You're playing newlyweds for real." Kristine didn't like Kelly's leer, but she'd asked for it.

"Something like that."

"Then, good. You know what I think?"

"What's that?" Kristine had a sudden feeling that she wasn't going to like whatever he said.

"I think you know a lot more than you're saying, and that your boyfriend does, too. It may be stuff that'll make our assignment here a bit easier—or not. But we'll find out. Won't we, Holt?"

They moved so fast that Kristine almost didn't anticipate it. Almost. But when Kelly grabbed her, she had already pulled something more useful than a camera out of her backpack: a Taser gun.

Before she could use it, though, Holt yanked it out of her grasp. "No way, bitch," he growled and aimed it toward her.

Quinn leaped out onto the pavement.

He had been watching from behind a nearby tree. He had wanted to act before. But if a wolf suddenly rushed out of the forest, they would assume at a minimum that they had found one of the animals that had killed the tourists.

Worse, with their knowledge—limited as it might be—about Alpha Force, he might not only make their job easier but confirm the true character of the covert military unit to feds who might not act in the force's best interests, only their own.

"What the hell?" Holt was clearly surprised by having canine teeth suddenly clamped around the arm that held the Taser. Maybe he actually didn't

suspect—or buy into—the true character of Alpha Force. Or maybe he simply hadn't suspected the nature of Quinn's involvement.

Quinn did not chomp down hard on the guy's sleeve-covered arm—just firmly enough to prevent Holt from using the gun. He did not want the guy to be able to show off bite marks. But Quinn would do what he had to, to protect Kristine.

"Shoot the damned wolf," Kelly shouted. "Dog. Whatever."

Kelly had Kristine by both arms, using her as a shield as he drew closer. Quinn needed to rid himself of Holt—fast. He had to help Kristine.

Growling, he made a quick, strong worrying motion with his head, forcing Holt to drop the Taser. Then he moved away just enough to spring onto the man's chest with all his weight, knocking him to the ground, using his leverage to ensure that Holt's head hit the pavement. Hard. Quinn heard the crack, and Holt went limp.

He leaped off and turned to help Kristine. But she didn't need assistance. She was suddenly a gorgeous, merciless epitome of military self-defense maneuvers. Kelly must have known some of those moves, too, but the lightning flash that was Kristine allowed him no leverage. Her arms and legs beat at him—his chest, his throat, his genitals—her limbs curved and vicious and full of power that he hadn't recognized were possible in such a sexy, appealing woman.

It was soon over. Kelly had fallen—also striking his head, thanks to Kristine's obviously calculated moves. He now lay on the ground not far from Holt. Neither man was stirring.

"Are they alive?" Kristine asked casually. She bent down, touched their necks. "Yeah, I feel pulses on both of them." She looked toward Quinn. He wished he was in human form now. He wanted—badly—to kiss her.

As if she read his mind, she said, "You'd better work on shifting back pretty damned fast. I have to call 911, and the local cops are likely to get involved. They're going to want to know where my new husband is."

She knelt beside him, where he remained in wolf form, and buried her face in his neck.

"Thanks for being there," she said. "But we still need answers that these bozos might have been able to provide."

He couldn't tell her—now—that he agreed with her. He also could not say that he had an idea how to get at least some of those answers.

Nor could he tell her how relieved he was...or how much he admired her.

Wanted her.

Most important now, he did not want her to face the EMTs or the authorities alone.

It was definitely time for him to shift back.

She should have kept her eyes on the two men who still lay motionless on the ground. In fact, Kristine continued to watch them relatively carefully. And check on them a lot. Their heads, both of them, had struck the dirt hard. Enough to kill them? Nope. They were definitely still alive.

But enough to affect their memories, or at least their credibility? That could work out well.

Meanwhile, she couldn't help it. As Quinn shifted back to human form just outside the range of the men's vision, had they been conscious, and not far beyond the nearest copse of trees, she had to glance at him. Often.

To make sure he had no trouble with his change, she told herself righteously.

Yeah, sure, her conscience contradicted. She just wanted to see him nude again.

Which she did. Too bad there was nearly no light. She would have loved a better view. He was so damned sexy.

And he had helped, in wolf form, to save her. Those feds had clearly wanted to grab her, take her somewhere else. Had they done that with Grace and Simon? If not, had some of their cronies?

Kristine was a damned good soldier. She knew that. But hand-to-hand combat with two equally well-trained men might have had a bad result. One-on-one was better—and that's what it had been, thanks to Quinn.

There. He was done. She'd left his clothes on the ground near where he had shifted back and he was donning them now. Too bad.

Well, she had seen what she had hoped to. At least a little of it. Or maybe it was mostly her imagination, viewing a hint of the silhouette of his hard and sexy body in the skimpy light in the area. His sinewy, muscular limbs.

The lower part of his body. His thick, full sex... no, that had to be her anticipation this time. Her yearning for another glimpse.

But she was too far away, and this wasn't the place for that. If she was lucky—as she was likely to be, thanks to her role here both undercover and as his aide—she actually would get to see more. Soon.

He rejoined her at the edge of the parking lot, eyes on the men, who remained motionless. One of his arms went around her waist. To steady himself? She didn't think so. His body, against hers, felt very steady. Very substantial.

Very good.

"You called 911." He didn't make it a question. He'd been nearby when she'd done it, still in wolf form.

"Yes. The operator indicated it would take a little while for the EMTs to get here when I described where we were."

"Good. Let's hope it takes a few more minutes."

He let go of Kristine, leaving her feeling a bit bereft. Ridiculous. She didn't need to be near him. He still had a job to do, and so did she.

"I'll start with Kelly," Quinn said. "See if you can get Holt anywhere near conscious."

She knelt beside the prone body, touched his neck to ensure he still had a pulse, then turned him onto his back.

He groaned, a good sign. But how near to waking up he was she didn't know.

She glanced at Quinn. He'd moved Kelly nearby, and the man's legs moved as if he was awake and attempting to sit up.

"Hold it." Quinn grabbed Kelly by the shoulders. "Stay where you are. You're too weak to get up. Help is on the way."

Kelly's eyes opened. "You're here," he said unnecessarily.

"That's right," Quinn said, his tone grim. "I was nearby when you attacked Kristine. Good thing I wasn't any closer."

Of course he couldn't have gotten much closer—

but these men didn't need confirmation that the wolf who'd helped to fend them off had been Quinn... though they might suspect it.

They apparently had some knowledge of the nature of Alpha Force, even if they didn't believe it—or hadn't before. To the extent possible, they had to be convinced that what they'd thought they had experienced had not been anything woo-woo, just a regular fight that they'd lost.

"The dog that attacked Holt...was that you?" Kelly's voice was barely a whisper.

"Me? Are you nuts? And I didn't see any dog." But Quinn knew he wouldn't convince this man of anything. Not now. Kelly had immediately lost consciousness once more.

Quinn heard sirens in the distance.

Chapter 12

Quinn watched—and listened—every moment while the EMTs worked the men over and before they were whisked away in the ambulance. Nothing was said about Alpha Force or possible shape-shifters or even a dog attack.

Nothing was said about anything.

Since Quinn had been careful, while shifted, to keep his bite firm on Holt's sleeve but not break skin, there would be no evidence of anything other than the two men having gotten beaten up.

He whispered quickly to Kristine to follow his lead as Chief Al Crane approached. Apparently, they were about to undergo interrogation by the local authorities rather than a fed, despite the alleged attack occurring in a national park. Not that Quinn gave a damn. That would get sorted out later by whoever was in charge.

The chief scowled in the bright headlights from the police vehicle. Idly, Quinn wondered if the guy even knew how to smile.

"You two want to tell me what happened?"

"Not really," Kristine said lightly. "But I'll bet you'll ask anyway, so here it is."

Quinn got up close and touched her shoulder lightly, preferring that she stay quiet and follow his lead. He didn't want the two men arrested. He also didn't want Kristine or himself in custody. He had already come up with a plausible scenario that he intended to use as their explanation.

But Kristine wasn't about to listen to him. He almost grabbed her to shake her—but she was talking. And everyone listened to the apparently frightened but brave and beautiful woman.

"I was here in the parking lot by myself while my sweet Quinn here was off peeing in the bushes, and those two attacked me. I figured they were drunk. What they don't know is that someone attacked me a long time ago, too—when I was a kid—so I've taken a lot of self-defense classes. And when Quinn heard what was going on, he rushed out. I met him in one of my more recent self-defense classes, so he knew what to do, too. And, well—I guess we got

a bit rough under the circumstances. I'm fine, and
as long as those men don't try to make any claims
against us for hurting them, I just want to drop it all.
I won't press charges, or anything like that. Right,
darling?" Only then did she look at Quinn, a look
of utter innocence on her lovely face.

He wanted to laugh. To hug her. The story he'd
come up with wasn't nearly as good.

He'd have to visit those feds in the hospital whenever they were awake and ready to talk. Make sure
their descriptions about what happened were similar—or that Kristine and he laughed about anything
they didn't want anyone else to believe.

Plus, Kristine and he needed to get the men's real
story. Why the hell had they attacked her?

And what else could they tell him?

They'd also better cooperate and not press
charges against Kristine or him—or he'd do more
than make them look stupid to their superiors.

"That's just what happened," he confirmed when
Crane looked at him. "I don't think either of us
meant to be so rough—but those guys deserved
it. They should never have touched my wonderful wife."

Crane looked skeptical. No wonder. But he didn't
press them. Maybe he didn't give a damn, since,
whoever attacked whom, it was done in the feds'
jurisdiction.

On the other hand, where had the local cops been that night—the ones Quinn had seen previously at the crime scene? Had they given up, or convinced their superiors that hanging out there was useless? If they had been around, things would be quite different now.

"Right," Crane said. "Well, since you're claiming self-defense, I won't arrest you now, but I'll get their version from those guys. In any case, don't even think about leaving town soon."

"We understand," Kristine said.

In short order, the two of them were the only ones remaining in the parking lot—along with their car and the feds'.

"I'm wired," she said, "after all this. Adrenaline, I suppose. But I should sleep well tonight. How about you?"

She tilted her head as she looked up at him in the near-darkness, her mouth set in a quizzical line. Adrenaline or not, he just had to kiss this amazing, imaginative, brave—and fierce—woman.

He bent down, intending only to skim his lips over hers, but suddenly he was holding her tightly. Tasting her. He concentrated on the feel of her arms around him, the sweet, alluring taste of her tongue that teased his right back, her tangy personal scent edged with the aroma of the soap from their hotel room and the few cosmetics she used.

Then there was the scent of the heat that kiss generated. Not to mention how his body hardened, suddenly becoming one massive ache of need. He pulled her even more tightly against him, reveling in the feel of her rubbing right back.

The overhead fluttering of wings from some creature of the night startled him. Only slightly, but it was enough to make him soften the intensity of the kiss, and she backed away.

Touching her lips, she looked up at him once more. "I was just about to ask how you figured we'd get those feds to play along with our little story."

He laughed. "Your little story, you mean. It was a good one. We'll visit them in the hospital tomorrow to express our 'apologies'—and to let them in on what they have to say for us all to stay out of police custody. For now, though, let's head back to the hotel."

He opened the car door for Kristine, then went around and slid into the driver's seat. She had her personal smartphone out and was examining the screen.

"No messages. We'll need to talk to Major Connell tomorrow so he knows what's going on here. I'll send him a text now to let him know there are developments, and that he should speak with us before discussing anything with the general or anyone else."

"You're pretty smart, aren't you?" He grinned at her, then returned his concentration to the twisting mountain road.

"Could be. And…well, I'm obsessing a little, too. I do that sometimes. What I'm wondering is…do I taste okay to a guy with a wolf's senses?"

He blinked, feeling his already stiff body parts grow even harder. Was she really asking that?

And did it mean what he hoped it did?

Once more he glanced her way. She was staring at him with a gaze as heated as if she'd set the car interior on fire.

He had an urge to pull the car over immediately and prove to her how good she tasted to him. Instead, he kept driving, ramping up the speed as much as he could and still stay safe.

"I'll demonstrate later just how good you taste," he finally answered with a growl.

Oh, lord. Had she really asked that? It must be that her adrenaline rush from earlier, as she'd fought so hard to take control of a potentially catastrophic situation, hadn't left her body, even after she'd spewed a fairy tale to the cops.

Not when she had previously seen, or imagined she'd seen, the tantalizing highlights of Quinn's naked and sexy form in the distance.

And not when her own body's stimulation had been so enhanced by his kiss.

She admitted to herself now that she had wanted him every night since they'd gotten here.

No, she had wanted him from the moment she had first begun acting as his Alpha Force aide— and seen his hard, perfect body nude.

And now...now, she would have to wait until they reached their room, despite every bit of heat from her insides flowing downward, taunting her, making her ache with need for the man beside her.

Man? Oh, yes, he was that...and more.

They reached one of the main park roads, then finally drove away from Acadia and into the outskirts of Bar Harbor. How much longer until they got to their hotel?

They spoke now and then, cracking jokes about the DSPA investigators and how easy they'd been to knock the crap out of. Good thing to think about now. It kept her mind centered just a little.

Then there it was— the charming Victorian hotel where they were staying. Quinn parked. Kristine grabbed her backpack.

Soon they were inside, after swiping their card key to get in the front door at this hour. They used it in the elevator, too, to get to their floor.

At last, they were in their room. This time, when

Kristine looked at that solo queen-size bed in its center, it didn't make her feel uneasy or defensive.

Instead, it called to her.

She didn't remember setting her backpack down, but suddenly she was in Quinn's arms again. His embrace now felt familiar, but what awaited her was brand-new.

"Kristine," Quinn whispered into her ear, as his hands lifted the back of her shirt, caressed her skin, caused her to push against him even more from the front.

But she was still dressed. So was he. She stepped back, using one fluid motion to pull her shirt over her head. She looked at him, daring him to do the same. She still wore her bra, but even so she almost melted as he directed his heated gaze toward her bust.

"Your turn," she said huskily.

"I get a lot of practice doing this around here." His joke made her smile, but she bit her lip as she watched him remove first his own shirt, then his boots and jeans.

He didn't discard his underwear but it did little to hide his straining maleness. She wanted to touch him but knew what he would want first. She took off all her remaining clothes, then shot a challenging look in his direction.

They were both naked when, in seconds, Quinn

took her arm and pulled her against him. His skin was as hot, his body as hard as she had anticipated. As they kissed again, she grabbed his buttocks to pull him closer, reveling in the feel of his maleness against her belly, wanting to touch it, too.

One of his hands moved between them to caress her breasts, cupping them, teasing at her nipples until they hardened.

They were on the bed suddenly. His hands moved lower, lower, caressing her female center. She writhed, pushing herself against those fingers until they thrust gently inside her, making her gasp with pleasure and need.

At the same time, she touched his cock, absorbing its tantalizing hardness. She grasped it as she had longed to do before. As she had wanted to do from the very first time she had seen him naked, before he shifted.

Slowly, she stroked it, reveling in the way it seemed to harden even more within her grip. She almost grinned as she heard Quinn's intake of breath, followed by even deeper breathing. A growl, not feral—or at least not wolflike this time. No, this time it came from deep in his throat, sounding all turned-on human male.

"Please, Quinn," she whispered. But he didn't enter her. Instead, he began kissing her, breasts first, even as his caress didn't stray from her heat. Then his mouth moved lower to follow those hands....

His tongue stroked her erotically. Her writhing before had only been preliminary to this, as she bucked gently, encouraging his every touch and taunt with that talented tongue.

He moved away suddenly, making her moan with frustration. That's when she heard the sound of plastic. He pulled out a condom. Her breathing raspy and uneven, she smiled, then held out her hand. "Let me," she managed to say.

He did.

And then, at last, he plunged inside her. Her eyes were open, her gaze captured by his heavy-lidded look so sensual that it helped to multiply her inevitable pleasure below.

Her need rose to a crescendo beyond anything she had ever felt before. His steady rocking motion stimulated her to rise with each thrust until she catapulted over the edge into completion, even as she heard him moan and felt him arch and grow still.

"You okay?" It took Quinn a while before he could talk, but he managed those words as he collapsed onto the bed beside Kristine.

He kept one hand on her, though, moving to her luscious, full breasts, not wanting to lose contact.

Wanting to remember every inch of her skin, every moment of their incredible sexual encounter.

Wanting to experience it again—soon. Sometime after his energy was restored.

"I'm good. Real good. You?" He was gratified to hear that she was as out of breath as he.

"Yeah. We fit well together, Mrs. Scott."

She laughed breathlessly. "You said it, Mr. Scott." She snuggled closer without moving his hand from her chest, then rested her head against his shoulder. "I think I'll sleep well tonight. Better than I have since we got here."

"Don't count on it," he said.

He only woke her twice more that night.

Barely awake the next morning, Quinn felt Kristine stir. He reached for her, but she moved out of his range. In a moment, he heard her talking on the phone, and he opened his eyes.

Good thing she was on the military-issue satellite phone and not on Skype or some other way of allowing people on both ends of a remote conversation to see one another. Even though her back was to him as she sat on the edge of the bed, Quinn absorbed one heck of a sexy view of Kristine, naked.

His body immediately woke up. But he realized at once who she was talking to and kept still.

"Yes, sir. Those guys attacked me—apparently

wanted to take me off somewhere else for interrogation…or something. Quinn was shifted at the time, in the forest, so they must have thought I was alone—or at least alone enough for them to take control of me."

"She did a hell of a job of showing them otherwise," Quinn called into the phone from over her shoulder.

She turned, and the movement put her lips within inches of his. But he restrained himself. Even if the major couldn't see them, he might, with his own enhanced senses, be able to make out the sounds of a kiss.

"Quinn did great, too, sir," Kristine put in. "Even though he was shifted, he made sure the one named Holt couldn't taze me, then he knocked the guy unconscious. Didn't leave any bite marks. I'm not sure what those guys'll say about the possible attack by a wolf, but with luck and the way we handled them, I suspect they'll doubt their own recollections."

She spoke for a couple minutes longer, then handed her phone to Quinn.

"I don't like what happened," Drew Connell told him, "though it sounds like you both dealt with it as well as possible under the circumstances. But go see those guys today, like Kristine said. Then report again to me. Something's off—way off. I'll inform General Yarrow and see what we can learn from here, but if there's any way of extracting information from those DSPA guys—without beating them up any more, especially now that the cops'll keep an even closer eye on this—I want you to do it. You and Kristine."

"Yes, sir." Quinn flipped the phone closed and handed it to Kristine. "He wants—"

"I know what the major wants." She smiled grimly as she shook her head. "He wants Simon and Grace found and this unofficial assignment over with. You know what?"

"He's not alone," Quinn responded. And as soon as Kristine had put the phone back on the bedside table, he reached for her.

It was time to move their minds—and bodies—in a much different direction. After all, it was still too early to accomplish anything else that day.

As Quinn lowered his body over Kristine's warm, willing and inviting one and kissed her full, smiling lips as his hands started a new encounter with the taut, sexy body he wanted to memorize, he figured this was a heck of a way to start what promised to be an eventful day.

Chapter 13

The men were both in the same room at Mount Desert Island Hospital. That was one good thing, Kristine thought, as Quinn and she walked down the sterile-looking hallway past other rooms filled with patients and their visiting friends and family members.

Another good thing was that the police hadn't restricted them from having visitors. That didn't mean they weren't under surveillance, so Quinn and she would have to be careful.

No one was obviously watching, nor standing guard outside their door, so Quinn and she entered.

Both men were lying in their beds tucked under sheets, with only the tops of their ugly, shapeless hospital gowns showing.

"Wondered if you were coming today to try to fix things with us," Kelly growled, twisting slightly to face the door. "Don't bother. We've already called in a preliminary report. In case it makes you happy, though, the doctors here want to keep us both here at least another day for observation. Guess they like to do that for concussions. So, thanks for that." His tone was clearly sarcastic.

"To the contrary, you owe me an apology." Kristine kept her voice cool. "And you need to report what really happened."

Quinn and she had already talked over how to handle this, and they would use an Alpha Force version of "good cop/bad cop." She had wanted to play the role of the baddy, but Quinn had convinced her otherwise. He couldn't flirt with them to get them to roll over and tell the truth—or at least some version of it—if threats didn't work.

"I'd really like to understand why you attacked me," she continued, trying to sound as if their actions hurt her to the core.

"So would I," Quinn growled. "Do you two thugs always attack ladies who happen to be alone in remote areas at night? Bet your superiors at your Department of Defense agency would love to hear all about that. Did you include that in your preliminary report?"

"Let me handle this," Kristine said sweetly to

Quinn. Then, to Kelly, she said, "I hate when Quinn gets all pissy and threatening. But he's not always easy for me to control."

"Why? Because he's not a P.I. but a member of Alpha Force?" Kelly's smile would have been snide, except that it apparently hurt him and he winced. "We've substantiated that."

"What do you know about Alpha Force?" Quinn demanded without either confirming or denying his involvement. "Or, what's more to the point, what do you think you know?"

Kristine sidled over to Holt's bed. He hadn't said anything, and he appeared zoned out as he lay there, as if he were under a lot heavier medication than Kelly.

Which could be a good thing. If he were less aware of what he was saying, maybe they could learn more from him.

"Holt, I really am sorry that you got hurt. But it's important that we understand why you attacked me. If you explain and it makes sense, I won't press charges."

"Can't tell you," he muttered.

Which made it all the more imperative that they get the truth from these guys, Kristine thought.

"And we're the ones who'll decide whether to press charges." Kelly sounded happy about the idea. "We're the ones who got our heads bashed in."

"Self-defense," countered Quinn. "You attacked Kristine first, and she fought back."

"But that wolf—" Holt said.

"What wolf?" Quinn demanded.

"The one that attacked me," Holt said. "Grabbed my wrist."

"You're kidding," Kristine said, planting an incredulous smile on her face.

"You know I'm not." Holt's shout made him wince and touch his head. He held out his arm. "It bit me here."

Kristine took his hand and looked at it, turned it over. "You're right," she said sarcastically. "Just look at all the bite marks."

Holt glanced down and grimaced. "Just because it didn't break my skin—"

"It would be more believable if either of us had seen it," Quinn countered. "But we didn't. Are you trying to capitalize on the fact that those tourists were attacked by something?"

"No, but—" Holt sounded confused now.

"What about the local cops?" Quinn continued pressing. "I've heard that some of them were keeping watch in the area of the attack on those tourists for a few nights. Did they see anything? In fact, maybe they were the ones who were around last night and set a dog on you that looked like a wolf, just for fun. Not while we were around, though, since we didn't see it."

Which didn't exactly make sense, Kristine knew, but she wasn't about to contradict Quinn.

"We knew they were sending observers to the park and told them to stop, that they didn't have jurisdiction. We didn't think they were listening to us, but we didn't see them last night. Just you."

"You sure?" Quinn demanded. "Maybe you ran them off first, before you decided to attack Kristine. I think we may ask them about that."

"No," Kelly repeated. "It was only you."

"You mean I'm the only one you attacked?" Kristine asked.

Even Kelly now looked as if his head was pounding in agony. "That's not what we were doing. But the fact that you were around the crime scene— we needed answers. About you and Alpha Force."

Kristine shared a glance with Quinn, willing him to let her continue this conversation. Fortunately, he did.

"You mentioned Alpha Force when we talked to you before," she told Kelly, "and now you've mentioned it again. Please tell us what it is. Are you members—is that it?" She faced Holt. "If so, what's its purpose? Is it why you came after me in the park?"

Holt looked even confused. "No, we're not the ones who're Alpha Force. You are—aren't you?"

"Enough of this," Kelly rasped from behind them.

Quinn took a step closer, as if he was about to give the guy a new concussion. Kristine slipped in front of him, nearer to the bed. She looked straight down into Kelly's obviously angry eyes.

"Look, Kelly," she said. "Tell us what you know about this supposed Alpha Force. If it was your excuse to attack me, I'd like to know. And—"

"And if you don't level with us, I'll make damned sure that whoever you work for at the Department of Defense knows how badly you screwed things up around here," Quinn interjected.

"You're the screw-up," Kelly said triumphantly despite the way his eyes shriveled with apparent pain. "No matter what, I'm gonna confirm in my report that you are Alpha Force. Don't try to deny it. You are—like those two folks who disappeared, right? The killers?"

"That's what you think?" Kristine wasn't really shocked, although she tried to make it sound that way. "And you believe we're somehow affiliated with them? Do you think we were involved with those killings?"

"Not you directly," Kelly said. "But your outfit—that damned Alpha Force, whatever it is. I've heard rumors..."

"Werewolves," piped up Holt in his low, confused voice.

Quinn laughed. "Really? That's what you think?"

"It would explain how those tourists were mauled to death. They were killed on the night of a full moon, for one thing." Kelly had fumbled with the switch on his bed and was now drawing up to a better sitting position. Apparently he wasn't drugged as much as his cohort. Which might be good for getting answers.

Or not, Kristine thought.

But whatever they thought they knew about Alpha Force, and shapeshifters—it couldn't be complete.

"Interesting theory," she said, letting scorn drift into her tone. "So you really think I'm affiliated with this Alpha Force, that I'm a werewolf or something, and you attacked me in the middle of the night? Why? Because you thought I'd turn into a wolf, even though it wasn't even a full moon? That's the supposed trigger, isn't it?" She hoped that whatever they believed, they hadn't heard of the shifting elixir.

Quinn was leaning against the wall near the door now, his arms folded and his expression snide. "These guys must have been on something even before they started getting good drugs in their IVs here."

"It doesn't make sense," Holt complained. "That's what I've said. It's just a cover story so they can act like terrorists, and—"

"Shut up, Holt," Kelly interrupted. "Look, we don't owe you any explanations. We—"

"But you do," Kristine countered. "You attacked me because you thought I was part of this group that pretends to have a woo-woo cover? But what is it that you're supposed to do even if you do find some members, if you're not affiliated with them?"

"Make 'em look bad," Kelly said. "Make *you* look bad, since we were already told you're part of that Alpha Force. Like I said, don't deny it."

"Who told you that?" Kristine demanded.

"Look, here's the deal. You're not pressing charges against us, and we won't make any complaints against you," Kelly said, apparently negotiating. "No talk outside this room about stupid stuff like werewolves, either."

"That's basically fine," Quinn agreed. "But I want more information first. Why are you supposed to make this Alpha Force look bad?"

"Orders," Kelly said.

"From who?" demanded Quinn.

"Wouldn't say even if I knew," Kelly responded. "But those two disappeared honeymooners were supposedly part of that outfit. We're here to figure out what really happened to the murdered tourists, and if we can tie it to those two missing people, all the better."

"Then where do you think those honeymooners are?" Quinn demanded. "Do you know? Did you attack Kristine because you thought she was getting close to them?"

"We don't know where they are," Kelly said. "Last we heard, they were spotted before the tourists were killed somewhere around one of Acadia's nature preserves. Around the Wild Gardens, I think. But they could have gone anywhere in the park. They had to have been there where the tourists died." He looked straight at Quinn. "Look, we were told that the two of you are part of that unit but you've gone rogue, looking into the killings yourselves against direct orders not to. We're supposed to figure out what really happened and at the same time make you look bad. That's all I know."

"But why?" Kristine asked. "And who told you to do that?"

And who knew they were countering direct orders besides Major Connell, who'd unofficially approved what they were up to?

"Like I said before—" Kelly now sounded exhausted, and he had collapsed back onto his raised bed "—I don't know where it came from. But now you know all I do. If you figure out who killed those damned tourists, let us know."

* * *

Before they left the hospital, Kristine had one more thing she wanted to do. Telling Quinn to keep his distance, she approached the nurses' station nearest the room they had just exited.

The golden-haired nurse behind the desk was named Bridget, according to the name tag pinned to the sweater over her white uniform.

"Hi," Kristine said. "My name is Kristine. I used to be a nurse before I got married and moved away."

She glanced behind her and shot Quinn a caring look. He didn't look happy, possibly because he wasn't pleased that she wasn't using a story fully conforming with their cover. But she had her reasons.

"I also—well, you might have heard that those two men attacked me, and I had to fight back, with some help. They said they both had concussions. Because of the situation, well...I know because of confidentiality that you can't say much, but do you think they'll be here awhile longer for observation? I never hurt anyone before, so I hope they'll be okay—especially since you never know if someone's going to sue because of claimed injuries. I'd also love to know how long they're likely to be here so I can watch out for them." She tried to look both rueful and upset.

The nurse frowned slightly, and her full cheeks

flattened a little. "I really shouldn't say," she said in a low voice, "but I don't think it'll hurt to let you know that it's the policy here to keep patients with possible concussions for at least a couple of days to try to ensure improvement. I did hear about what happened, and so did a lot of others on staff here. Glad you're okay, at least. You can always notify the authorities that you're worried when those guys are released. I'd imagine the cops will be keeping an eye on them, too."

"Thanks." Kristine beamed at the woman. "I really appreciate your help. I'm so worried about the situation, even though I did nothing wrong. It was self-defense on my part and—well, I'd be grateful if you'd try to keep them under observation as long as possible to make sure there's no permanent damage…and to keep me from having to worry about where they are."

Not that a nurse had much to do with treatment or length of stay, Kristine thought, as she finally walked out with Quinn. But doctors did sometimes listen when a nurse expressed concern. And Bridget had at least acted simpatico.

Maybe Quinn and she would know, at least for a while, where Kelly and Holt were.

Quinn drove their rental car out of the hospital parking lot into the nearest lane. As he turned onto

Main Street, the satellite phone rang. Kristine pulled it out of her purse and answered.

"What the hell is going on there?" demanded Maj. Drew Connell.

"What do you mean, sir?" Kristine asked. As Quinn glanced at her, he saw how wide her blue eyes were as she stared at the phone now lying on the dashboard between them. "We just spoke to those two DSPA operatives in the hospital and—"

"You'd better have gotten something good from them," the major interjected, his angry tone filling the entire rental car. "It's just been made very clear to me that your injuring them, putting them into the hospital, has jeopardized the entire operation. Even the ongoing viability of Alpha Force."

"But, sir," Kristine began, "like I told you, they attacked me. What I did was self-defense. Quinn was shifted, but what he did wasn't out of line. Since we knocked the guys unconscious, they're not pushing too hard with their claims that one of those they fought with was a wolf. I'm guessing they don't really believe in shapeshifters at all, let alone outside of a full moon. Plus, Quinn didn't hurt the guy he attacked any differently from the way a human would. So why is Alpha Force in trouble?"

Quinn wanted to interrupt with his own angry questions, but Kristine was doing fine...for now.

"Because it is," Drew responded. "Because we

were under orders not to get involved at all with the investigation of those tourist maulings, and I didn't discourage you from doing it on your own. I should have, though. I just got reamed by the general, and I'm on my way to D.C. now. He was called to a meeting at the Pentagon to discuss Alpha Force, what it really is and the involvement of its members in the ugly attacks that have occurred in Acadia recently—including the DSPA's own agents. He says there's more to it, too, that he can't reveal yet. But even more, there are additional ugly rumors that too many Alpha Force members have been acting way out of line."

"You mean like Simon and Grace supposedly did?" Quinn finally jumped into the conversation. "That's exactly why we were on those two DSPA guys. They acted like they're sure the honeymooners were responsible for the attacks on the civilians. They didn't seem entirely convinced about shapeshifting, though—a good thing. But I gathered that they may consider that just some kind of odd cover story to allow Alpha Force to engage in some terrorist acts without repercussions. What we need to do now—"

"What you need to do is back off," Drew said. "Immediately." His voice was lower, but the tone was unambiguous. They were under orders.

Quinn had continued driving when the conversation began. But as it progressed he had pulled into a grocery mart parking lot so he could concentrate on what was being said.

And counter it if necessary.

"I understand," he said, "but something is going on here that we haven't figured out yet. Maybe I'm just feeling paranoid as a new member of Alpha Force who hasn't even been assigned an official mission yet, but there are too many complaints about our unit—and too many people gunning for us who don't even know what we're about. Something about that seems very fishy to me. I thought that the military is more discreet than that, that *covert* means *covert*."

He glanced at Kristine. She didn't look happy.

"It has nothing to do with the military," she said, "but there appear to be a lot of people willing to believe that Simon and Grace—on their honeymoon, yet—decided to do something really nasty and kill people. Those with even a hint of knowledge about Alpha Force seem sure they grew violent while shifted, and others may think they simply mutilated the tourists to make people think wild animals did it. But no one has come up with a motive for them."

"No one has found them yet, either," Quinn added. He watched out the windshield as people pushed grocery carts past them. Hardly anyone glanced toward their car, which was a good thing. "But those DSPA guys—they gave us a possible clue when we were in their hospital room just now."

"What's that?" Drew demanded.

"They told us the last place anyone appears to have seen Simon and Grace—near a nature preserve within Acadia." Quinn paused, then continued, "We still have nearly three weeks until the next full moon, when they'll have to shift at least part of the time whether they want to or not, even if they've got some version of Simon's imperfect meds or the newest form of the Alpha Force elixir with them. In case they do, or there's some evidence still around, I want to check that area out while in wolf form and also look for any clues that people would miss. I plan to do it tonight."

Drew said nothing for a few seconds. "All right," he finally said. "I won't order you home immediately. But be careful. And report to me first thing in the morning—and right away if you find any sign of them."

"Yes, sir," Quinn said. Kristine echoed the words.

Quinn reached up to the dashboard and turned off the phone. He shook his head. "This kind of investigation is hard enough without—" He stopped, knowing that Kristine realized he was about to criticize the military again. Instead, he said, "Looks like tonight's going to be even more significant than we thought."

"And we already thought it would be critical," she replied. "Let's go somewhere private to discuss strategy."

They walked slowly near the brookside area, one of twelve habitats within the Wild Gardens of Acadia. Kristine had taken Quinn's hand and held on tightly—and not entirely to maintain their cover as newlyweds. She wondered if she needed to control him—or herself.

"They can't still be near here," Kristine said dejectedly. "Presumably, since the moon was full, they were shifted the night those tourists were killed, but they'd have changed back to human form by dawn. And if they had no elixir or other meds along—"

"They'd have stayed in human form," Quinn finished. He looked down at the park brochure he held in his other hand. "The Nature Center's just over there." He pointed to their right. "It's housed in a building, at least."

"And you don't think any of the park personnel would have noticed a couple of strangers hanging around there? Or wolves?" Kristine used sarcasm to hide the sadness—and hint of panic—that she had begun to feel.

"Who knows? My bro is a pretty resourceful guy, and I suspect his bride is, too."

"*That* resourceful?" Kristine demanded, even as they began walking in the direction of the Nature Center.

Quinn stopped. She looked up into his face as he planted himself in front of her on the path. "Look, I don't want to think they really had anything to do with killing those people. But if they did, and they needed to hide…well, yeah, they could be that resourceful. Otherwise…"

He tapered off, but Kristine finished the thought—something they had not even discussed. Hadn't wanted to discuss.

But one reason no one had seen her former boss and her new husband could be because they were off the radar altogether.

Dead.

And that was something Kristine could not accept. Not unless there was evidence.

She could only pray that, whatever Quinn learned around here tonight, it wasn't that.

A while later that afternoon, Quinn called the hospital. The DSPA men were still there.

The time was right, then. That night, she drove him back to the Wild Gardens and parked in the lot closest to that area and the nearby Nature

Center. There weren't many people around there at that hour.

It was time for him to shift again.

He was deep in the forest, beyond the multiple, diverse plant communities of the Wild Gardens. He crept slowly on his sensitive paws, his ears alert, his nose, too, taking in all the diverse scents around the area and searching for more.

He had hated to leave Kristine. The last time she was alone while he was shifted, she had been attacked. Those who attacked her remained in the hospital, but other people in their organization might be under orders to assist in the downfall of Alpha Force.

Finding anything tonight would be a long shot. But he had to at least attempt to take advantage of what those men had told him.

Was there any possibility that Simon and Grace remained in this area? It was more than a week ago when they had been spotted here, so Quinn knew how unlikely it was.

Even so...he began circling, still slowly, senses alert for all wildlife.

As before, there were nocturnal rodents. Birds. Even reptiles.

No wolves.

He waited, circling even more for long minutes

that turned into an hour, or so he believed. That night's moon wasn't so visible overhead any longer.

And still he scented and listened. And hoped.

More time passed. He had sensed no human presences save for Kristine—whom he checked on often as she remained locked in their vehicle. She seemed fine.

Nor did he sense any other canines in the area, not coyotes or wild dogs or anything else. Still, he continued to prowl.

Daylight would return soon. He would change back then, or earlier if he chose.

He moved further and farther from the area where he had begun his hopeful quest, continuing to circle, to try to sense any unusual presence. Any other wolf.

Finally, he could resist no longer. There had been no humans but Kristine around for hours. Only she would hear...

He sat on his haunches, lifted his muzzle in the air.

And howled.

Then, he listened. If there were other wolves around within their keen earshot, they would respond.

Nothing.

Not surprising, of course. Especially when he had no belief that his brother and his brother's bride would be shifted tonight, when the moon was far from being full and they were outside the aegis of their military unit.

But though he had found no indication of their having been here, he had also found no sign that they had died here.

He could maintain hope that they were still alive.

Chapter 14

What was Quinn doing? *How* was he doing?

From the car's driver's seat in the parking lot, surrounded by trees and the almost hidden walls of a couple of buildings, Kristine heard the howl of a wolf nearby. It had to be Quinn.

No responsive howls, though. Not that she had really expected to hear any, not even from any local coyotes or wild dogs. Even so, she was eager to see Quinn and make sure he was all right. And, as doubtful as it was, to hear if he had found any sign at all of Simon and Grace.

Kristine moved in her seat, peering out through the windshield. The parking lot near the Nature Center and other park visitor sites was illuminated only by the moon, which had begun to slip down below the top of the tree line. That meant she would be in darkness soon.

Of course she had come prepared for that—and more.

She was no fool. For one thing, she had kept fully alert as she sat in the car waiting for Quinn to return.

She kept the doors locked, too. Her cell phone was near her hand. Her Taser was still in her hotel room, this time.

But her military-issue weapon was right beneath her seat.

Sure, she could have let Quinn out of the vehicle, waited for him to shift, then driven off, planning to come back at daybreak for him.

That was what he'd told her to do, in fact, just before the sun went down. She'd be safer. But though his concern had turned her warm and fuzzy inside, she had kept her demeanor neutral. She had thanked him and left his clothes hidden behind a building, where he'd wanted them, but made no promises.

Within the last hour, she had seen the wolf that was him poke his nose into the parking lot every once in a while, in the moonlight, so she knew he was aware she remained there.

Fortunately, although the spring night was cool,

the fleece jacket she had brought was heavy enough to keep her warm. She felt comfortable.

She also felt alert. And concerned. What had that howl meant? Should she go see? Surely, Quinn was all right.

Before she could decide what to do, she saw headlights approaching along the road toward the parking lot. Rangers patrolling for security? Tourists arriving to see dawn in Acadia?

The car pulled onto the pavement nearby, and Kristine felt her blood start to freeze. The vehicle was much too familiar.

It was the one that had been driven by those DSPA guys.

So they were out of the hospital? That wasn't what they'd been told, but she shouldn't be surprised. Doctors didn't tend to keep people for long in hospitals. Kelly and Holt might still be in pain, but if they'd insisted on leaving and their physical condition was nonthreatening, they might have been released.

But what were they doing here?

Had they set Quinn and her up—again—by mentioning the area around this nature preserve?

Memories of their assailing her the last time made her consider turning on the engine to flee. But she'd come out of that okay. They hadn't. Would they really want to try again to harm her?

Of course, this time they'd be prepared.

Well, so was she.

She stuck her phone into her left pocket, then bent down for the gun beneath the seat. That would only be a last resort. Maybe the Taser would have been a better idea, but it hadn't done much good last time.

She placed the gun inside a tote bag she'd brought to look like a tourist. She picked up her camera, then slung the tote over her shoulder and exited the car.

She saw the men get out of their vehicle, too, and braced herself. Was this going to be friendly... or ugly?

Either way, she'd handle it.

First thing, she again took their photos. If things went south, at least there would be a record of this latest confrontation—as long as she managed to keep the camera safe.

"Hi," she called. "Didn't know you two were out of the hospital this fast. This looks a lot like the last situation. You planning on attacking me again?"

"No," Kelly said. He was wearing dark clothes once more, though, and managed to look menacing with his tall, rangy body and glaring hazel eyes. "To the contrary, are you planning on attacking us? Where's your buddy Quinn? Is he a wolf out there somewhere?"

Kristine laughed, taking one more picture of them. As she slipped the camera into her tote, she felt the reassuring cold metal of her gun. "That's a lot of questions. Here are my answers. No, I won't attack you but I will defend myself again if I have to. Quinn? He's been looking in this area for any sign of those honeymooners because you told him that they were last seen around here. And that wolf question? Weird. Even if you believe in those silly rumors you mentioned about Alpha Force, the moon's not full tonight."

"And I guess you would know if they're just rumors or a cover story." That was Holt. Both men had approached Kristine and now stood just a few feet away. She felt uneasy, especially since stocky Holt, also dressed in black once more, seemed to clench and unclench his fists at his side. Was he planning on attacking?

And what about Quinn? Had they come here after him? Had they found—and harmed—him?

No use thinking about that. He was okay. He had to be.

"So would you," she countered. "Weren't you briefed on what you were looking for as part of your mission here?"

"Yeah," Kelly said. "That's exactly it. We're looking for proof, one way or another, about the nature of that unit—and if those two members were involved in the killings, whatever shape they happened to be in. Like you, I guess, but our mission's official. We've checked again and had it confirmed that not only are you part of Alpha Force, but you're acting contrary to orders. You're not supposed to be in this area. So what are you doing here?"

Who confirmed it? And it wasn't exactly true, since their commanding officer had unofficially approved their presence—before, at least.

But that was not a question she wanted to answer. "Like we've said, we're vacationing," she said lightly.

"With Quinn, who claims still to be a P.I. and not a member of Alpha Force," Kelly scoffed. "And you came as honeymooners because—"

"Do I have to give you a detailed description of why we chose to use a cover—especially that one?" This was old territory.

"Maybe not." Kelly's leering gaze traveled up and down her body and Kristine wanted to throw up.

Instead, she pretended nonchalance. "I'd have thought that the two of you would be sleeping in your hotel rooms tonight, since you just got released from the hospital."

"Yeah, well, first thing, we looked again at the crime scene and saw the local cops were there again. Unofficially, of course, or so they claimed. Didn't stop to argue with them this time, but we'll talk to

them later. Tonight, we just couldn't resist checking things out after mentioning this area to you
and your supposed hubby, just in case you decided
to look for your buddies here tonight," Kelly said.

"Well, you were right about that, at least. We're
following up on all leads, no matter how remote.
Too bad there aren't werewolves. Maybe they could
help us. Only—oh, yeah. Like I said, it's not a full
moon."

"Right." Kelly's tone was scornful. He looked
around in the dim light. "So...where's Quinn?"

"He's looking around, too. We decided to split up
for a while. He and I can stop in at your hotel once
he gets back here."

"Oh, I think we'll wait."

That was exactly what Kristine didn't want. Not
that Quinn was likely to enter this area while still in
wolf form if he saw she had company—unless she
needed physical assistance once again—but still...

"Hey," called a familiar voice from the shadows
near the Nature Center. Quinn emerged onto the
pavement—a fully clothed man. "You guys feeling
okay now? What are you doing here?"

She hid her grin. He was all right.

And he was in human form.

Quinn approached. In the faint light that remained from the disappearing moon, Kristine met
his gaze. It was warm. And concerned.

"These two…gentlemen…were here hunting werewolves," Kristine said with a laugh. "They figured you were one of them."

"Interesting thought," Quinn said. He looked up into the black night sky and turned toward the only area of illumination. "That doesn't look like a full moon to me. So what legend are you buying into? It must not be the same as I've heard. For me to show up as a werewolf, how would I do it?"

Kelly's thin face appeared almost skeletal in the faint light, and his frown was apparent. "Good question. Did you find any clues about your fellow Alpha Forcers—I mean, honeymooners—out there?"

Now it was Quinn's turn to frown. "Unsurprisingly, there was no sign of the missing people." He didn't address their IDs this time. "Of course I was pretty sure that was just a story to get me out here. But why? You didn't attack either of us this time."

"Like you, we're trying all angles," Kelly said somewhat cryptically—but Kristine figured they might believe Quinn and she were somehow conspiring with the newlywed Parrans. If that was their rationale, though, it made no sense. Why would Quinn and she meet up with them here, in the area where the DSPA guys might be primed to look for them?

"Look, we could trade information," Quinn said.

"Even work together. If you have any idea of where they really are, I want to know."

"I'll bet you do," Holt countered. "But that's our official assignment—finding them. Not yours. Why don't you just go back to Ft. Lukman and start following orders like the good little military types you're supposed to be?"

"I think it's time for all of us to head for our hotels and go to bed," Kristine said. She grabbed Quinn's hand and started leading him to their car.

While remaining on alert, listening, in case those men decided to jump them from behind.

Quinn must have had the same idea since, despite his keener hearing, he turned without releasing her hand and stared at them. Kristine did the same.

They hadn't moved toward their vehicle but remained in the middle of the parking lot, watching Quinn and Kristine. Their expressions were similarly suspicious and adversarial.

Kristine wondered what they were thinking.

Whatever it was, she was afraid that their report to their superiors at the DSPA would not bode well for the longevity of Alpha Force.

"How long were they there?" Quinn demanded. He was in the passenger's seat of the car while Kristine drove them back to their hotel. He was exhausted. The quick shift back to human form had taken a lot out of him.

"They arrived only a short while before you did," Kristine said. They were about to pull onto one of the roads outside the park, and she looked over at him. "They said they'd seen some of the local cops back again—guess they figure whoever or whatever killed the tourists will return to the scene of the crime." She paused. "You look awful. Are you all right?"

He laughed. "Nice thing to say to your husband, dear. Or are we giving up on our cover story with everyone, not just those DSPA freaks?"

"Nope. We're still honeymooners." They were under a streetlight now, and her glance toward him was warm. No, hot. The way she pursed her lips and looked at him from beneath partly lowered eyelids…

"Sounds good to me," he said, smiling.

He was curious enough to consider asking Kristine to drive by the area where the tourists were killed to check up on the local cops and what they were up to, but figured they'd be long gone by then. Instead, he didn't comment on their destination.

He kept checking in the rearview mirror as she drove to their hotel, but he didn't see the DSPA guys' dark van. There were only a few vehicles at all out at this hour. Dawn was just starting to break.

Kristine finally pulled their car into the hotel parking lot. It was nearly full, but no one else appeared to be up and about. "You look beat," she told him after she'd parked.

"Oh, I'm awake enough." He unfastened his seat belt and leaned over.

The kiss they shared was hot. Her taste was tantalizing, her lips wide and open for his tongue to enter her mouth.

After a long, sensual interlude, she leaned back. "Let's go to bed," she said breathlessly.

"Yeah."

They hurried through the Victorian building and up the elevator, barely making it to their room and closing the door before Kristine began pulling at his shirt, his jeans, his shorts…and kissing him where it really mattered.

He managed to get them both to the bed, taking her clothes off on the way. "Late nights at Acadia turn you on?" he managed to say.

"Having you turn up as a human when I was damned worried about you…that turns me on," she said.

He climbed gently on top of her, then touched her. Stroked her hot, firm body all over, starting with those enticing full breasts of hers. Kissing them. Sucking them, even as she moaned—and grasped his cock with her steady, slowly pumping grip.

Then he stroked her down below, confirmed she was ready—more than ready for him.

And that was pretty much all they said for the rest of the night.

Quinn hated to keep his hands off Kristine for even a minute. But he'd fallen asleep, and when he awoke at the sound of some people talking in the hallway outside he glanced at the clock near the bed. Seven-thirty. A reasonable time to report in to Drew Connell.

He roused Kristine, who immediately sat up. She, too, checked the time. "He'll want to know what happened last night."

She placed the call from the satellite phone— after donning a thick hotel robe. "I don't understand what they're up to or what their orders really are, sir," she said to Major Connell. "They left the hospital faster than we believed they would, so maybe they were ordered to. They claim to know what Alpha Force is really about but still act like they don't believe it. They gave us information about where they'd supposedly last seen Grace and Simon, but now I think it was just a setup so they'd know where to find us last night."

"Did you see any sign of the Parrans?" Drew demanded. Quinn raised his head as Kristine glanced at him as if wanting him to respond.

"No, not even after prowling around a fairly extensive area in the park near where these guys claimed they'd actually been seen," Quinn said. "No scents or visuals, although—well, I did try testing them by howling." He didn't mention that the DoD guys had mentioned seeing cops again at the crime scene. If the cops had found anything this time, they would have had to report it, and that would have involved notifying the federal agency in charge.

A pause, as if the major was trying to decide if he liked what Quinn had said or intended to chew him out. "And?" he finally said.

"Nothing."

"That's too bad—since right now I have to insist that you stand down and obey my orders. Stop your investigation. I haven't had my official meeting at the Pentagon yet—that was postponed until later today—but I have talked to the general. I still won't insist that you return here, although I'm sure that'll come soon from him. He's defending Alpha Force to the max right now. We're running out of time and options. But I'll have his back at the meeting. I'll call you afterward, and we'll talk about what's next."

If anything. He didn't say that, but Quinn heard it anyhow.

And didn't like it.

"For now, though, I don't want you to do anything

but wait. Nothing. No looking around for our missing honeymooners, and definitely no further contact with those Department Special Projects guys. Sightseeing like real tourists is okay, but nothing else. Got it, both of you?"

"Yes, sir," Kristine said.

"I repeat, that's an order," Drew emphasized. "Stand down. You got that, Parran?"

Quinn wanted to argue. To tell the major what he really thought. What he really wanted to do.

But he was the major, and Quinn reported to him.

And there was more. They were both shifters. They hadn't discussed that part of their situation. Hadn't needed to.

As his commanding officer, Connell was also the tacit alpha of their pack.

No matter what Quinn thought of that idea. Or anything else about the military. At the moment, he believed his enlistment had been a mistake.

Quinn exchanged glances with Kristine as she hung up. He had a strong hunch that their outing as honeymooners was about to come to a screeching halt. They'd have to return to Ft. Lukman as failures.

Worse, his bro would still be missing with his bride.

Twiddling his thumbs wasn't in Quinn's nature.

But using up some time in having hot, memorable sex—

When they hung up from talking to the major, he caressed Kristine once more. Maybe for the last time, if what he feared was true.

They might as well enjoy it while they could.

It was midmorning before Kristine awoke again. Quinn lay sound asleep at her side. He was mostly under the covers, but she could see his gorgeous, masculine face with its sharp features now enhanced by dark stubble. His broad shoulders, too, peeked from beneath the sheet, and she held herself still to keep from touching him.

He undoubtedly was exhausted after last night— and not just because of his shifting.

They'd made love a few times, not a record but a lot, considering the early morning hour when they'd gotten here. The last had been after their call to Drew Connell.

Quinn was sexy. Damned sexy. She couldn't get enough of making love with him.

But what would happen when they got back to Ft. Lukman? She prayed that they would somehow have Grace and Simon with them. If not, that would be even harder on Quinn than on her, since Simon was his brother and Grace was only her superior officer and friend. *Only?* Well, hell, it would be damned difficult for her, too.

In any event, Kristine couldn't continue being the assistant to a male shifter. That would change no matter what.

And the fact that he was a shifter? She hadn't anticipated it before joining Alpha Force but she admired shifters. Liked them. Always enjoyed the secrecy and adventure and more while part of this really special military unit, even now.

Actually revered Alpha Force and all it stood for.

She had become a nurse years ago because she had wanted to help people. Make a difference. Maybe even be recognized for it—after a childhood of being abandoned first by her father, then by her mother after she'd remarried. Kristine's aunt had taken over her guardianship by default, and Kristine had felt even more alone until she'd become a nurse.

Later, she had sought even more—the boundaries and camaraderie of the military.

When Alpha Force had started recruiting without initial explanation of what it was, she had jumped at it—because it had been made clear that the unit approved and recognized ingenuity and team mentality.

She loved it.

But have an ongoing relationship with a shifter—especially one like Quinn?

She had become all military. Had chosen it, felt that it had chosen her. Yes, she was sort of ignoring that here, because of the importance of what they were doing. But Quinn? He would probably never be a career, order-following soldier, at least not willingly.

No, she might as well enjoy his incredible body now, while she could.

Their unofficial mission here would end soon. Immediately, if they listened to Major Connell.

They needed answers fast.

When they returned to Ft. Lukman, no matter what they learned or didn't learn here, she would be assigned to help a female shifter—assuming Alpha Force continued as a viable covert unit.

Which it had to. No matter what came out of this terrible situation, Alpha Force had to go on.

And if Quinn remained a member, he would be assisted by a male aide.

They would see each other, perhaps even go on the same missions in the future.

But whatever they had personally, what they had shared here?

It would be over.

Chapter 15

Quinn pulled a nice knit shirt and casual slacks from his suitcase, then dressed quickly while Kristine was in the shower. He pictured her beautiful, irresistible nude body beneath the spray.

Which was why he stayed out of the bathroom—to avoid temptation. As much as he regretted it, he was out of time. He had things to accomplish.

He wasn't going to shift today. However, he did intend to take some risks.

Risks he had no intention of inflicting on Kristine.

Risks that included going against a very clear order from a commanding officer to essentially do nothing but wait.

Doing nothing went against everything within him. Plus, he had an idea, one that might yield nothing, but he had to try it.

He had to do something, whatever was necessary, to find his brother and sister-in-law—if that was still possible—as well to help the outfit that their commanding officer also wanted to protect. Not to mention all the other shifters who belonged to it. And Kristine.

If she knew what he'd be up to, she would tell him that he, too, had to obey the order they were under. That was her military mind-set. But if he made it clear he was going to do it anyway, she would insist on coming along to help—as much as she'd hate disobeying. She would resent him for it—and she might even impede him.

So, instead, to cover his trail, he'd tell her he was doing something else she'd want to avoid.

He'd already sounded her out about her interest in sports. She had very little, if any.

The Bar Harbor Golf Course had an excellent reputation. He'd make up a story about how they paired up groups at the course. And that was where he would claim to go, alone.

As long as he felt comfortable that Kristine would be safe, of course.

On impulse, he drew his cell phone out of his pocket. As he had so many times before, he pressed first the button that would automatically call Simon's number.

As always these days, it went right to voice mail.

Even so, he tried Grace's number, too.

The same. Not that he expected anything different. If they were in trouble somewhere, there was no reason to think that they'd suddenly gotten access to their phones again.

If they had, surely Simon would have called him.

He still refused to dwell on the obvious alternative—that they were dead.

Instead, he allowed this moment of frustration to bolster his resolve to do as he'd planned today. After all, it would result in his visiting possibly one of the last places Simon had mentioned in one of the couple of conversations they'd had when the honeymooners reached this area.

He slipped his phone back into his pocket and got back to putting together a story to distract Kristine.

When she finally exited the bathroom, he was sitting on the bed poring over touristy materials they'd picked up to support their cover story. He looked up.

How could a woman look so sexy in a huge white robe with her hair tucked into a towel?

He made himself stay cool as he said casually, "Since we're supposed to do nothing, I've got an idea. I'll go play a round of golf."

Her face was as beautiful without makeup as with

it, even when she frowned, like now. "I could watch you, I suppose..."

Damn. That wasn't the idea.

"But, you know," she continued, "I think I could do more good just wandering around Bar Harbor. Not doing any investigating, of course. I won't do anything against the major's orders, so I'll just be waiting. But wandering around this town, observing as a tourist...if I happen to see anything helpful, I'll call him to get the okay before I act on it, but—"

"Call me first," he said fiercely. "I don't want you doing anything dangerous."

She laughed. "That's sweet, but you've seen how I can protect myself if I have to."

"And you've seen how good I am as your backup."

"Yes, you've proven yourself. I especially like you as a wolf...except around here." She looked tellingly at the bed. He laughed.

"Okay, no need to lay it on so thick. But you promise to stay out of trouble? And to stay away from those DSPA guys?"

"I promise."

Of course her fingers had been crossed behind the folds in her robe. Kristine would play it all as it came, she thought as she changed into her jeans and T-shirt. She kept her back to Quinn, not just for modesty. She loved the way his eyes watched her as she dressed—or undressed. She didn't need the distraction.

She had never disobeyed direct military orders. She wouldn't—exactly—now.

She was glad, though, that Quinn was being a good boy and going off to play golf. Or at least that was his story. She hoped it was true—or that he at least wasn't doing anything foolish. Or dangerous.

This way, he wouldn't be around to see it if she herself did something not strictly in accordance with what the major had directed, beyond simply looking at local sights, like a normal tourist.

That would grate on her conscience, but at least no one else would ever know. Especially Quinn.

No need to tempt him to reciprocate if he wasn't already.

"I'm ready." She turned...to see he'd been watching her anyway. She felt her face redden, even as her blood began heating inside.

No time for that now. She grabbed her purse. "Let's go."

Quinn joined Kristine in the coffee shop and bought a large brewed coffee to go. She sat down with her laptop at a table.

"Do you plan to hang out here all day?"

"Don't know yet." Her too-innocent expression suggested she might bolt as soon as he was gone.

"Call me when you're ready to leave. I'll check in with you when I can from the golf course." Or wherever he really happened to be.

"Sounds good." She smiled up at him.

He bent down to kiss those obviously perfidious lips. They were still, after all, playing the roles of newlyweds.

Good thing that he was taking the car. She could always hop a tourist bus or whatever, but there would still be other people around. Less chance of something nasty happening to her.

Unless...

"Be sure to call me if you run into those guys," he said, knowing she would understand which guys he meant. "If they show up anywhere you happen to be, be sure you've got plenty of other people nearby."

"Witnesses when I deck them the next time?" She laughed.

"Something like that." He hesitated. "You know, maybe I'll just forget the golf. You and I could do more sightseeing together. See what other plans we come up with." He'd have to forgo the latest idea he'd had for attempting to track down Simon and Grace, but so be it.

"I'll be fine." Kristine looked peeved. "I know how to stay out of trouble."

He knew how well she could get into it, too. But this would possibly be his last chance to do what he intended to—and leaving Kristine here, even without him as backup, would be less dangerous to her.

Besides, she wasn't likely to do too much to get into trouble. She would never disobey a direct military order. She would at least have to appear as if she had listened and was standing down. Looking around for answers? Maybe. Acting on suspicions? No.

"Okay," he said. "But be sure to stay in touch."

First thing, as Quinn directly disobeyed orders, was to rent a small boat.

With all the touring they had done on Mount Desert Island, Quinn felt fairly certain he'd have sensed his quarry sooner if they'd been in a hotel or hidden somewhere in Acadia National Park.

But one place Kristine and he hadn't searched was the coastline.

Simon and Grace had talked about wanting to tour the New England coast on their honeymoon, and his brother had actually called from one of the spots to gloat about being there, about the incredible seaside location complete with wild waves crashing into the thick, eroded cliffs of the shoreline. Could they be hiding in a place like that?

Might they even have shifted somewhere along the shoreline, using some of Simon's pills or the Alpha Force elixir?

Maybe this would be fruitless, too. Quinn had to try, though, in case this vast area held answers.

If not, he had a backup plan for surveilling other parts of the island later.

Now, he edged the tiny motor craft between the towering rocks and lower reeflike crannies that constituted the edges of the island. There were undoubtedly caves hidden along the shore. In fact, he spotted some openings in the cliffs that suggested hollowed-out areas where people—or shifters— could hide.

Or be hidden, dead or alive.

He aimed his craft as close to the shore as he dared. This spring day threatened a storm, and it was windy—which made the surface of the ocean rise and fall in waves of unpredictable height and ferocity.

He could swim, if he had to. But saving himself from being battered against the rocks if he fell into the surf—well, that was less certain.

It felt chilly here. He'd intended to bring along the beige hoodie he'd packed but hadn't found it during his quick search of their hotel room and rental car. No matter. He could always buy another one, and the coolness now was far from unbearable.

He again felt glad he had left Kristine behind. As a longtime soldier, she probably could swim well, like she did everything else. Even so...

Good thing she hadn't questioned his ability to play golf today, though. He supposed she'd figured he would simply stop if the weather got too bad.

At the moment, his surroundings smelled like salt water and sea life, fishy and strong and not his favorite scents. Over the cracking of waves against the shore, he heard the calls of birds overhead, other watercraft in the distance.

No howls, although he didn't expect to hear them, in daylight, outside the full moon. Even so, he every once in a while uttered his own soft call as similar to a shifted wolf as he could, just in case.

No responses.

Maybe he should come back while shifted, lope along the beach, duck into even smaller openings. But there were too many areas where the cliffside reached the water, where wolves would be unable to run.

Twice, he maneuvered the boat to the shore, beached it and walked into caves nearly at the waterline, good caches for people or animals. He found moldering seaweed, occasional dead seals or fish. No people. No bodies of mammals that were not usually found at the shore.

Even so, he had rented the boat for the day, and it was barely midafternoon. This was a long shot, sure. But it was something he had to try.

At one of his stops, he called Kristine. He could

barely hear her, although his phone had a satellite connection so he did get through.

"Everything okay?" he asked loudly.

"Yes, but where are you?" she shouted. "There's so much background noise. Are you on the golf course?"

Good thing she didn't have a tracker on him.

"Inside the clubhouse. In the bathroom, actually—near the showers. Sorry. I should have called from outside. I'm enjoying this, though."

"Good. I'm having a good day, too."

He smiled as he hung up, glad he had checked in with her.

He got back into the boat and sailed on.

So where the hell was he—really?

She shouldn't feel so peeved that Quinn had abandoned her to go against direct orders and continue his investigation, but she was certain now that was what he had done.

Kristine had been a good girl so far, mostly retracing steps, stopping in shops where newlyweds might go for souvenirs or clothes or stuff that they could ship home to start furnishing their living quarters at Ft. Lukman. She, at least, wasn't exactly disobeying orders this way. If anyone asked, she was just having fun. Being a tourist.

But in each place, she talked up how she'd just gotten married and wondering aloud, as she had so many other times before in this town, if other new couples frequented the shop. The answers varied. It sounded as if a couple resembling Grace and Simon had gone a couple of times into a nice-size bookstore and browsed. Had they bought anything? The clerk Kristine talked to was unsure, although she remembered them because they seemed interested in books about Bar Harbor nature and wildlife.

Yes, it was probably them. But this didn't get Kristine anywhere beyond confirming the presence of the people she'd known had been in town.

She was already butting up against the major's orders, at least somewhat. But she needed to do more. Her time here was undoubtedly limited, and so far Quinn and she only had questions, not answers.

She had to do more, right now. Before Quinn returned from his claimed golf game, or Major Connell called again with more orders—like telling them to return to Ft. Lukman right away.

Fleetingly, she recalled her promise to Quinn to be careful, stay safe and not do anything to put herself in danger.

Well, she would at least be careful.

But it was time to implement her current—and perhaps last—idea to try to find Grace and Simon.

"Oh, they're gone?" Kristine acted both surprised and sorry after stopping at the nurses' station on the floor of the hospital where Kelly and Holt had been patients.

Once again, the nurse she'd caught there between patient visits was Bridget, the same one who had acted so friendly to Kristine before.

"Left late yesterday." Bridget looked up from where she sat behind the desk. Her nod caused her bright golden hair to crimp around her pudgy cheeks.

"I'd talked with them again and thought they were still having some pretty bad headaches," Kristine said, leaning over the cubicle that formed the station. She would play the nurse card again, since it had gotten her some empathy when she spoke with Bridget before. "When I've dealt with people with severe head trauma, they can remain hospitalized for a lot longer than this. Do they have follow-ups scheduled with any doctors?"

"That's getting into possible patient confidentiality issues again." Bridget's lips pursed as she pulled back.

"Sorry," Kristine said. "Like I said before, because of my... involvement in their injuries, I want to make sure they'll be okay."

From the last time, she knew that the staff was aware that the two men had been injured in an altercation. Kristine could always hint more strongly that she was a little worried that the guys would sue for compensation for their injuries—and if so, that she'd need to gather evidence that they attacked her first.

Bridget studied Kristine for a long moment with soft brown eyes. Then she stood and drew closer. "You know I don't have all the facts, but there was some more talk around here. Whatever happened... well, from what you told me those guys deserved all they got, and more." She stopped for a moment, regarding Kristine shrewdly, as if assessing her reaction.

Kristine sucked in her lips in a way she hoped looked sad yet resolute. "That's my position," she said.

"Well, whatever the circumstances, they still needed medical attention and seemed to know it. When they insisted on leaving yesterday, though, it was like they'd had a bomb lit under them—figuratively, of course. They suddenly had to get out, never mind their short-term prognoses."

As if they'd received orders, Kristine thought.

"But did you think they were progressing adequately? I'm not asking for a medical opinion, of course. But as I said, I'd like to believe they're healing as well and as quickly as possible."

"Oh, I think so. In fact—"

Kristine took a step closer at Bridget's hesitation. A doctor and nurse walked by behind her, conversing so earnestly that Kristine doubted they were paying any attention to what went on at the nurses' station, but whatever Bridget had been about to say, she obviously didn't want anyone to hear it.

"In fact?" Kristine prompted quietly.

"Well, don't let this go any farther, but...well, I heard those guys talking now and then when I went in to check their vitals. They spoke only in generalities, so I wasn't sure what they meant, but they seemed to be discussing some work assignment they were on that had gone bad. They weren't sure what would come next, but staying in the hospital as long as they could sounded like a good idea at that moment. Of course, I could be all wrong."

Or all right, Kristine thought. If the DSPA guys had wanted to stay here, it could mean their investigation hadn't been going any better than Quinn's and hers.

Maybe they had no better idea of the newlywed Parrans' location and were happy to stop looking.

Until they got orders to leave the hospital. Because they weren't permitted to give up—just as Quinn and Kristine were under orders that they *had* to give up?

Or were they given more information?

This was something she'd discuss with Quinn... after she followed up on it herself.

Where was he now? Had he found anything helpful during his "golf game"?

Was he staying safe?

This outing hadn't been useless, Quinn told himself as he turned the wheel to aim the small, rocking boat around the last craggy areas he intended to investigate today. The sun had started its descent in the sky long ago, and the surrounding odors of water and fish somehow seemed enhanced—maybe because he had endured them for so long.

He had at a minimum eliminated a lot of areas of the shoreline from his suspicions about where Simon and Grace might be hiding out, or where they'd been stashed.

He hadn't eliminated the surrounding ocean itself, though, despite how unlikely it was that his brother and sister-in-law were being held captive on a boat.

But they could have been killed and their bodies tossed into the water.

Damn. He definitely hated to think like that. But if they were alive, Kristine and he would have found at least some sign of them, wouldn't they?

On impulse, he dialed her number on his phone. Amazingly, despite how sporadic even his satellite reception had been out here, it went through.

"Hi," he said. "You still at the coffee shop?"

"No, but I'll be back there shortly."

"Where are you?"

"Wandering the town. And you?"

"Wandering the golf course. I'll rejoin you soon, though. Think about where you want to grab dinner."

"Okay."

It sounded like such a mundane conversation. As if they really were newlyweds.

But Quinn knew better. He knew *Kristine* better. "Where are you headed right now?" he asked.

"I'm just figuring that out," she said. "See you later. Bye." And then she was gone.

Leaving Quinn unreasonably worried.

Why, suddenly, did he have a feeling that, obeying military orders or not, she was going straight into danger?

Chapter 16

The hotel where Kelly and Holt were staying hadn't seemed far when Kristine rode there with Quinn. Now, though, she realized she had a distance to walk.

No matter. She enjoyed the exercise—both for her body and her mind. She had her purse with her, but not her backpack. She didn't need to carry the shifting equipment. She did, however, have her gun.

While she walked, she would use the time to consider how to approach the two DSPA guys and what to say to them—notwithstanding Quinn's insisting that she stay away from them.

The direction she took led her past the police station. She couldn't help herself. She walked into the lobby area.

Did she dare ask anything about their investigation into the killings of the tourists?

Not that they'd be likely to admit anything...

There were a few people standing around inside, and she had to wait a couple of minutes before she could approach the receiving desk. The same uniformed officer she'd seen there before, Officer Canfield, stood to greet visitors. "Can I help you?" he asked.

"I was just wondering..." From the corner of her eye, she noticed a couple of uniformed cops exiting a door near the caged-in welcome area. They both looked familiar—the ones Quinn had confronted after their last visit here.

The ones he had seen, while shifted, right at the crime scene.

The ones she really wanted to talk to—much better than talking to that Chief Crane again and trying to ask questions without answering any of his.

"Sorry," she told Officer Canfield. "I've got to run." She ignored the combination of puzzlement and irritation on the young cop's face and moved away from the line that had grown behind her.

She approached the nearest cop. "Hello, Officer Angsburg." Kristine made herself smile at the slim, uniformed woman with an expressionless face. "Good to see you again. You know, I'm still hoping to hear some kind of resolution on the killing of those tourists in Acadia." She looked toward the male cop who stood beside her, Officer Sidell. The squat, large-chested guy frowned, and since he was nearly bald his entire forehead became a plane of parallel wrinkles.

"It's not our jurisdiction," the male cop said, his tone filled with irony.

Kristine shrugged one shoulder. "I just thought you were interested enough to keep looking…and, since you know this area better, you'd do a better job than the feds."

"Yeah? Tell that to them," he retorted.

"Sorry, we've got to go." Officer Angsburg touched her partner's arm as if to give him a message. Kristine could guess what it was.

"I'm still rooting for answers soon," Kristine called after them in the crowded lobby. "My husband is, too." She added that just as a reminder to them of the persona under which she had previously met, and been questioned by, their superior officer.

Unfortunately, this brief meeting hadn't gained her any knowledge—other than to have her assumption about the frustration of the local authorities confirmed. Which wasn't surprising, considering their apparently hanging out sometimes, maybe unofficially, at the crime scene.

Now, it was time to continue with the investigation she had planned today to take advantage of Quinn's absence.

She wondered about him, though, and where he really was.

Worried about him. Couldn't help thinking about him, especially since she had mentioned her "husband."

She stepped back onto the Bar Harbor sidewalk outside the police station. The weather was as iffy as many New England spring days. A strong breeze was blowing, and a storm threatened. Not a great day for golf, she surmised. Another reason to doubt that was what Quinn was up to.

Would what she now was about to do cause lightning of a different kind? Even just the idea bothered her.

She had definitely come to appreciate the charm of Bar Harbor and its quaint shops, its parks and its proximity to the water, not to mention its myriad of happy tourists that surrounded her on the sidewalk and meandered in and out of the stores.

If only she were here as a real tourist.

Or as a real honeymooner, like Grace had been… Not that Kristine had any intention of getting more involved with the other Parran brother, let alone considering anything as foolish as marrying him.

Never mind that she was hooked on the guy sexually.

But he held a higher military ranking than she did—when he didn't even like, or relate to, the military. Their fraternizing here wasn't any big deal since they weren't acting officially, but they couldn't continue it even if they wanted to.

Even more critical—he was a shapeshifter.

Simon and Grace were both werewolves, and Kristine figured that would lead to a lasting relationship. Mates for life.

Of course other Alpha Force couples consisted of pairs where one person shifted and the other didn't—Major Connell and his veterinarian wife, for one, and they had a young child. Then there was Lt. Patrick Worley, whose wife wrote for a nature magazine.

Kristine stopped abruptly at an intersection and castigated herself for the way her mind was racing in the wrong direction. Quinn hadn't given any indication of interest in a real relationship, even if she wanted one. Which she didn't.

But she had wanted to succeed on their completely unofficial mission, and what she still intended to accomplish today could make a heck of a lot of difference in what Quinn and she had come here to do.

Maybe she would be excused from violating a direct order by continuing her investigation, talking to the cops—and more—if she succeeded. Then, she might also excuse herself.

She might even admit the lapse to Quinn—although she didn't really want him to think she condoned ignoring orders.

But what difference would that really make, considering how little he thought of the military?

And his attitude wouldn't prevent her from trying to seduce him tonight in celebration—if all went well.

Quinn had finally circled the entire island, after starting out toward the north. The last area he passed on the loop back to his starting point was perhaps the most interesting—the area south of Bar Harbor. A while ago, he had passed the Coast Guard installation that Major Connell had mentioned, but had decided not to go in. He doubted that the DSPA guys would be there now, and felt certain that the Coast Guard members on duty wouldn't share information even if they had any.

He had just gone by Seal Harbor, a small, somewhat upscale village with a small port for recreational vessels. Beyond the town were Otter Cove, Otter Cliff and Thunder Cove—all shoreline phenomena that were majestic and magnetic. If he had actually been a sightseer, he would have stopped and explored the area by land a lot more than he had

while looking for any sign of Simon and Grace—
or canine wildlife.

But he wasn't a sightseer. And slowing down
wouldn't help to alleviate his fear, as irrational as
it might be, about Kristine. The longer he was away
from her, the more he believed she might be doing
something she would only regret.

Him, too.

He kept his boat on course toward Bar Harbor.

On impulse, he called Kristine, but his signal,
unsurprisingly, wasn't strong. He'd try her again
when he reached the shore.

Only...okay, he was acting like some teenager
with a crush. Or maybe like a real honeymooner.
But being away from her this long? It didn't seem
right.

Especially because he somehow had a gut feeling. She hadn't seemed at all worried that they were
going in different directions today.

That probably meant she had something on her
mind, just as he had.

Something that could put her in danger?

Hell. He had to go find out.

Their SUV wasn't in the parking lot.

That might be a good thing, Kristine thought.
She'd been weighing ideas in her mind for getting
someone to reveal the room number of the DSPA

guys so she could knock on their door and surprise them—or sneak in and lie in wait if they weren't there. But in these days of enhanced privacy, she wasn't sure any of her schemes would work.

At least she could do as Quinn and she had done before—treat herself to a decent meal in the hotel restaurant while keeping an eye on the parking lot.

A hostess in a silky dress showed her to a seat near the window, as she requested, despite how busy the place was once again. Kristine looked outside as much as she studied the menu. No DSPA guys.

Were they even still registered at the hotel? Still in the area?

She tried to be surreptitious as she took her cell phone from her purse and called the front desk and asked for Mr. Kelly's room. The operator didn't say that he was no longer there, so apparently Kristine's fears were ungrounded. Nor did either Mr. Kelly or Mr. Holt answer the phone—probably a good thing since Kristine's plans hadn't included calling them to schedule a meeting.

Unless nothing else worked.

Their time here was limited, hers and Quinn's. She had to make a move, push the feds to give up more information. This could be her last opportunity, and she was desperate to learn more about Grace and Simon—no matter what the cost.

And if they were dead, as she feared, or had gone

rogue—well, Kristine would do all she had to do to protect Alpha Force. That was paramount to anything else.

She'd be cautious, of course. Learning something would do her no good if she didn't survive to tell about it.

But those feds had to know something. Why else would they still be here?

Although they did keep saying that they, too, were looking for answers...

She ordered a glass of white wine, then considered either Maine steamers or lobster—but both might be too time-consuming to wait for, or to eat, if she spotted her quarries. Plus, she really wasn't very hungry. Instead, she requested crab cakes.

She ate slowly, savoring her food while keeping watch. But no black SUV. Not until she had taken her last bite and considered ordering another glass of wine.

Then the vehicle pulled into the parking lot. Frantically, Kristine glanced around and found her server nearby. She made the universal sign in the air of wanting her check. But the men moved fast. Maybe she should have just taken something to read and sat out there waiting.

She paid quickly and hurried from the restaurant. Fortunately, she spotted the men walking through the crowded hotel lobby. Maneuvering around other people, she dashed over to them. "Well, Mr. Kelly, Mr. Holt, fancy seeing you here."

Kelly's smile looked so snide that it sent shivers up Kristine's back. "No surprise to see you here, Kristine." But he looked around. "Where's your... husband?"

Holt's expression, too, looked almost triumphant as he also grinned. "I'll find him. Is he letting you be our bait again?"

"What do you mean?" she demanded.

Holt sidestepped around her and seemed to be scanning the busy lobby—for Quinn, no doubt.

"He's not here," she called. "I'm on my own today. Care to join me for a drink?"

"Thanks to you and your guy we're off alcohol for a few more days," Kelly growled. "Not good for concussions."

"Coffee, then. Is caffeine okay? I know you've been combing the area for the two missing people, and as I told you before, I want to collaborate with you."

"And why should we do that?" Holt demanded. He was now standing at Kristine's side. Kelly was directly in front of her. They seemed much too close. At least, with all these people around, they were unlikely to try to grab her again.

Did they plan to coerce her some other way? She no longer felt in charge of this situation. She took a step back. It was time to walk away—fast. But she knew both men would stay with her if she tried.

Hell, she was in the military, trained for combat. A little confrontation like this was nothing. She could handle it.

"Because we have the same goals," she told Holt, keeping her eyes level, her voice hard. "We can help each other. I may have a little information about Alpha Force that I can share with you that could be of assistance." Or not. She'd have to figure out what she could allude to without giving up any secrets. But enticing them with possibilities was a good thing.

"Fine," Kelly said. "Why don't you just come along and tell us what you know." He took her arm, and when she attempted to wrest it away he grasped it even tighter.

"I don't think you want to make a scene here," Kristine said, her gaze traveling around the lobby. "The security guys wouldn't like it, for one thing. I'd imagine there are plenty of cameras around."

"We won't be the ones making a scene if you just come along."

"Why is it that you keep trying to get me to go with you?" she demanded.

"Like you said, we might have information to share. And since you talk about it so much, we're fairly sure you do." There was a cruelty in Kelly's nasty smile that made Kristine shudder inside—not that she showed it. But he looked like a grinning skeleton, and his hand on her arm felt like a tightening vise. "Let's go," he finished.

"I don't think so." Kristine stood still, readying herself for self-defense moves, if necessary. In this crowd, she wouldn't be able to get much leverage. And Kelly had apparently learned his lesson. He was now positioned almost sideways, which would make it a lot harder for her to aim nasty kicks at his genital area.

But where was Holt? Kristine glanced sideways and didn't see him—but then she felt another hand, this one creeping around her waist.

Damn! This was getting ugly. She could shout, but calling attention to herself wasn't ideal—especially when Quinn and she weren't supposed to be here and her presence could be deemed counter to their direct order to stand down. Another incident with these guys could hurt the military career that was so important to her...not to mention how it could negatively affect Alpha Force.

What was she going to do?

And then, as if this was some kind of adventure movie where heroes appeared out of the blue to save the poor, frightened girl—there he was.

Quinn.

He strode up to them as if he'd been choreographed to be there. "Hello, gentlemen," he said, the nasty grin illuminating his gorgeous—and absolutely welcome—face apparently dismaying the two feds. "I think we all need to talk."

They didn't talk long. It seemed that Holt and Kelly had pressing government business to take care of that evening. What a surprise.

"What were you doing with them?" Quinn demanded after Kristine sat down in the passenger seat of their rental car.

"Where were you?" she countered, figuring that the best defense was a strong offense. Especially since she realized that she hadn't handled this right after all her planning...

She should have had a much better backup plan. One that didn't require that she be the maiden in distress waiting for her champion to arrive.

They were still sitting in the hotel parking lot. Kristine watched Quinn stare straight ahead for a long moment as if controlling his temper.

She should have felt equally angry with him. She shouldn't feel attracted to him as he clearly criticized her, internally even if he was wise enough not to vocalize it.

But she understood his anger. She would have felt the same way if she had discovered him in a dangerous situation from which he'd have had a hard time extracting himself.

"I'm sorry," she heard herself saying. "I just thought that I'd take advantage of being on my own to conduct my own investigation without involving you—without your having to act against direct orders."

He laughed and looked straight at her. His mood had clearly changed. "You know what I was doing when I left you in town?"

She couldn't help smiling back. "Disobeying orders? Conducting your own investigation?"

"Exactly."

The tension between them had clearly eased.

"You hungry?" she asked him. "I'd like a light dinner now. How about you?"

After a quick meal at a local seafood restaurant, Quinn drove back to their hotel.

"I'm still hungry," he said when they were in their room together. "Besides, you owe me some penance for making me worry the way I did this afternoon."

"No, you owe me—"

He didn't let her finish. He lowered his mouth down onto hers and used his tongue to tease away any words that she might be forming to contradict him.

The contact, that kiss as it deepened, made his

cock harden so fast and so tautly that he had no choice but to quickly take off her clothes—even as she pulled at his.

They were soon in bed together, naked and hungry and ready for their hottest sex yet, or so he anticipated.

He was right. He nearly had an orgasm the moment she gripped him and pulled him toward her own center, but he controlled it until he was deep inside her. After somehow managing to tear open and pull on a condom.

After all, she was all woman. Human woman. No need to take chances on starting something they couldn't control—like a baby.

How he was able to focus on that while pounding into her, watching the hazy need in her eyes, hearing her gasps of pleasure...well, who knew?

And when he climaxed, it was all-consuming, especially since she reached orgasm at the same time.

Kristine felt sated. And confused. And she simply wouldn't think about her foolishness that day, confronting those two feds on her own.

Her current foolishness, thinking that she might be falling in love with a superior officer, a shifter... impossible.

It had to be.

But her confusion didn't prevent her from making love with him twice more that night.

In the morning, she wasn't sure what to think. How to react. And so, as soon as he left their bed to head for the bathroom, she turned on the television.

And gasped. "Quinn. Come here!"

They both watched the rest of the newscast. There had been another killing in Acadia last night. More maulings of humans by some kind of animal.

The dead victim was Officer Emily Angsburg, one of the cops who'd been looking into the prior killing.

The cop Kristine had spoken with only the day before.

Chapter 17

"It wasn't a night of a full moon," Kristine said right away, grasping Quinn's hand as they continued to watch the news. "At least everyone who knows the situation will back off from thinking that Grace and Simon could be the killers."

"If people really know the situation, they'll also know about the Alpha Force elixir," Quinn reminded her grimly. Not that she, of all people, really needed the reminder.

They stood beside the bed. Quinn had tied a towel around his waist, and Kristine remained highly aware of his sexy physique despite the extra worry that now permeated her mind. She had pulled on a tank top over panties. This was not a time to be naked and aware of one another, remembering yet another night of incredible passion.

But she couldn't help thinking about it, however briefly.

The news jumped to a commercial, and Kristine picked up the remote control from the end table beside the bed to turn it off.

"Two cops were there," Quinn said unnecessarily. "One survived. Sidell, they said." Kristine had caught that—even as she thought about the officer who'd been killed.

"I wonder if he's in condition to give them any information about the attack—and what the attacker looked like."

"I doubt it'll do us much good, but we're going to take a little trip to the hospital to see what we can find out." Quinn looked down at her with his golden-brown eyes, not in query but in command.

She wasn't about to disagree. In fact, the same idea had crossed her mind.

They parked in the outside lot and hurried inside via the hospital's emergency room.

Quinn was determined to avoid the media jackals who festered outside, waving cameras at everyone who wasn't among their fraternity. He hated comparing them with other canines, even jackals, but those creatures had a reputation of being ruthless scavengers that far exceeded wolves'.

Even so, Kristine and he had dressed up, in case they had to pretend to represent some kind of publication to wend their way into the hospital with the crowd.

Presuming, at that point, no one recognized them.

They were lucky—unlike a couple of auto accident victims who were brought in around the same time Kristine and he inched their way inside. Everyone was involved in checking them over, stabilizing them.

The good news, from what Quinn heard as Kristine and he reached the door at the far end of the E.R. facility that led to the rest of the hospital, was that the two teenaged accident victims who'd been brought in would apparently survive.

The better news was that Kristine and he soon found themselves in the nearly empty hospital lobby.

They didn't stop at the desk to check in but strode to the elevator bank as though they belonged there.

When they were alone inside the climbing elevator, Kristine turned to him. "What if they have Sidell someplace different from where the two feds were?"

"Good question. We'll play it by ear. Let's see—our cover story for the moment is that we honeymooners heard that the guys who attacked you—those damned feds—might have been involved in this situation, too, and we're here seeking more information. For our own safety."

"Sounds pretty ridiculous to me."

"You got anything better? Look, we'll try it and improvise more if—"

He ended what he was saying as the elevator stopped on the third floor, the level where Holt and Kelly had been hospitalized during their stay here. Nodding to Kristine, he walked quickly out of the car.

The nurses' station was right there. Several female nurses sat behind the long, empty counter with tables lining its inner area. Two were talking to one another and the others apparently were involved in administrative work.

Once again, Quinn was concerned as Kristine took the lead...but he let her. She approached the far end, where a familiar-looking woman stared at a computer screen as she typed on the keyboard. Quinn just followed Kristine, ready to listen to her—and prepared to jump in if she led things in a direction that could harm their current investigation.

"Hi, Bridget," Kristine said.

The woman looked up. She had bright blond hair and narrow lips folded between thick cheeks. "Yes? Oh—are you looking for those men who were here a while ago? Mr. Holt and Mr. Kelly? To my knowledge, they haven't been back."

"That's probably a good thing," Kristine said. She stood stiffly now, looking like some kind of official investigator, lawyer—or media representative—in her white button-down blouse and black skirt. He felt proud of her professional appearance. He'd chosen to dress similarly, in a suit, but he'd left the jacket in their rental car.

"No, I'm here looking for some answers." Kristine leaned over the counter as if she was preparing to share a secret with the nurse. "As I told you before, I'm a nurse by background. The news is full of another death in Acadia, and the reporters are saying the means of death was similar to those tourists—only this time a police officer died. They also said another one was injured but survived. Is he here?"

The nurse frowned, pursing those thin lips. "You know I can't discuss our patients due to confidentiality issues. We talked about that before."

"Yes, but the thing is, well—I have my suspicions that those two men who attacked me were involved with this, too."

Interesting angle, Quinn thought, wondering if this nurse would buy into it. If she did, that would mean she might think the feds had something to do with the other deaths in Acadia.

Instead, she shook her head. "You mean those guys bit and clawed you like wild animals before you somehow got control and knocked them out? I don't think so. What is it that you're really after? Are you some kind of reporter—and is that why they jumped on you in the first place?"

Kristine laughed. "Me? Not hardly. But—"

The phone on the desk beside Nurse Bridget rang just then. She raised one chubby finger, as if telling Kristine to wait a minute.

But Kristine turned away. She looked up at Quinn with her brilliant blue eyes and whispered, "From her lack of denial, I'll bet that surviving cop is on this floor. Can you tell where he is?"

Quinn had already considered that. He'd been near the cop a couple of times, but even with his special abilities it was hard to distinguish scents in a hospital setting like this, where everyone and everything was doused often with antiseptics to minimize the risk of infection. He had also kept an eye on comings and goings, assuming that there could be a guard assigned to monitor the cop's room. He had seen nothing—although he had heard some distant discussion in a room at the far end of the hall.

"Not sure," he said, "but let's check it out."

He started down the hallway. Kristine joined him. They were passed by a couple of the nurses' aides going the opposite direction, but no one questioned them.

As they passed a multilevel cart with food baskets and other gifty things on it, he picked up a couple of items and handed one to Kristine. "In case we need a cover story."

"And you're good at those." Her tone sounded ironic, but she lifted that strong chin of hers and smiled, making him smile back.

"Yep," he said, then stopped as they reached the door that was his target.

He knocked once but didn't wait for a response before opening it.

"What the hell are you doing here?" demanded Chief Al Crane. The sterile-looking room held two beds, but he sat on a chair near the only one that was occupied.

In it lay the cop who'd been mauled during this last episode—the same officer who'd been hanging out at the scene of the first killing in Acadia. Sidell.

Crane rose and stalked up to them, confronting Quinn, who held himself in check and responded, "We heard about what happened and the similarities to the deaths of those tourists. As visiting honeymooners—"

"Oh, forget that crap," Crane spat. "We're beyond that. Honeymooners don't show up everywhere asking all those damned questions. You with the feds, or what?"

"We're not at liberty to say," Kristine said primly. He wanted to hug her. Without any prompting by him, she was assuming an undercover role as…well, as whatever. He felt comfortable that they'd work together, following each other's leads.

"Then get the hell out of here," Crane commanded.

That was when Sidell stirred in the bed. Since the chief was confronting Quinn, that gave Kristine the opportunity to approach the injured man. He was hooked up to all kinds of monitors, and there were bandages over every part of his body that was visible from beneath the sheets—his neck, both arms, part of his face.

"I'm a nurse," she told him, "although I don't work here. Is there anything I can do for you? Anything I can get for you?"

"Painkiller," the man managed to say between gritted teeth.

"I'll check with those on call to see what we can do for you. Tell me exactly what happened, will you? That'll help in determining your treatment."

"Leave him the hell alone." Crane moved away from Quinn to confront Kristine instead. He reached out a hand as if to grab her arm, but Quinn interposed himself between them.

"Dunno," said the voice from the bed. "Someone—something—attacked. Knocked me onto the ground, grabbed my neck. Sharp teeth or...I don't know. I fought." Tears were running down the poor sap's face, dampening his bandages. "But then... nothing."

"Which was probably a good thing," Crane grumbled. "Whatever it was thought you were dead already."

"But I couldn't save Emily." The guy was weeping even more now. Even Quinn felt moved by his anguish.

But sympathy wouldn't get the answers he needed.

"Did you see what attacked you? Hear anything?" Like, could it have looked like, sounded like a wolf—or, hopefully, something else?

"It happened so fast—and then..." His voice tapered off.

The door burst open and the two feds, Holt and Kelly, barged into the room.

"What the hell are you two doing here?" Kelly demanded.

"This sounds like a chorus," Quinn responded calmly. "Chief Crane, here, asked us the same thing. And here's our response...again. We're looking for answers."

"But you're violating your—" Holt all but

shouted, but he stopped as Kristine stalked toward him and looked straight up into his face.

Quinn wanted to grab and shake her for putting herself in harm's way, but Kelly was in his path.

"That's on a need-to-know basis," she hissed softly at the fed. "If you violate national security by saying too much here, I'll report you."

"What national security?" Crane demanded. "You with the feds, too?" he asked Quinn. "Just because Acadia's a national park it doesn't mean that there're no repercussions for people getting killed there. Especially when local cops are attacked. You understand?"

"You're talking to the wrong person here," Quinn retorted. "Talk to these guys. They're with the government. Not me."

That wasn't exactly true, and Quinn caught the distressed look on Kristine's lovely face before she resumed a serious but neutral expression. Well, neither of them was representing the government at the moment.

Neither was acting under the aegis of Alpha Force.

"We're conducting our own investigation into what happened in Acadia this time," Holt said in a calm and reassuring voice to the police chief. "We'll want your input, too, of course. We can share what we learn so both of our organizations can reach a mutually satisfactory solution here."

"Mutually satisfactory?" Crane all but spit. "One of my officers was killed. Another—" he pointed at the bed where Sidell lay with his eyes wide, his mouth open as he breathed heavily "—was gravely injured. There can be no satisfactory solution for us till we catch whoever or whatever did this, and you're gonna help us. You are going to share with us. Got it?"

"We understand," Holt said soothingly without agreeing to anything.

"I think it's time for us to leave," Kelly said. "All of us." He looked commandingly toward Kristine first. Quinn saw her nod slightly. He hated the idea of following this government jerk's orders, but perhaps talking with the two DoD guys would lead to more answers than the locals had.

"Good idea," he said, apparently startling Kristine, who glanced at him inquisitively.

"Okay," she said.

Maybe that hadn't been such a good idea after all, Kristine thought, as she preceded the men into the hallway. All they had learned was how badly mauled Officer Sidell had been—and that he didn't remember anything.

Shades of her self-defense attack on these two

Defense Special Projects Agency guys, with Quinn's help while shifted.

Did that mean that a shifter had been involved in these latest attacks in Acadia? In the first attacks? If so, who?

The answer seemed so obvious, since they hadn't yet found Grace and Simon.

But that only led to further questions...like, why?

A nurse walked by and glanced at the four of them curiously while they stood outside the closed door to the room they had exited. Maybe the antagonism created some kind of electrical charge in the area. Or maybe it was just the way the three men glared at one another.

Counterproductive, Kristine thought. Not that she wanted to become best friends with these miserable, secretive and aggressive feds.

But they still probably had information that Quinn and she wanted.

Like more about what had actually occurred this last time in Acadia.

What the feds currently thought about it.

What did they officially perceive could be the involvement of Simon and Grace?

And where the hell was the newlywed couple?

"Okay, guys," she finally said in a totally sweet but firm voice. "We're not getting anywhere by standing here. What do you say we go..." She pulled her cell phone out of her pocket and looked at the time. "Let's have dinner together and talk."

"Can't tonight," Kelly asserted. "We have plans."

Kristine caught the look between him and Holt. It seemed to speak volumes—none of which she could understand.

But she wanted to know what they were thinking. *Really* wanted to know.

Quinn must have caught that, too.

"I think it would be good for all of us and what we're doing here—" He raised his hand at the glare the two feds leveled at him. "Officially or not, I think we have the same goals. And I also think that we could help each other by talking. So, if we can't do dinner tonight, how does breakfast look on your agenda?"

He actually sounded calm and convincing. Kristine felt proud of him and readied herself to back him up.

She didn't need to.

"Okay," Holt said slowly. "Let's plan on breakfast. How's 7:00 a.m. tomorrow at the BarHar Bistro?"

Chapter 18

Kristine felt inexplicably nervous that night.

Heck, of course it was explainable, she realized, as she lay awake under the covers in the firm hotel room bed, her eyes wide-open in the dark after another bout of incredible lovemaking with Quinn.

It had been so hot and intense and consuming that it felt to Kristine as if they both feared it would be their last.

But as she knew well, each experience of incredible sex with Quinn could be their last. They were here in Bar Harbor on borrowed time and could be forced to leave on a moment's notice. There was no way they'd ever be able to get together like this again in real life, as members of the military. As an officer and an NCO, both members of Alpha Force.

Kristine didn't dwell on it—or at least she tried not to. Instead, what made her nervous was her pondering of their next confrontation with those feds who thought they knew about Alpha Force—and the fact that Quinn and she were defying orders by conducting their own investigation.

Although...Kelly and Holt might have some jurisdiction here, but they were really just flunkies, doing whatever they were under orders to do by their superiors at the DSPA.

And unlike Quinn and her, they did not seem inclined to disobey orders. Why should they? They weren't emotionally involved in their assignment here. They were just doing their jobs.

Somehow, during their discussion at breakfast today, Kristine had to finally figure out how to make the two men believe that their interests coincided with Quinn's and hers. That by sharing information about the latest attack—and anything so far unrevealed about the first one—would be useful to them.

"You awake?" came a throaty whisper from behind her. She turned over and found herself in Quinn's arms, under his hard body, almost instantaneously.

And for that exquisite moment, all thoughts fled once more.

* * *

The BarHar Bistro's claim to fame must mostly be at night, Quinn thought as Kristine and he walked in. All the tables still sported red-and-white-checked tablecloths, and now they were a lot more visible among the scanty breakfast crowd.

The people who sat at the few occupied tables looked like tourists—overeager ones, ready to tour Bar Harbor from dawn till dusk.

All of the tables but one. There, in the farthest corner, Kelly and Holt were already there. Staring toward the doorway.

At Kristine and him.

"Over there." He pointed toward them, then gently touched Kristine's arm to guide her in that direction. Bad idea. Touching her at all reminded him of last night. Hell, just being with her, inhaling her fresh yet sexy scent, it all reminded him of being with her and sharing yet another amazing night filled with delicious and memorable sex.

He quickly cleared his mind. He had to. He needed his wits fully about him for the upcoming conversation.

They both wore jeans that day with generic T-shirts, his green and hers black. He loved the way hers hugged her curves…but that was something else he cast to the back of his mind.

"Gentlemen," he said, holding his hand out as

they reached the table. Both Kelly and Holt stood and shook hands with Kristine and him. They, too, were dressed casually, as if they were not acting officially for the feds.

Which Quinn didn't believe for an instant.

They all sat down and just looked at one another.

"So…how can we all work together to solve this situation?" That was his congenial Kristine, of course. She'd want this meeting to result in win-win situations for all of them.

So did he, but he doubted it would happen.

Even so, he said, "That's right. Do you two have any ideas?"

"Yeah," Kelly said, his hazel eyes darting from one to the other of them from his skeletal face. "You two can follow orders and go home, and leave it to the people with real authority to find whatever's killing people here—even if they have something to do with your damned Alpha Force."

"That's still your position?" Quinn tried to keep his voice calm but knew he wasn't succeeding. "You're blaming Alpha Force?"

Kristine clearly caught the tension that was rising among the men at the table. She rose slightly. "Please remember that Alpha Force members are victims here. At least until we know otherwise. Simon and Grace are still missing, and it's been so long now, with no one finding any evidence of where they are—there's no reason to assume they're involved in the killings. They might have been killed, too, and their bodies not yet found."

The server came over then, brought coffee and menus. That seemed to ease some of the tension at the table.

Especially since Quinn had noticed Kelly and Holt exchanging glances that appeared to communicate something about what Kristine had said. Agreeing with it? No way.

But if they disagreed...why?

He decided to ask—obliquely. "I suspect that there's an official position on their disappearance, isn't there?" He looked directly at Kelly. "Look, I don't want to make any trouble. That was never my intention. But I need to know what's going on with my brother and his bride."

"And you really don't know what it is." Holt didn't make it a question, but something in what he said, and the way he stated it, suggested that he believed otherwise.

"No," Quinn said, trying not to let the gritting of his teeth seem too obvious. "If I knew, why would I be here, especially under these difficult circumstances?" Which he didn't have to elaborate on. They all knew that Kristine and he weren't officially supposed to be here.

"Good question," said Holt, a small smile puffing out his round cheeks even more.

"Why did you agree to talk to us this morning?" Kristine sounded upset and frustrated, but she had to hold it while they gave their orders to the server—an older lady this time, not the young babe who'd waited on them the night they'd been here.

Eventually, they were alone again, and Kristine repeated her question.

"Just wanted to find out your take on who attacked those cops and killed one," Kelly said. He was smiling, too, and it seemed condescending, as though he knew the truth and wanted to find out if they did.

"We have no idea," Kristine said. "Do you?"

"Nope," Kelly said too quickly, looking straight at Quinn with his eyebrows raised. "Do you?"

"Of course he doesn't," Kristine said. But Kelly's response left Quinn certain that he knew something—something that the two of them from Alpha Force didn't know and wouldn't like.

"I know it was off-limits to the locals, but did you have DNA tests conducted after the first maulings?" Quinn asked. "Any indication of what kind of animal killed those tourists, and if there was more than one that attacked?" It was way too soon for any results if they'd done any testing after the cops were attacked.

"Yeah, there were tests, but no conclusive re-sults," Kelly said. "Looked maybe like one animal, but we're not sure."

One? When they were trying to frame both Simon and Grace?

On the other hand, if the DNA testing wasn't conclusive, maybe whoever it was didn't have access to either of them.

Where were they? That question continued to burn through Quinn, but he knew he wouldn't get his answers here.

Even so, he continued to push for information about what the feds knew—or at least suspected. But the games continued through breakfast. Mostly, they talked about what had already appeared in the news, how the media likened the more recent attacks to the prior ones. How they called for better animal control in Acadia. Of course it had been some kind of wild beast—only one?—that was on a rampage, killing humans.

But everyone at this table suspected otherwise.

Problem was, it seemed clear that no matter what the limited evidence said, Kelly and Holt held on to their prior beliefs, that somehow Simon and Grace had gone rogue, were out to disgrace and bring down Alpha Force. Didn't make sense to them, though, since they apparently only had heard rumors about the special shifting elixir. But that wouldn't have stopped the couple from making it appear that the attacks were done by wild animals.

Quinn, on the other hand, knew it had to be someone else with that very goal: bringing down Alpha Force. Someone controlling actual wild animals? Another shifter outside the unit with some other kind of shifting formula?

When they were done eating, Kelly excused himself to go to the restroom. As he stood, he leveled a really odd look toward Quinn, along with a tiny nod of his head, as if he wanted Quinn to accompany him.

Which he did, through the rows of tables and down the hall.

In the restroom, Kelly glanced around as if assuring himself that they were alone. Then he said, "We're not accomplishing anything here, are we?"

"No," Quinn agreed.

"Then how 'bout if I show you something that will assure you that our position is right? Just you, though. Since you're related to one of the 'missing' people—or whatever they are—you have more of a stake in this." He made it clear from his tone that he didn't consider the honeymooners missing at all.

"Fine," Quinn said. He'd be wary, of course. He didn't trust anything Kelly said. But whatever it was that Kelly wanted to show him, he'd keep Kristine out of it. Keep her safe.

* * *

Quinn recognized that Kristine wasn't thrilled when they separated after breakfast. He would have been amused by the irritated look on her face, that belligerent lift of her chin, if he'd had time. But Kelly was clearly in a hurry.

In fact, they left while Holt and Kristine were still finishing their food, with just a cockamamy story about checking out a lead Kelly received on his cell while they were off peeing at the same time.

Quinn didn't like leaving her with Holt, but she'd be safe here, in public. He was taking their rental car, following Kelly toward Acadia, although the guy still wouldn't explain where they were going, damn him.

But at least this way Kristine would need to stay in town. Holt had already described where he was going when they were done eating, and it involved going to talk to the cops again—nothing that would include Kristine.

Quinn followed Kelly's car through Bar Harbor onto twisty roads leading to the shoreline, then upward along the outer perimeter of Acadia.

Eventually, Kelly pulled into a remote turnoff and parked. Quinn did the same.

When they both had exited their cars, Quinn stood on the gravel and looked around. The forest was thick enough here that all he could see was trees, not the water below.

"Why are we here?" he demanded of Kelly.

"Follow me. I'll show you." Kelly marched off onto a path that led into the forest.

Good thing Quinn was wearing athletic shoes. The undergrowth was thick and, since it had rained recently, slippery. But he had no trouble keeping up with the thin fed who clearly kept in good condition.

Surprisingly, in this remote area, they soon got to a small log cabin. It looked old and weathered, as if it had been there for a long time without any work being done on it.

"What's this?" Quinn asked.

Kelly just beckoned for him to follow as he twisted open the rusty metal knob on the front door and walked in.

Quinn wondered if the place was ready to fall down on anyone entering—but he was too curious not to follow the fed inside.

Kelly flicked a switch, and a light appeared in the middle of the room from a naked bulb hanging from the ceiling.

It was as worn-out inside as out, with the bare wood walls looking rotted, a single room with a toilet at one end, a sink at the other and not much in between except for two cots with what appeared to be clean sheets on them.

There was also a suitcase along one wall. A generic-looking one to be sure, but it was black and appeared to be of the same brand as one owned by Simon. But Quinn figured he thought about that only because he was here to be shown something that could prove Simon's involvement in whatever was happening. Maybe Grace's, too.

"This look familiar?" Kelly asked with a snide grin. He bent down and opened it.

Inside were clothes. Jeans and T-shirts, underwear, an extra pair of shoes.

And a camo uniform that looked like the kind worn by Alpha Force.

That didn't prove anything.

But the name tag Kelly pulled out that read Simon Parran? That was another story.

And what was even odder?

He also yanked from the suitcase a hoodie that looked a lot like the one Quinn had misplaced. He put out his hand and felt the fabric, then took it from Kelly.

"You looking for this?" Kelly asked, holding out a small piece of paper. "I got it out of the pocket."

Quinn looked at it.

It was one of his P.I. business cards.

Kristine was worried.

She remained with Holt in the restaurant, still

sipping on coffee and taunting her with planning on revealing something to her—in a while.

But not just yet, damn him.

She'd asked Holt immediately, after Quinn left with Kelly, "Where are they going—and why?"

"That's between them," he'd replied with a snide grin. "But I bet your *husband* isn't going to enjoy it."

"Is he in danger?" Kristine had reached down for her purse, which rested on the floor beside her, wondering why she'd stayed in that dratted restaurant with Holt. She should have followed Quinn.

But her curiosity had kept her there.

"Oh, danger is everywhere, don't you think?" Damn the guy even more. He seemed to be enjoying himself by irritating her this way.

"I'll make sure it is," she'd replied through gritted teeth.

That had gotten to him. His expression segued from snideness to anger. "I need a drink," he said. Never mind that it was still morning, she wanted to tell him. But she didn't have to. "I'm not going to order one, though. Know why?" He didn't wait for her to hazard a guess. "Because, thanks to you and your guy, we're still off alcohol."

"Obviously caffeine doesn't hurt you," she'd responded with a snide grin of her own. "This morning, you seem to be drinking even more coffee than last time."

"Yeah, it's fine." Holt took another sip, then scanned the restaurant with his gaze before looking at his watch.

That had been almost forty-five minutes ago, and they were still there. He was still holding the carrot of additional information out to her without letting her nibble on it.

She was getting damned tired of that.

Time for her to go find Quinn.

"Well, it's been fun," she said, reaching down to gather her purse. She looked around the place, too. It was getting more crowded, perhaps with people after brunch or an early lunch. With their current slow sipping of coffee and no additional purchases behind it, she felt certain the restaurant would be happy to have them leave.

"Okay, let's walk," Holt said. Not exactly what she wanted to do, but at least the feds had been generous enough to pay for their breakfasts.

Out on the street, Holt began strolling slowly, as if he was one of the sightseeing tourists surrounding them, which only annoyed Kristine.

"Look, unless you give me a good reason to hang out with you, I'm leaving." Dread suddenly coursed through her. "Did you hang out with me to keep me from going with Quinn? You never really answered my question about danger."

"Could be," he said. "But there's more to it than that." He took hold of her arm and kept her from slipping away through the crowd of tourists meandering around them and window shopping at some of the nearby stores.

She'd stopped feeling in charge of this situation. She stopped, ignoring Holt's tug on her arm. "Let me go," she commanded, staring up into his rotund face.

"Oh, I don't think so. Do you really want me not to reveal the information I'd planned to tell you?"

"I don't believe there is any information," Kristine spat at him, tugging again, still fairly gently. But if she had to, she would use stronger, more skillful techniques on him. Hell, she was in the military, trained for combat. A little confrontation like this was nothing. She could handle it.

"Fine," Holt said. "Maybe you can tell me something interesting instead."

"Forget that."

"Fine." He looked beyond her down the street.

She turned. A familiar-looking figure was heading toward them.

The team leader for special projects within the Defense Special Projects Agency, Darren Olivante? Here?

This couldn't be good.

Kelly and Holt obviously reported to him, but she'd figured it was indirect, that there were other lower-ranking government employees between them in their official chain of command.

But here he was. Why?

"Sorry I'm late, Holt," Olivante said. "And Staff Sergeant Norwood, isn't it? So glad to see you— even though I didn't think anyone from Alpha Force was authorized to be here just now." His gaze was steely from beneath his thick glasses, but his flabby lips were pursed in an expression that looked almost amused.

Kristine stood frozen in place. What should she do now? Wasn't this one of the people opposing General Yarrow—wanting to shut down Alpha Force?

"I'm here on vacation," she said lightly, repeating yet again the lie that had become so natural to her. She didn't bother trying to refute his identification of her. No way would he buy that she was the new Mrs. Scott on her honeymoon, not any more than these other DSPA guys had.

"Right. Well, from what I've gathered my men, here, have had a difficult time doing their job thanks to you and Lt. Parran—Quinn Parran, that is. Is he with you? Oh, yes, right. I understand he's with Mr. Kelly right now." He grinned almost maliciously, which sent shivers of concern down Kristine's back. His salt-and-pepper hair seemed a bit longer now, deemphasizing the roundness of his face. He wore a white shirt and dressy gray slacks, but if they were part of his uniform—a suit—he'd at least removed the jacket and tie.

"I guess so," Kristine said. What should she do? Retreating seemed the best option. "Well, very nice to see you, sir. I'll be leaving now."

"I know you've already had breakfast, but why don't we grab another cup of coffee?" the deputy said. "Holt, you can get on your way to that other assignment I gave you for today. I have something to discuss with Sgt. Norwood."

Kristine wondered what was on the guy's mind but didn't necessarily want to find out.

"Thanks anyway," she began, but he interrupted her.

"If you were going to say no, don't. I think you'll be very interested in what I have to tell you." He bent down toward her and whispered, "It's about Quinn Parran. And it goes to the very core of saving Alpha Force."

Chapter 19

Needing a break from his cat-and-mouse discussion with Kelly, Quinn had claimed to need to go outside—not wanting to use the bathroom facilities in the one-room cabin, with its lack of privacy. He stood outside simply drinking in the sounds and scents for a moment, until he saw Kelly staring out a window at him. He walked away.

The next thing he did was to call Kristine. Fortunately, there was a phone signal in this area so close to the park, although it wasn't very strong.

"Everything okay, Kristine?" he asked.

"Fine," she said. "And with you?" Her voice sounded a bit strained, although that could just be the bad connection they had, with him off in the boonies like this.

"Fine," he repeated. "You still with Holt?"

"No," she said quickly.

"Then where are you?"

"Taking a walk. You?"

This conversation wasn't yielding anything useful but reassuring him that Kristine was safe. And that had to be good enough.

"Still having a discussion with Kelly. I'll tell you about it later."

"Good. I'll look forward to it."

Of course Kristine wasn't going to tell Quinn what was really going on—and who she was really with just then. Not till Olivante had explained what he'd been talking about.

Olivante and she had just sat down inside a coffee shop, at a table in a corner. Surprisingly, the place wasn't very crowded for being near lunchtime. Maybe that was because this was a local shop, not part of a large chain.

Olivante was getting their order. After all the coffee she had drunk before, Kristine had asked for something cold and loaded with sugar—not her favorite drink, but she'd be able to sip it while chatting with him.

And hearing what he had to say.

When she hung up with Quinn she looked up to find Olivante just arriving with two cups in hand.

"Were you talking to your 'hubby'?" he asked in a mocking tone.

She shrugged a shoulder. "Could be. Now, what did you want to tell me about him?"

Quinn went back inside the decrepit old cabin to talk some more with Kelly. But only for a short while.

Kristine's attitude had bothered him. He had to go back to join her again, soon.

First, though, he wanted more answers here. But Kelly resumed playing games with him, laughing, as he had before, at Quinn's demands to tell him what was really going on.

"I think it's pretty obvious that I should be asking that," the skinny fed said, waving Quinn's card practically in his face as they knelt again beside the open suitcase.

"I think it's pretty obvious," Quinn had said in a mocking tone, "that I'm being set up." Then he grew more serious. "But what I think is in both of our best interests—not to mention my brother's and his wife's—is to figure out how this bag and its contents got here and where my family members are right now."

Their conversation went nowhere.

Kelly had made it clear, though, that, given his preferences he would have taken Quinn into federal custody immediately, demanding that he tell them where the missing, and obviously rogue, members of Alpha Force had gone. Oh, and by the way, had he physically helped them in their attacks on first the civilians, and then the cops? Or had he just helped to cover their trails, so to speak?

But apparently Kelly was under orders just to find what information he could and keep his superiors informed, at least for now.

A short while later, he was the one who left the cabin first, to Quinn's relief.

Apparently Kelly had taken extensive photographs of this site but didn't consider it a crime scene. He left Quinn there with no protest.

Which only puzzled Quinn all the more.

He nevertheless spent an additional few minutes examining that suitcase without Kelly's interference.

Was this somehow part of the setup against him, along with his brother and sister-in-law? Or was there even more to it than he currently imagined?

Now, no more than ten minutes after he had watched Kelly's rented car head back down the dirt road through Acadia, he took off after him—still with no answers.

No.

Whatever Kristine had expected this horrible government suit to come up with, it wasn't this.

For a long moment, she stared at the sweet, almost untouched drink in front of her as she sat at the table with Olivante.

Sure, she'd figured before that Kelly and Holt could suspect that Quinn and she were somehow collaborating with Simon and Grace in their disappearance, but of course that was absurd.

At least it was as to her. But could Olivante be right about Quinn?

She looked up again at Olivante. Then, keeping her voice low as they had both been doing in this conversation, she asked, "What evidence do you have of any of that?"

"Some of it's circumstantial. We haven't found any indication of where the honeymooners currently are—not even their bodies—despite a fairly thorough search of areas where they'd been spotted or were otherwise likely to have been. We have come across some of their belongings in a remote part of Acadia that could indicate they were harmed, but there was no real proof of that. It was more like they had to flee before being found there—and there was some evidence that Quinn might have been with them. All we can extract from that so far is that they are probably in hiding somewhere. Since your 'husband,' Quinn, insisted on going against direct orders and coming here to look for them—and since what we found indicates he might have been with them at least at some point—that suggests he's part of the conspiracy."

"That's a stretch," Kristine countered, trying to keep her temper. "And if it were true, why on earth would he bring me along? I might figure it out and expose it all."

"You're a distraction," Olivante said calmly. "Part of the role he's playing to hide whatever is going on. He must believe he can control you, or at least point you in different directions to ensure that you don't learn the truth."

"That makes no sense!" she countered, even as her mind started dissecting the possibilities.

Of course Quinn would have wanted to come here when his brother and sister-in-law disappeared, to learn what had happened to them—as well as to try to figure out any involvement, real or manufactured, with the tourists' deaths.

Could Simon and Grace really be involved in something else, something they hadn't revealed to Major Connell or anyone else at Alpha Force—something to help the unit? Kristine knew them well enough, especially Grace, to be sure they wouldn't intentionally do anything to harm it.

Kristine had been like Grace's right arm on their last assignment together. Her backup and advisor. Her friend.

She couldn't believe that Grace had gone rogue, nor Simon, either.

But if they were doing something to benefit Alpha Force?

And if so, might Quinn really know what they were up to? Be involved, too?

Of the four of them, Kristine was the only one who wasn't a shapeshifter. Had they chosen her as a patsy to help with their cover because she was the outsider and couldn't fully relate to what they were up to?

With his werewolf mentality, he'd consider his place in his family's pack, his loyalty to them, a lot more important than anything he might feel about Alpha Force.

But surely she'd have known. She would have sensed something in Grace's attitude, or Quinn's. She had worked so closely with Grace before. And now, with Quinn...well, two people couldn't get a whole lot closer, physically, at least, than they had.

But did she read him well enough to know if there was something beneath the surface that he was hiding from her?

"We'd appreciate it if you'd keep an open mind, Kristine," Olivante said. "For one thing...well, we've gotten a warrant and traced calls to and from Quinn's phone. All the times he claimed not to have reached Simon? False. There was even a text message he received yesterday from Simon that said 'Thanks, bro.'"

Kristine's body froze. That simply couldn't be.

But before she could voice her incredulity, Olivante continued. "There are some things I'd like to show you. They may convince you I'm telling the truth—or at least that what I'm saying may be real. If so, we'd like you to work with us. We'll devise a scenario that you can play out with Quinn, gauge his reactions. Maybe even get him to lead us to the other Parrans, if what we suspect is true. Okay?"

"I'd like some time to think about this," she said.

"Time is something we don't have," he countered. "Besides, do you think you could just get back together with Quinn, continue to play the games you've been playing—and not have him realize that you're at least a little suspicious now?"

"I...I'm not sure," she said. But she was sure. Quinn was an investigator by profession. He was trained to spot people in lies, or at least to suspect them.

Plus, they'd been close in so many ways, working together.

Sleeping together.

Could she just walk away from Olivante, spend the night with Quinn again and keep him from figuring out that something was on her mind? Something that could change their relationship—

professional and, to the extent they had one, personal—forever?

"All right," she said reluctantly. "Show me what you've got." At least that way, if it had no credibility, she could return to Quinn's presence without qualms. Maybe even tell him about it so they could use whatever it was in their own investigation.

"Okay," Olivante said. "Let's go."

She took a restroom break first, mostly because she knew she had to get in touch with Quinn.

She wasn't stupid enough to fully trust Olivante and everything he said. Not until she saw the supposed proof that Simon and Grace had gone bad and Quinn was joining them.

But she had to act as if she bought, or at least didn't completely reject, Olivante's story, in case he did reveal something helpful.

The smart thing for her to do was to keep in touch with Quinn, at least act as if she trusted him fully until, and if, she had some proof otherwise. But right now, she didn't want a long conversation with him. He'd tell her to get out of there, or at least wait till he caught up. He would give her his version, true or false.

And then she would get nothing from Olivante.

So, to avoid any issues, she sent Quinn a text message.

* * *

Quinn was in his car, hurrying back to Bar Harbor, when his cell phone beeped, the signal for a text message. He pulled it from his pocket. He wasn't surprised that it was from Kristine—but he didn't like what it said: Interesting development. Don't call me. Will report when I can.

What development? How?

And did she really think he would just sit back somewhere, grab a beer and wait for her next communication?

No, whatever she was up to, he had to know about it. With all the unknown factors, with those feds acting so confrontational, she could be putting herself into danger.

Good thing he was nearly out of Acadia.

The winding roads made speeding difficult—but not impossible.

Olivante's silver sedan was apparently a rental. It resembled the one Quinn and she had hired.

"I flew up here in a chopper from D.C.," he acknowledged when she commented on the vehicle. He sat in the driver's seat with his flabby hands on the steering wheel, the seat pushed back to accommodate his extended gut. His white shirt was wrinkled now, but she had been right about the suit. She saw the jacket and tie on the backseat. "Rented this when I got here."

Kristine continually assessed both the driver and the direction in which they were driving. Best she could tell, it was south. They were already on an extension of Bar Harbor's Main Street that led into Acadia National Park.

"Where are we heading?" she asked, not for the first time. He had skillfully changed the subject each time before. Irritating? Yes. And disturbing.

He laughed. "When you get a question in your mind, you're definitely determined to get an answer, aren't you? What I want to show you is at the house I rented here."

"You rented a house?" Why hadn't he just taken a room at the same hotel as his minions?

"Yeah. The guys who report to me are moving in there, too. They were staying at that nice hotel since we thought their visit here would be fast—figure out what happened to those dead folks and the involvement of the Parrans, and return to D.C. to report. But it's taking longer, so I've leased a house. I can stay there, too, and bring in more people to help in the investigation if necessary. Renting by the month will save money in the long run."

Sounded logical—if one could believe that anybody working for the government would try to minimize expenses. She'd reserve judgment.

"As a taxpayer, I appreciate that," she said lightly. "But where is it? We're out of Bar Harbor now. Did you rent a cabin in the park somewhere?"

He glanced at her with a huge grin on his face. His apparent amusement made Kristine feel anything but amused. "No, and as a taxpayer you shouldn't be entirely pleased. It's outside the major town on this island, but the place still isn't cheap. It's a fairly nice house just outside Seal Harbor."

"So let's talk on the way. What do you want to show me? It must appear to tie Simon and Grace to the killings or you wouldn't consider it useful, right?"

"I'm a good soldier, Sgt. Norwood." The sudden nastiness of his tone startled Kristine. He leaned over the steering wheel, his gaze straight out the windshield. "Or I was. Now, as a civilian member of the Department of Defense, I'm a different kind of public servant. I don't make assumptions—not without proof."

"I didn't say—"

"You don't have to."

Kristine felt even more ill at ease than before. Though she was damned good at using self-defense measures, she certainly didn't want to do something while they were on the road. Not unless she had to.

But her sense of wanting to hear what Olivante

had to say was growing, too. Something definitely didn't feel right, and she needed to know more.

Too bad she hadn't waited for Quinn. She might need his backup even more than she'd imagined.

Especially since Olivante kept glancing in the rearview mirror. Maybe he figured she'd gotten Quinn to follow, and he expected Quinn to pull up behind them.

Was this a trap for her? For both of them? But why?

For now, she would change the subject, get Olivante talking about something neutral. Something he liked.

What better than himself?

"You said you used to be a soldier," she said lightly. "Which branch?"

"Not special ops or anything outside the regular military," he responded through gritted teeth. "Nothing like your Alpha Force. No, I was in the Marines. Liked it there. Learned a lot, and rose through the ranks pretty fast. Made it to Chief Warrant Officer 5, and it looked good for me to rise even higher. But I saw that the real authority didn't always come from our officers, not even our generals, but from the civilians they had to report to and satisfy, so I decided to go that way."

Which meant he no longer went on field exercises

or otherwise had to stay in shape, Kristine noted. That might work in her favor.

Although…despite his thick gut, she noticed that his upper arms filled out his white shirt very well, and as he drove along the twisty road she saw his muscles flex.

The guy could be strong. And with a Marine's training behind him, he might not be a pushover if she had to engage in hand-to-hand combat with him.

No, it would be better if she could just use her brain to come out of this with the information she wanted. And her life.

"That sounds good," she told Olivante. "I'm a nurse by background, but I liked the idea of the military so I enlisted." That had to be neutral enough.

"Then why did you decide to join a unit as irregular as Alpha Force?" He seemed to spit the words at her.

Once again she glanced around. They were inside the park now, on Route 3, called Otter Creek Road. The road wasn't very wide, and cars were passing the other direction. There was no good way to escape this guy, even if she decided that was wise.

For right now, she would continue to play along.

"It just sounded interesting," she said carefully. "I gather that you know of the unusual background of Alpha Force. It sounded like you did while we were at Ft. Lukman, and you spoke with General Yarrow."

"It's ludicrous!" he exclaimed. "Maybe. Tell me, Sgt. Norwood, are you a shapeshifter?"

Kristine laughed. She had anticipated the question, but not so fast and directly. "Not hardly."

"But some members of Alpha Force are." Although his tone was fairly neutral, she sensed that he was holding back what he really wanted to say.

"Is this some kind of test?" she asked lightly. "You know enough about Alpha Force to understand that we all have very high security clearances—and that we're all under very strict orders not to discuss who we are or what we do with anybody outside Alpha Force. That includes anyone in the Department of Defense."

"Of course I know that. And maybe I was testing you. But I admit I don't like the idea of a unit so full of secrets even from those charged with its oversight. It's a farce and unprofessional, unmilitary, to have a unit that's so covert that its very existence is all based on sly references to activities that most people consider paranormal—and to use those claims, and those very real abilities, as a means of getting control in combat and other serious situations."

"But it's so cool, sir. At least I think so. And it's all to the advantage of our country."

"Not if—" he began, then stopped.

Not if what? Was Olivante upset because he wasn't within the elite central group given actual knowledge of more than the basic character of Alpha Force? Or was he truly acting in what he considered the best interests of the country in possibly opposing a rare and unique—and therefore potentially difficult-to-control—military unit?

"I believe in the damned things," he hissed. "I know they're real. That's one reason I wanted jurisdiction over this particularly bizarre troop. I know of a lot of personnel within the Department of Defense who just laugh at the whole idea."

Maybe that was a good thing—although for continued funding, for continued existence, Alpha Force had to keep up its good work, meet its goals, go where more usual military units could not succeed. And if those they reported to had doubts about them… Although Olivante claimed he believed. And Kristine was aware that at least one member of the House Armed Services Committee—Congressman Crandall Crowther—knew exactly what they were and how they achieved their accomplishments.

In fact, one of his aides, Alec Landerson, was involved with one of their shifters—Lt. Nella Reyes, who shifted into a lynx.

But knowledge of Alpha Force was on a need-to-know basis, and not everyone in any part of the

DoD was considered to have that need, no matter how highly they were placed.

"But you buy into the possibilities? You don't laugh?" Maybe she was pushing too much, but—

"Oh, yeah. I buy into it. Too much. The unit's clearly out of control, and something needs to be done about that." His tone made her blood turn to ice.

This was definitely not a man who should have jurisdiction over Alpha Force—not when he obviously had conflicts about its existence.

But Kristine already knew that. Major Connell had talked about a meeting in the Pentagon. Kristine now surmised that Team Leader Olivante was one of the suits who wanted to disband Alpha Force.

They were now out of the national park and had reached the outskirts of the village of Seal Harbor. Olivante made a few turns on narrow roads, and Kristine attempted to recall the names of each, as long as she saw the street signs.

Then, Olivante drove onto a street off Upland Road, and then up a driveway.

At the top was a large house, imposing with its dormers and curved windows, an example of attractive New England architecture.

"Here we are," he said, turning off the engine. "Come in and I'll show you around."

"And you'll show me the evidence you were talking about."

"Right," he said in a tone that gave Kristine no confidence at all.

Okay, she might have made a mistake in agreeing to come here. But she would do more than survive this.

She would pay attention to Olivante. Outwit him. Get answers.

She thought again of Quinn. He'd be furious with her for acting on her own.

Or would he be glad for an excuse to allow harm to come to her? Could Olivante be right about his involvement?

She wouldn't believe that until she had more evidence than the word of this man she didn't trust. But, right or wrong, she did trust Quinn. Mostly.

Although that pack mentality thing bothered her. Might he be conspiring with Simon and Grace?

But why? And to do what?

Somehow, she would let Quinn know where she was, let him come in. See if he tried to help.

And wouldn't it be great, considering Olivante's attitude, if Quinn showed up here changed into a wolf?

Chapter 20

Quinn was walking fast along the narrow Bar Harbor sidewalk, edging around the people strolling more leisurely.

He nearly missed them: the two DSPA men, sitting at a table in a small but crowded café.

Quinn hadn't gotten any further responses to text messages or calls to Kristine, which concerned him. He'd gathered that she had stayed in town—partly because he had checked with tour companies and no scheduled sightseeing would have taken off after he'd spoken with her.

Nor was she in their hotel room. He'd checked.

Now, preparing another text message, he peered into all the retail and eating establishments he passed while looking for her. He was so focused on finding her that he was initially surprised that he even recognized the guys, let alone zeroed in on them.

But despite her hard-line military attitude, he feared that Kristine was doing something he wouldn't like in furtherance of their now really unauthorized investigation. And these men were definitely involved.

Quinn hurried inside despite not really wanting to talk to Kelly again. But Holt had been with Kristine after he'd left. Maybe he would have some information.

"Hi," he said to Kelly and Holt, both with sandwiches on plates in front of them as well as glasses of beer. Apparently their ban on alcohol was over. "Mind if I join you?" He didn't wait for their answer before asking the people at a nearby table for their unoccupied chair.

But he didn't even know if they had that knowledge.

"Have you seen Kristine?" he asked Holt. "She's not answering her phone."

"Yeah, I saw her."

Quinn didn't like the snide look on Holt's puffy red face, but he did forbear from punching it. "Do you know where she is now?"

"Not really—not after she went off with Team Leader Olivante."

"Hell, Holt," Kelly growled. "You ever heard of being discreet?"

"We're not under orders to keep quiet about one of our bosses showing up," Holt responded, glaring at his cohort. "I didn't like playing games about it then, don't like it now." He took a large swig of beer.

"Then he didn't approve of the great job you gentlemen are doing?" Quinn didn't hold back his sarcasm. Like accusing innocent people like his brother, sister-in-law—and him—of murder and more.

"He told us when he arrived that unless things change around here fast he's pulling it out from under us," Holt grumbled. "This job sucks sometimes."

"Don't worry about that," Kelly countered, sounding malicious. "After this, you won't have it much longer."

Holt met his gaze. "You, neither."

This wasn't getting Quinn anywhere. "Well, if you both like what you're doing, I hope you can work it out. Meantime, do you happen to know if Kristine is with Olivante now?" He looked at Kelly.

"Probably." He sounded indifferent.

"Then do you know where they went?" Quinn spoke through gritted teeth to the man who'd been so difficult to deal with in the rotting cabin, although he made himself smile as if he felt friendly to him.

"Nope," Kelly said. "Sorry." But he didn't look at all sorry.

The server returned with coffee. Quinn took a large swig of the bitter, hot brew, then pulled out a few bills, laid them on the table and stomped out.

Outside, he yanked his phone from his pocket and called the hotel where these clowns were staying. He asked not for their rooms, but for Darren Olivante's.

"Sorry, no one by that name registered here," said the operator.

Damn. Was Olivante just visiting for the day rather than taking over the investigation like the flunky DSPA men apparently thought? Or was he staying somewhere else?

And, most important, where was he now?

Quinn's next call was to his commanding officer.

"This is one hell of a puzzle," he told Drew Connell. He gave a brief rundown of all that had happened that day so far, including Kelly's leading him to that remote cabin that contained some of Simon's and Grace's belongings.

"And you didn't call to tell me this before?" Drew demanded.

Hell, Quinn had thought about it. But now that

their presence here was even more precarious, with even their commanding officer demanding that they end their investigation and making it clear he wouldn't have their backs if they didn't, he figured he'd give a report only when he had something useful—and positive. But Olivante's presence, and Kristine's being with him, were things Drew needed to know about.

Especially in case Quinn wound up needing backup to find her. If it wasn't Kristine in danger, he would plan on just using his normal P.I. skills. But it was Kristine. And if assistance would let him find her faster—and figure out what really was going on—then he'd have to avail himself of it.

"I just learned from those two Defense Special Projects Agency operatives here that their superior, Darren Olivante, showed up," Quinn told Drew. "Kristine's apparently with him, and I'm hunting them both but don't have a lot of ideas."

"Let me contact the general, have him use his resources to check what Olivante is up to," Drew said. "I'll get back to you. And Quinn?"

"Yes…sir," he added.

"This is potentially a major screwup. You know already that your continued unofficial mission is only adding to the charges being made against Alpha Force. Your presence there, too, after the latest attack on those cops. Right now, just find Kristine and get out of there. Both of you."

"Yes, sir," Quinn asserted, grimacing.

"For now, I'll be waiting for whatever information you can provide." Quinn hung up before Drew could ream him any further.

But waiting wasn't the equivalent of taking action.

As Quinn continued to hurry to where he had parked the rental car, his mind weighed what he should do next.

They were inside the house now, entering from the rear through the kitchen. It smelled of cleaning products but appeared run-down, as if it needed a major renovation.

Kristine didn't like this. She immediately surveyed her surroundings for exits, other means of escape—and possible weapons. Nothing obvious like sharpened knives sat on the old laminate counters, but at least there were a couple of other doors from the kitchen. Not to mention a fairly wide window that probably looked out on the backyard.

She hugged her purse more closely to her side. She already had a weapon.

"Come this way," Olivante said. "To the living room. I'll get you something to drink. A soda? Something stronger? Unfortunately, I don't have the ingredients around to make you another of those coffee drinks."

"Just water, please." She followed him down the short hallway to a sparsely furnished room that was a bit more elegant, with its paneling and wainscoting in keeping with the attractive exterior of the house, but had little charm.

It had a large-screen TV, though. Not that she would ever watch it.

Except...Olivante turned it on. "I'll be right back with your water," he said. "Meantime, make yourself at home."

Something in his innocuous expression suggested to Kristine that he was about to do more than merely get her a drink. But she simply thanked him.

She waited for a couple of minutes after he left, then walked from the living room and into the hall. She thought she heard a door close somewhere near the kitchen and headed that way.

Olivante wasn't in the kitchen, nor could she find him right away. Since he could be taking a restroom break, she wouldn't knock on doors looking for him.

She only wished she had some of the enhanced senses that Quinn had, even in human form. Better yet, she wished Quinn were here with her, to watch her back.

But she needed to hear what Olivante had to say about him.

She thought she heard voices, very low and very distant, and they didn't seem to come from the TV. Olivante must be talking on his phone with the speaker on.

She wished she knew who he was speaking with, and what they were saying. But she needed to take advantage of this opportunity.

She didn't want him to hear her talking, too, though, so when she pulled out her phone she decided to text Quinn again. She had to trust him, no matter what Olivante had claimed. Didn't she? At least she'd stay aware if he didn't, in fact, watch her back—and not let their sexual attraction be a factor.

Not when her life could hang in the balance.

But she only got part of the directions to get there entered when she heard that door open and close again, and then Olivante's footsteps in the kitchen.

She wasn't sure there was enough detail for Quinn to find her—or even if she'd gotten everything right. She'd try again later, when she was alone once more.

For now, she quickly returned to the living room and sat on the musty gray fabric sofa. When Olivante walked in and handed her a glass of water, she shot him a perfectly innocent smile.

"Hey, Quinn." Chief Al Crane strode up to him just as Quinn got to his car.

"Hi," he responded. "How is Officer Sidell?"

"Surviving. Where are those damned feds? I need to talk to them. We're at a dead end as far as evidence goes in that last attack and I need to talk to them. Neither's responding to phone calls."

"I just left them." With pleasure, Quinn gave the name of the coffee shop. He hoped this cop would give them a hard time. Maybe even extract some useful information from the uncooperative men. Unlike Quinn.

"So...you aren't leaving town, are you?" the cop asked, scowling so much that his shaggy gray brows nearly met in the middle.

"Not immediately." Quinn paused. "I assume I'm not a suspect in any of the attacks."

"Don't assume anything."

"Then if you have any evidence that seems to implicate me, please let me know." Like that damned business card in the stuff that had apparently been stolen from his brother and sister-in-law by whoever had made them disappear. Or that was what he had chosen to believe.

"When I arrest you," the cop muttered.

Quinn said nothing more but slipped into the car. He was driving when his phone beeped. He grabbed it from his pocket. Was it legal to talk on the phone or text while driving in Maine? He didn't know. Didn't care.

He checked the screen and almost cheered. As he'd hoped, it was from Kristine.

But then he scowled. Her message was short: With olivante. House near seal harbor. Ocean view off upland. And that was all.

Ocean view? Was that a description or a street name?

Good thing he had brought his GPS. He aimed for the nearest parking lot to set it.

He didn't think that he could track Kristine's cell phone with it, and she probably didn't have the military satellite phone with her.

He just hoped the system included a good map of Seal Harbor.

"So where's the evidence you wanted to show me?" Kristine asked Olivante.

They still sat in the living room. The TV was muted. Kristine glanced that way every once in a while to see the talk-show hostess chatting with her guests—one publicity seeker talking to others. Why bother?

"I'll show it to you soon," Olivante promised.

"Why not now? I'd like to see it and get back to town. Quinn and I have dinner plans. I can pretend I still don't know his involvement but sound him out about what he knows."

They didn't have any dinner plans, but she wanted

Olivante's commitment to get her back there, the sooner the better.

"Just need to figure out the best way to present it to you."

What a load of BS. She was about to tell him to cut out the crap and show it now or take her back, when a voice from beside her said, "Hi."

Startled, Kristine jumped in her seat. A man stood there, someone she didn't know.

"Hi, Mel," Olivante said, standing. "Kristine, I'd like you to meet my brother Mel."

The taller, thinner man wore jeans and a loose, untucked blue shirt. He held out his hand as he approached her. "Good to meet you. I've heard a lot about you, Kristine. The rest of Alpha Force, too."

Kristine glanced at Olivante, whose smile resembled the traditional cat-got-the-canary grin. Was this brother an employee of some Department of Defense agency, too? If not, why would Olivante discuss the classified military unit with him—brother or not?

"And what have you heard?" She made her own expression bright and receptive, as if having a stranger learn about Alpha Force was no big deal.

"Very interesting things." His gaze suggested that he was assessing her, trying to determine if she was a shifter.

She stood and rounded on Olivante. "May I speak to you in private?"

"We can talk in front of Mel," he said.

There were now two of them and only one of her. Not good.

"Okay," she said to Olivante with a shrug, then turned back to Mel. "Do you work for the government, too?"

"Me? Not hardly. I just sell cars."

"No kidding? I'm in the market for a new one. Are you from around the D.C. area?" She knew she sounded like a naive ditz, but she would extract information any way she had to.

"No, I stayed in Montana after Darren left."

That was something new, even if it wasn't particularly useful—was it? Olivante was apparently from Montana.

"That's a pretty far distance for me to go just to get a new car. What brings you here?"

"Just helping my brother." The two men exchanged glances.

"Really? That's so nice. I was an only child, so I don't have that kind of relationship with anyone. What do you need help with, Darren? Maybe I can do something, too."

Both pairs of eyes turned to her. "Maybe you can," Olivante said. "Although you'll need to prove that we can trust you. That the whole U.S. government can trust you."

"Absolutely," she said. "I've been a member of the military for years. I'd do anything for my country."

Especially to figure out what these men were really up to, then fix it.

"Let's start with what I said I'd show you," Olivante said. "Then we'll see how cooperative you really are."

That didn't sound good.

"Okay," she agreed.

He motioned for her to follow him. "Down the hall."

Mel waited for her to catch up with his brother, then he followed. She was sandwiched between. Was this a trap?

Her heart thumped crazily inside her chest. She could handle two adversaries if she had to, especially nonmilitary types.

As she'd thought before, maybe she should have waited for Quinn. Unless Olivante's claims had been true...

Hell, she was a soldier. She knew better than to act without her unit—usually.

Well, at least she had her purse, and its handy contents.

The hallway was wide but the gray walls could have used a coat of paint. The carpeting on the floor was dingy, too. Not a place she'd have wanted to rent, even on a budget. So why had this guy, whose expense account was undoubtedly generous, resorted to living here?

Another thing that didn't smell right.

Olivante reached the end of the hall and pushed open a door. He flicked on a light, and Kristine realized that the afternoon had segued into evening. How would she get out of here before nightfall?

"Here we are, Kristine. I'll be interested in your reaction."

She wasn't about to just walk in and let him slam the door behind her. "After you," she said with a smile.

"Sure." Both men, in fact, preceded her. Maybe she could slam the door on them.

But Mel remained in the doorway.

She walked up beside Olivante—and gasped.

The whole room appeared to be full of wolves.

Dead ones.

Chapter 21

He'd found it—maybe. The GPS showed that there was a street called Ocean View off Upland Road in Seal Harbor.

But were there homes there? If so, he needed to know which one Olivante was taking her to.

Well, hell, he was a private investigator.

He pulled off the road into a parking lot and grabbed his laptop computer from the backseat.

And stared for just a second at Kristine's ubiquitous backpack. Yes, he'd picked it up when he had gone to their hotel room to look for her, then brought it along. Even without her assistance, he could use its contents to shift if it made sense to do so.

He started to boot up the computer, which he'd

been smart enough to equip with a satellite chip. Then it dawned on him. He had even better resources than that. He grabbed his cell phone and called Drew Connell again.

"Hey, Major," he said when the phone was immediately answered.

"What's up, Parran? You found Kristine yet? I'm still fighting here, and—"

"I've got a fight of another kind I'm dealing with," Quinn said, "but they're related. Right now, I'm following up on a cryptic, incomplete text message from Kristine. She's still with Olivante, and they're somewhere in Seal Harbor here on Mount Desert Island. Maybe on a road called Ocean View, off Upland. Could you get one of the computer geeks at your disposal to check into whether Olivante or someone he knows owns or rents a house there, or something else that would give me a lead on where to go?"

"Sure thing. You need backup?"

"I might, but right now I just need information."

He rang off, then, just for the hell of it, tried calling Simon's phone yet again. As always, it went immediately into voice mail, and the recorded voice said the mailbox was full.

He only hoped that Simon would, one of these days, have an opportunity to listen to the messages and empty it. And return the calls to him.

Shoving his phone back into his pocket, he once more started the engine. He wouldn't wait for Drew to get back to him.

He needed to find Kristine. Right away.

"What is all that?" Kristine stammered. There were wolfen creatures of all sizes. Most looked real, as if they'd been killed, then stuffed by a very skilled taxidermist.

There were also some heads hanging on the wall. They didn't look quite so real. Were they actual wolves or were they masks?

There were also facsimiles of wolflike legs, with horrendously sharp claws at their ends. They hung beside the fake heads—and appeared damned dangerous.

The one thing she didn't dare ask herself, didn't want to face, was whether some of the creatures who appeared to be real canines were actual wolves...or whether they were werewolves who'd been killed while in wolfen form and hadn't returned to their human shapes.

She shuddered. At least none of these could be Quinn. Olivante couldn't possibly have had time to kill him and get him stuffed. Besides, as smart as Quinn was, he would never be captured while in wolf form and harmed this way.

But was what Olivante had said about him true—

that he had conspired with his brother and sister-in-law to make Alpha Force look bad? To bring it down?

And could any of these be Grace or Simon?

"I thought you'd appreciate this," Olivante said, "thanks to your affiliation with Alpha Force. You said you were making no claims to being a shapeshifter, right?" He stood sideways, arm outstretched as if he were a game show host showing off the latest prizes.

Kristine would have to move around his prominent gut to go farther into the room. She just stood there, gaping. "You know I can't talk—"

"Yes, I know. But my interests diverge from yours and your Alpha Force's. I'm mostly charged with doing what's right for our country. So here we are. This is my Alpha Force display."

Kristine took a deep breath.

"Interesting," she said. "But you said you had proof of a conspiracy in which Quinn was involved. Something harmful to Alpha Force. What does this stuff have to do with it?"

"If you only knew," Mel called from behind her.

She had moved through the doorway far enough that Olivante's brother was now at her back. She was trapped as well as stunned.

"The ironic thing, though," Olivante said, then stopped. He approached Kristine, his smug gaze making her shudder inside, even as she fought to maintain a cool expression. "Do you actually believe in werewolves, Kristine?"

What was the right answer here? The truth? A lie? "I'm a member of Alpha Force," she said. "I'm paid to believe in them."

"Very tactful. So tell me this. Is your partner Quinn one?"

"Does it matter?" she countered. "You've said that his brother and sister-in-law got together and killed those tourists and that cop, and that he was involved. I don't care whether they were shapeshifted demons or people with fake claws like these." She gestured around the room. "I want to know how and why you think they did it."

His smile looked rueful, as if she had given the wrong answer. "Come here and look at these, Kristine," he said. "They're evidence. I've collected them, brought them here. Mel has kept them safe."

Which made Kristine's heart plummet. Were these wolf-related things actual evidence about who attacked those tourists and cops? They could have been used to create the gouges and wounds that had appeared as if a wolf had mutilated them. She had seen some of the photos on the news that had been censored but still appeared gory. And the saliva found on the victims? Olivante could have collected that from dogs, or even real wolves.

Or not.

"These are genuine wolves, Kristine," Olivante continued. "At least a few are. Some of the body parts are fakes meant to look like them. When you've gotten your fill of observing them, let's adjourn back to the living room. I'll answer some of your questions—then ask you a few of my own. And don't worry. I won't report you to anyone. And if anyone should suspect that you've cooperated with me, I'll be able, with my position, to protect you. All right?"

What else could she say? "Of course. I'm really looking forward to learning the truth."

"Got anything?" Quinn had answered the call from Drew Connell without saying hello. Without slowing down. Not many people on this road anyway, and he was driving in near darkness.

"Well, first thing you should know is that the local Bar Harbor cops are really pushing the feds to find Simon and Grace. No indication of what evidence they think they have, but the cops are sure that our missing couple was at the site where the cops were attacked."

"In what form?"

"Unknown," Drew said. "Presumably human, since they wouldn't know how to check for shifters who'd changed—or that's what we think. Meantime, here's something else for you. We're still looking into hotel records for Olivante, and so far nothing. But we also had our guys check out local real estate agents, and one transaction showed promise."

"What's that?"

"Nothing under the name Olivante, but there was one deal under Oliver. Mel Oliver. And our DSPA team leader just happens to have a brother named Mel."

"That's a stretch, isn't it?"

"No guarantees, but the property that was leased is on Ocean View, a small street that runs off Upland Road."

Definitely worth checking out. Without slowing down, he carefully grabbed a receipt and pen from his shirt pocket to jot down the address.

"One more thing. I don't know if it strengthens or weakens the possibilities, but the property was leased out to Mr. Mel Oliver the week before Simon and Grace got married."

The three of them returned to the living room with its minimal furniture but big-screen TV. Olivante waved Kristine to an end of a once elegant but now worn red sofa and she took a seat, placing her purse on the floor beside her. He sat at its other end while Mel took a seat on a less comfortable-looking wooden chair with torn cushions.

"Before I tell you more about your partner

Quinn," Olivante said, "I want you to tell me all *you* know about him. We need to cooperate to make sure justice is done here."

She would feel more like cooperating if she felt she could trust this man.

"I really don't know him very well," she said. Which was true—except for in the carnal sense. "I was assigned as an aide to Lt. Grace Andreas-Parran, now. Quinn was a new recruit into Alpha Force, like his brother Simon. When Simon and Grace got married and went off on their honeymoon, no one had been assigned as Quinn's aide, so I was given that job temporarily."

"Simon and Quinn—they're both lieutenants, too?"

She nodded. That, at least, would be in regular military records.

"What do you do as an assistant to one of those officers?"

This could present a problem. She wasn't about to tell the actual truth.

She glanced at Mel—and found he was leaning forward in his chair, his hands clasped and his expression as expectant as if he believed she would tell all, and that it would be both lurid and disgusting. His face was not as round as his brother's, just like his body was thinner. But his cheeks still puffed out beneath his crafty, small eyes.

"I still feel uncomfortable talking about this," she said.

"I'll use my position within the Department to protect you," Olivante reminded her. But did she want that kind of protection?

More important, did she want this guy to know the truth? His brother?

No way.

"Okay," she finally said with a sigh. "I can't really get into what within Alpha Force is real and what is just intentionally directed rumors." Boy, did that obfuscate reality. "But whatever the officer I report to says or does, I back it up. I appear at their meetings, take notes, do what's necessary on the computer or in person to make sure it's memorialized and followed up on. And then I start the follow-up, make sure it's completed. That kind of thing." Not to mention watching their backs when they shifted—her main job.

"I don't follow that."

"Well," she said, grasping a bit at the idea, "when I was on an assignment recently with Grace at a hospital out West, I worked with her and her therapy dog. She's a doctor as well as a member of Alpha Force. Since I'm a nurse, I was able to use those skills to be there to help out, too. Alpha Force was assigned to look into some alleged terrorist threats there, and I acted as Grace's backup in her investigation. I'm sure that the Alpha Force records show we were successful."

But not necessarily how they succeeded. That involved both Grace and Simon, who was also a doctor, already on staff at that hospital.

Plus, they were both shapeshifters. Grace and he bonded well, in many ways. Grace recruited Simon—and Quinn—into Alpha Force.

That should have been the end of the story.

"Interesting," Olivante said. "But I want to hear more about the shapeshifter end of things. In case you think I'm going to use what you say to ridicule Alpha Force, to the contrary. As I said, I believe in shifters. Know why?"

"No," Kristine said, actually interested in the answer.

"Would you like to tell her, Mel?"

"Why not?"

Kristine looked at the man still staring at her. He was leaning back in the chair now. She couldn't quite read the expression on his face, but it appeared studiedly blank. As if whatever he was about to say was so upsetting that he erased any indication from his demeanor. She waited with interest.

"Darren and I, we're brothers," Mel said unnecessarily. "We had another brother, too. He was Darren's twin, in fact."

Kristine darted a glance at Olivante and saw that

his expression, too, was empty. All except for his eyes, and they looked furious, but only for a second, as if he suddenly got them under control.

"He's dead now—Daniel. He was killed when we were all teenagers, back in Montana."

Kristine suddenly stiffened. She thought she knew where this was going, at least one of two ways. Either Daniel had been mistaken somehow for a shapeshifter, or—

"He was attacked on a night of a full moon by a werewolf that slashed his throat with some really horrible, sharp fangs. He died from those wounds."

"I'm sorry for your loss," Kristine said. "But in Montana, real wolves sometimes prowl." She didn't think they attacked people without provocation, but of course she hadn't heard the entire story. "Couldn't it have been a real wolf that attacked your brother?"

"No," Olivante said. "Because I saw the attack, but I wasn't close enough to stop it. When I got there, though, I shot the damned wolf. It was too late to help my brother. And the creature that I shot?"

Kristine knew exactly what he was about to say. "It was—"

"It was a dead human being, or at least that's the way it looked a few minutes after I shot it, draped over the body of our poor, dead brother."

Chapter 22

Kristine's mind was racing. She had continued to ask questions of Olivante, ones intended to sound understanding, as if she didn't blame him for what he had done.

But the guy had just admitted to killing someone. A person, even though he had allegedly been in wolf form when he was shot on the night of a full moon.

Yes, the dead man had supposedly first killed their brother. Olivante might be vindicated in a court of law because of that, or perhaps even on a self-defense theory. Plus, he'd been a minor.

Had he been tried for homicide? Had he gotten off under the combination of circumstances?

True or not, this definitely explained his apparent hatred of the idea of shapeshifters. And it also explained why he was sure they existed.

But why had they told her this story—to garner her sympathy? To prove it was humans against shapeshifters?

Or simply because they intended to kill her, so it didn't matter what she knew?

"I'm so sorry all of this happened to you, Darren," she said. "You, too, Mel." She looked at the brother in the chair across from her whose usually sardonic expression was now blank.

She actually was sorry. She was also full of those additional questions but unsure how to ask them in a tactful enough way not to raise their ire.

She wasn't a cop, nor did she want to be one, or even a P.I. This interrogation thing would be much better for Quinn to do.

But she suspected that he wouldn't act as sympathetic as she was pretending to be. She'd seen on TV and in the movies that interrogators often acted like buddies to get those they were questioning to confess. True? She wasn't sure.

"What happened then?" she probed. "With two dead bodies like that—was there an investigation into how your brother had died?" *Or your shooting of his killer?*

"Of course," Mel said. "Good thing it was a small town. People knew one another. But they figured

Darren here had gone nuts when he started talking about the werewolf attacking Daniel."

Kristine kept her gaze on Darren. "That must have hurt even more, to have people think you were crazy." *But didn't the evidence of bites or whatever help to convince them? And did it get you out of a murder charge?*

"It might have if I hadn't known the truth. And—well, I had help afterward, so all of it, including what I said and did, was hushed up for my protection."

"Really? What—?" But Kristine heard a noise from somewhere in the house. She caught the look that passed between the brothers.

"Excuse me for a minute," Mel said. He glanced at his watch. "Time got away from me."

"Know what?" Olivante said. "I think it's time that Kristine learns more about what's going on here."

She didn't like the sound of that—particularly because of his falsely jovial tone.

"You know," she said, "I really think it's time instead for me to head back to Bar Harbor. I've enjoyed talking with you both, but—"

"Don't you get it yet?" Olivante growled. "You've seen and heard too much. You surely understand that you're not just heading back to your supposed husband for more fun and games on behalf of that miserable excuse for a military unit. Military unit? Shapeshifters? Hell, our country deserves a lot better than that mockery of our military system."

Was that the basis of his actions against Alpha Force? He hated shapeshifters, presumably loved his country and didn't like to see the type of people he despised have any degree of success?

Kristine would have loved to ask—but not now. He had answered her questions about why he had told her so much. He had also said she couldn't go back to Quinn.

He would learn otherwise.

But what if they wanted to use her for some kind of leverage? To lure Quinn in?

She wouldn't allow that.

"Sorry you feel that way," she said icily. "But if you had kept an open mind, you'd recognize how much good Alpha Force does in helping our country out of unusual situations."

"I know more than you're aware of. But—"

The noise sounded again. Mel remained standing in the doorway, observing them with apparent interest.

"Go take care of that!" Olivante exploded.

"It might help convince Kristine about how things are around here if I took her to see our guests."

Guests? Kristine knew who he must be talking

about. Her hands on her hips to prevent herself from lashing out in fury, she began, "Do you—?"

"You're right." Olivante grabbed her by the arm and started dragging her toward the door.

Mel had started down the musty hall. He opened a door at the end and disappeared, his feet clomping on a flight of wooden steps.

Olivante propelled Kristine that way, too. She didn't fight him. Not when she wanted to see what was at the bottom of that precarious-looking stairway. But she did toss the strap of her purse over her shoulder.

And was shocked, as she neared the stairway entrance, to see a face in the window at the far end of the hall. Only for a moment. She blinked, and it was gone.

Warmth flooded through her, but she forced it to dissipate just as quickly. Had she conjured up his image in her mind, or was Quinn really there?

She'd texted him info to find the place, but had he located it this soon? And if so, was it a good thing? After what Olivante had told her...

Was Quinn involved with the killings? Of course not.

But his coming here, following her—ready to protect her?—had probably put him in danger.

As if reading her thoughts, Olivante, behind her,

gave her a brief shove. Fortunately, he must not have seen Quinn.

Assuming Kristine hadn't just imagined seeing him.

But Olivante surely would have reacted in some other way—like rage? Or…smugness?

Kristine hurried down the steps and stopped at the bottom.

The light was dim, but not too low for her to see the bars of two cages along the far side of the moderate-size room. One was occupied.

"Kristine!" shouted Grace's voice. The woman who peered from between the bars didn't look much like the alert, well-dressed military lieutenant who had been Kristine's superior officer. She was dressed in a torn white T-shirt and ratty jeans, and sagged as she held on to the metal cage, as if she had no energy anywhere in her emaciated body. "Run!"

"You bastards." Simon Parran stood in the same cage as Grace, looking equally shabby and gaunt.

The couple held hands, though, as if giving each other strength…and reassuring each other of their love.

Sweet. And inspirational.

Kristine would get them all out of this, somehow. Seeing them there made it clear to her that Olivante had been playing them all. Quinn needed to get inside here, to see this.

He needed to help her get his family freed and safe.

But for the moment, she was on her own.

Could she shoot both men at once? She hugged her purse closer.

"Time for your next medication, doctors," Mel Olivante chortled. "And I think we have enough for your friend Kristine, too."

Quinn had parked some distance away, in case the car was noticed by a curious neighbor. He had Kristine's backpack over his shoulder as he hiked into the hills.

Fortunately, in this area, the houses weren't close together. Also, the address was not along the main part of the street and was shadowed by surrounding hills that secluded one lot from another.

He was damned pleased at his timing. He had been there for only a few minutes, cased the place, initially found some windows he could peer into easily.

Had somehow chosen the right one for catching Kristine's attention.

But now she had disappeared through a doorway.

He needed to get inside.

Backing up, he continued his surveillance and

discovered what he had hoped to find: an open window.

Not on the ground floor, unfortunately. But it was near a gabled roof over a porch.

Quinn could get in that way. Easily.

As long as he was in wolf form.

He had become used to Kristine being there as his aide. To set up his shift when it wasn't under a full moon, like now.

Well, this time, she couldn't watch his back—but he would damn sure get in there and watch hers.

"I don't understand," Kristine said. "Why are you keeping Simon and Grace here? Let them go."

She stood off to the side of the decrepit stairway, her back intentionally against the filthy stone wall. That way, neither man could sneak up on her.

But neither could she easily sneak out of there.

"You know we won't do that, Kristine." Olivante's tone sounded utterly reasonable, as if he spoke to an obstinate child who needed reality to be explained. Both he and Mel stood at the base of the stairway, preventing her from bolting up it. She hadn't thought that the bulky form of Olivante would ever seem ominous, but it did now—especially when reinforced by the more muscular presence of his brother. "Would you like to join them?"

"Of course not," she spat. "Let them go." Would

they pay any attention if she kept repeating that? She doubted it. "Quinn knows where I am." Boy, did he ever—but she wasn't about to reveal anything about that. "It'll go easier on you if you start cooperating now."

"Oh, I don't think he does," Olivante said. "I wish it were true, though. The more members of Alpha Force that I can involve in my plan, the better."

"What is your plan?" Kristine demanded. Maybe it wasn't such a good thing for Quinn to be here. Was this a trap?

Mel laughed. "It's so rich. She's not leaving here," he said to his brother, "so I want to tell her. Okay? I can brag about it to these fools since they won't be able to tell anyone."

"It's a total setup," Simon interjected from behind the bars of the cage, underscoring Kristine's fear.

"They killed those poor people and are blaming it on us, as members of Alpha Force," Grace said. "They claimed we shapeshifted and did it, since it was the night of the full moon, but you know we didn't harm them."

She was talking about the tourists, and not the cops. "I do know," Kristine said. "And you'll be exonerated as soon as we get out of here. For the mauling of those two cops, too, and the death of one of them."

"They attacked cops the same way?" Simon

yelled. "Locals? But there hasn't been another full moon. No one will think it could be shapeshifters."

"Oh, they just might," Olivante said much too sweetly. "Those who really count will. Those who know about Alpha Force and its nature and the enhanced abilities of some of its members. And the rumors about more. We did a damned good job of using our collection of wolf claws and fangs. Not to mention the canine saliva we'd saved up, too."

"And like I said," Mel added, "you're not leaving, Kristine, and neither are these two. But they have to stay alive till the next full moon so we can complete all our plans. We want even people who don't know about Alpha Force to believe in shapeshifters—murdering ones. If you're not a shifter, though, you don't need to be alive then."

Kristine shuddered. What could she do? She had to get them all out of this somehow. Carefully, she began to move her purse around so she could reach inside.

"If you're looking for this, don't bother," Olivante said casually. He waved her gun in front of him.

How had he gotten it? She'd had her purse with her since she'd arrived. And yet—well, there had been times her eyes had been on Mel instead of his brother.

She shrugged without commenting, letting her hand drop to her side. She touched the outside of the pocket of her slacks. Could she surreptitiously push some button on her phone to make it call someone and broadcast all of this?

If only she could reach Quinn so he could hear everything before coming inside.

"They blindsided us," Simon continued. "Olivante invited us to join him for breakfast the day after the full moon. We'd already recovered from the moon's effects and thought it would be a good idea, but the juice was drugged. We woke up here, but his brother keeps knocking us out. They apparently even checked us out of our hotel and took our belongings away."

"Hey, bro," Mel said. "Take our dear Kristine upstairs. I can't drug these two with her looking on. Unless you want me to drug her, too."

"Not yet," Olivante said. "There's more I want to milk from her about Alpha Force before she joins these two. Although…" He aimed Kristine's gun at her. "I'll let her have the choice of either going back upstairs like a good girl, staying here and getting a small shot in the arm or getting a real shot." He brandished the weapon.

"Not much choice," Kristine said. She wished she could reassure Grace and Simon that all would be well. She had to make that happen.

But she'd have a better chance one-on-one with Olivante upstairs.

Olivante motioned with the gun toward the stairway. "Then after you, my dear," he said.

He had done it.

It was much easier when Kristine was there, facilitating the change.

More enjoyable, too, when he could tease her with his naked human form.

But he had set up the light first, then drunk the elixir, removed his clothes, then stood in the glow.

And now he was ready.

Slowly, carefully, he approached the house once more, glad of the near utter darkness except for some lights through the windows. Despite the seclusion here, he did not want neighbors to see a wolf prowling their hillside.

He heard voices from inside. Kristine! And that SOB Olivante.

At least she was still alive. Maybe she'd even taken charge of the situation, knowing his Kristine.

And even if she wasn't in control now, he would be. Soon.

He positioned himself carefully, knowing he would have only one chance to do this correctly. The porch roof was, fortunately, very pointed, with portions of it not far from the ground.

It was time. He leaped.

* * *

"What was that noise?" Olivante stood in front of Kristine in the living room once more, still brandishing the pistol. He looked upset. Frantic, even, which didn't bode well for her longevity if he accidentally pulled the trigger.

"It came from downstairs," she lied. "Sounded like your brother swung that cage door shut too hard."

She knew it came from somewhere else around the house, maybe above it.

Could it be Quinn?

She prevented herself from smiling, but she allowed herself to hope.

And then—

A canine form leaped into the room, pouncing on Olivante even as the man got off a shot.

"Quinn!" Kristine exclaimed. He had to be okay, but she couldn't tell where the shot went.

At least there was now a distraction. She picked up the chair where Mel had been sitting before and swung it—straight at Olivante's arm.

He dropped the gun, even as Quinn clamped his teeth around Olivante's throat.

Chapter 23

Kristine had never been happier to see Quinn.

Well, not exactly true. There were times when she had been thrilled to see him, all human and all naked. But she was definitely relieved that he had come to her assistance now in wolfen form.

The gun was on the floor. Kristine grabbed it. Quinn remained at Olivante's neck. His ferocious growls filled the room as the DSPA man struggled against him, arms flailing, legs kicking—and neither making Quinn release his fangs.

Kristine saw where the bullet had gone—into the floor, fortunately. Quinn was not injured.

Olivante's struggles soon grew fainter.

"Damn you, Parran," he gasped. "And damn that elixir. I thought it was only a rumor."

Good thing Kristine had possession of the gun. She was tempted to shoot Olivante but resisted. He was subdued now, and she wouldn't take any chances on hitting Quinn.

But she heard Mel shouting as he raced up the stairs.

He burst through the door—and Kristine pointed the gun at him. "Good to see you, Mel," she said with a grin. "Know what? It's over."

"What the hell?" His eyes were on the wolf at his brother's throat. "Is that a real wolf or a shifter?"

"What do you think?" Kristine asked. Apparently, whatever information Olivante had been given about Alpha Force, its makeup and its abilities, the successful formulation of the special elixir that allowed shifting outside the full moon hadn't been confirmed despite his decision to act, with his horrible wolflike weapons, as if it were true. And his brother might not even have heard rumors about it.

Kristine worried now about Grace and Simon, downstairs and alone and quiet. Mel must have administered the drugs he'd been threatening them and her with. She could only hope they would be okay.

Right now, though, she needed to call for help. Still aiming the gun at Mel, she pulled her phone from her pocket and called 911. She quickly described a kidnapping situation and asked for both cops and EMTs.

But things needed to be rearranged here before their arrival. That Chief Crane of the local police department wouldn't be pleased to see a werewolf in the flesh.

If he believed his eyes, he would probably shoot Quinn on the spot and claim he had to be the one who'd attacked the cops.

"Watch Olivante for another minute, Quinn," she said, then waved the gun at Mel. "You come with me." She had him precede her down the stairs to the basement.

As she'd anticipated, Simon and Grace were sleeping on blankets on the floor of their cage, as if they were animals on display in an old-fashioned nonhabitat zoo.

Fortunately, there was a second, empty cage. Kristine had noticed it before. Had these two SOBs planned to put her in there?

Her teeth were gritted as she motioned for Mel to pull open the door to that one. "Get inside," she commanded. He didn't argue but regarded her warily. Was he about to attack? She again brandished the gun while glancing at the lock that dangled at the opening. She smiled to see that it was one with a key rather than a combination. She used her free hand to pat him down, looking for weapons as she kept her gun pointed at him. Then she secured him inside, tested the lock and stuck the key in her pocket. "See ya later," she said. One down.

She returned upstairs and looked around for an exit besides the front door. There was one in the kitchen at the back of the house, and she left it open. "Let me lock him up downstairs with his brother, Quinn," she said to the canine, who remained on guard. "You need to go shift back fast, before help arrives. The nearest houses aren't too close, but be careful when you leave. We don't want any neighbors to see you. Assuming they didn't see you when you got here."

Quinn moved back, and Olivante groaned, rubbing his neck.

"Let's move." Kristine waved the gun in Olivante's face. As the man slowly stood, Kristine looked into Quinn's golden canine eyes and smiled. "We did good. Now go."

He gave a small nod of his wolfen head, then headed out. As with his brother, Kristine got Olivante down the steps and into the spare cage.

When the police arrived a while later, she was waiting. One was Chief Crane, and the portly cop scowled in the way she remembered. "What's going on here?" he demanded.

"I've solved the murder of the tourists and attack on your officers for you, and more," Kristine replied with a grin.

She showed them the cage downstairs with Simon and Grace sleeping in it, along with the enclosure holding the two fuming men.

"She's the one, Officers," Olivante shouted. "Look at my neck. That whole werewolf situation before..."

"I'll show you how I subdued him before his brother came upstairs," Kristine interrupted. "They set this all up to make it look like woo-woo nonsense. I used some of his own weaponry on him— pretend wolf fangs. That's how he attacked your police officers, too."

"Get those unconscious people to the hospital," Crane said. "We'll take these two into custody and sort this out later."

"Thank you, Officers," said the wonderful, familiar voice of Quinn, who had just arrived in human form, wearing his own clothes. "I wish I had been here to see everything that Kristine did. We all owe her."

Kristine smiled at him. His golden eyes were glowing hotly, sensually, as he smiled back. She wanted to throw herself into his arms to thank him. And more.

She realized that it was partly adrenaline pulsing through her. Partly relief.

But she ached to show her gratitude in a personal way.

Very personal.

Kristine sat in the living room with Chief Crane while a local crime scene team canvassed the place, taking photographs and collecting evidence.

The local cops allowed Quinn to remain with his brother and sister-in-law until help arrived for them in the form of a military helicopter. While Kristine was still with him, Quinn had gotten permission from Chief Crane to call his commanding officer to have emergency aid brought in immediately.

Kristine could hardly wait to talk to Maj. Drew Connell and give him a full rundown on what had happened here.

And also to hear how he would talk to General Yarrow and give their highest commanding officer ammunition to torpedo that entire horrible Defense Special Projects Agency and keep them from investigating, and undermining, Alpha Force any longer.

For now, Kristine gave Chief Crane a rundown on what had occurred here—putting her own spin on it, of course: the way Olivante had essentially kidnapped her, given her a totally weird tale of wanting the world to believe that there were werewolves, of all things, in Acadia National Park. How he'd apparently decided to kidnap a couple of honeymooners, whom he'd kept drugged, to frame for his incredible murderous spree.

He'd brought his own brother into it.

And then, to harm the U.S. military, make it look inept and absurd, he set things up with nasty, potentially lethal paraphernalia he had collected to make his story of a unit of combative werewolves, of all things, appear true.

"For the sake of national security," Kristine concluded, "we'll need your discretion in all this. I'm certain that General Greg Yarrow, who's headquartered in Washington, D.C., will send official media relations advisors to help put the right spin on this amazing, ridiculous story, and your cooperation would be greatly appreciated."

Eventually, Quinn and she were released.

Simon and Grace were, by then, undoubtedly under appropriate medical care.

This assignment was over. Their mission had been accomplished, most successfully.

It was time for them to head back to Ft. Lukman.

First, they had to return to their hotel to check out. That meant packing up the clothing and few personal items they had left there.

Quinn watched as Kristine collected her stuff and tossed it into the carry-on bag she'd place on a luggage stand. "I'm so glad this is over," she said, her back to him.

"I'm just happy that Simon and Grace are okay," he responded. "And that those damned Olivante brothers will get what's coming to them."

They were civilians, of course, but Olivante himself had had clout within the Department of Defense. Clout over Alpha Force and its members.

The ability to give them orders. Control them. Make them look bad.

That only emphasized to Quinn the problems with remaining in the military. Would he?

He would be considering the pros and cons very carefully from now on. And at the moment, considering the lack of support and backup Kristine and he had been provided, the cons were definitely in the lead.

One thing had particularly surprised him as Kristine had recapped what had happened. She had told him that Olivante and his brother had lost a relative who was murdered by a shapeshifter.

Quinn and his family had lost a relative because he was a shapeshifter.

Interesting similarity—and even more interesting to see how the Olivantes had attempted revenge against all shifters.

Now, Kristine turned to look at Quinn, a troubled

expression on her face. "Did Major Connell think they'd get off on some kind of insanity plea?"

"Not likely. Most of their crimes were committed on federal property and they harmed U.S. soldiers as well as civilian police officers. They'll be tried for their crimes in federal court with prosecutors just waiting to throw the book at them. And the evidence collected at the crime scenes, the place they were held prisoner, their testimony, ours..."

"They'll be incarcerated for life?" Kristine finished with such a delighted smile on her face that Quinn almost laughed. Almost. But he was distracted by the bra she held in her hands to pack.

Which encouraged him to take a quick look at the part of her body where such clothing was generally worn. Well, not so quick.

And when he looked up, Kristine's smile had become heated. Longing.

He dropped the jacket he'd been about to throw in his own bag and quickly crossed the room. He took her into his arms and kissed her, hard and deep, using his tongue to incite her to the kind of heat that had started permeating his body.

"One for the road?" he demanded against her mouth.

"Oh, yes." But she really hadn't had to answer him in words.

Her hands were already unbuckling his belt, pulling down his pants.

And then her mouth moved away from his, downward, to his hard cock…and after a few exquisitely enticing minutes, they both rushed onto the bed.

Chapter 24

A week had passed. Kristine and Quinn were back at Ft. Lukman. Grace and Simon remained in the nearby military hospital where they'd been flown, but they would be released in another day—substantially before the next full moon. They were doing well.

Kristine had checked on Tilly, Grace's cover dog, and her own dog, Bailey. In the absence of their humans, they had been spoiled in the base kennel with all the other dogs that weren't currently living with their masters. Kristine had retrieved Bailey, who now occupied her base housing with her once more.

They spent time with Tilly whenever they could. Right now, though, Kristine looked at the others meeting in General Yarrow's office. They were all dressed in their standard military camo uniforms. No more undercover role as newlyweds or anything else. Not any longer.

She sat between Quinn and Major Connell. After all the initial interrogations and the arrival of backup from Alpha Force, Quinn and she had only remained in Bar Harbor for that afternoon—when they'd packed, and more. The hours before they left their hotel room had been extraordinary, even better than she had anticipated when their passion had once more started to erupt.

But it hadn't been repeated. She had hardly seen him since their return.

Which hurt. More than it should. She understood how things were, how they'd continue to be.

"That whole situation with Olivante seems to be coming to light," the general was saying. "Our champion within Congress, Crandall Crowther, is conducting a quiet hearing with members of the Department of Defense. Plus, we're being kept informed about the Olivante brothers' interrogations. Interesting stuff."

"I assume that they've talked about how their other brother was killed by a shapeshifter when they were in their teens, and that when Darren shot him the wolf turned back into human form," Kristine said. She had told Major Connell and Quinn about it, but of course had not mentioned any of that during her discussion with the local cops.

"Right," the general said. "Plus, the whole thing was kept quiet thanks to the intervention of another shifter, a neighbor of theirs who'd hated that the killer had gone rogue. The guy made up something to explain why the Olivante brother looked like he had been attacked by an animal, and even protected Darren Olivante and kept him from further interrogations or arrest for killing the other 'man.'"

"So even if Darren holds a grudge because of the death of his brother," Quinn said, "shifters should have earned at least a few points in his book for having helped him."

"You'd think so," Drew said. "But he apparently went over the edge when he spent time redeeming himself in the military, got ambition and rose within DoD agencies, only to learn that shapeshifters were being given a major, if covert, role in protecting this country. He vowed to stop Alpha Force, bring down the whole unit, and enlisted his brother to help. The whole thing with killing the tourists using pseudo wolf fangs and claws was planned for months, and when he heard about two Alpha Force members marrying and taking their honeymoon in a relatively remote location, he took his opportunity. He had his brother rent that house as soon as he heard the plans."

Kristine knew a lot of this, but not everything. "If he was so smart, and was digging into the background of Alpha Force, why was he so uncertain about the existence of the rumored elixir, and how well it actually works to allow you guys to shift outside a full moon?"

"Parts of our cover are even more restricted and covert than the rest," Drew said with a grin. "Especially my work with the elixir and its continuously evolving formula." He paused. "The guy went about his scheme really methodically, though, from planting clothes in that old cabin where his subordinate Kelly took you, Quinn, to show you the stuff—as well as your old business card to implicate you. He had his own brother sneaking around, too—he's the one who stole your hoodie from your hotel room to plant there."

Quinn had told her about how Kelly had taken him to that run-down place and showed him stuff that had really concerned him—mostly because, though false, it could have implicated his brother, sister-in-law and him as at least getting together while they were in this area, if not conspiring together. That could have supported the story that Simon and Grace were loose—and rogue.

And that Quinn, and perhaps Alpha Force, were involved.

"His claim about his getting a warrant to check

out Quinn's phone calls was a lie, though," Drew continued. "There was, of course, no text message on it from Simon, thanking him for whatever."

Not that Kristine was surprised, but she was glad to hear the truth.

"And Simon and Grace?" she asked. "How are they taking everything?" Kristine had been told that Grace would rejoin the rest of the unit in a few days, and Kristine's assignment as her aide remained in effect.

"They're fascinated by it all," Quinn said. A pleased smile lit up his handsome face in a way that Kristine hadn't seen since the wedding. "You know, during their honeymoon, on that night of the full moon, they'd been prowling in Acadia without knowing they were being set up—but a lot of what happened could have been avoided if they'd run into Olivante before the night was over." He turned to Drew. "Your newest formulation that incorporates some of what Simon was working on let them shift back to human form for a short time while the moon was still full, and they were happily wandering around Bar Harbor showing that off—not that anyone else would have gotten their message, of course."

"Olivante would have freaked out," Kristine chortled. "He was trying to frame those people he thought were shifters, and there they were, looking like normal people even before he'd have expected it."

"That's correct," the general said. "The Olivantes' debriefing is continuing. Despite their having defense counsel, their interrogators are making them look like total fools on the record—so when they testify at their trials, even if they try to deny their claims about shapeshifters, they'll even look dumber."

"Then they will be brought to trial?" Kristine was concerned, although not surprised.

"For murder," General Yarrow confirmed. "No doubt about it. The Olivante brothers killed those animal-loving tourists with their false wolf paraphernalia and attacked the cops, too, when the investigation seemed stalled and sliding from the forefront of the authorities' and media attention. At least Officer Sidell will survive, and he's starting to remember a little more about the attack that night. Unsurprisingly, local authorities aren't pleased that the investigation and prosecution will all be done at the federal level."

"Do you know how the testimony will be handled?" Once again, Kristine knew she was asking questions way beyond her authority, but she cared about Alpha Force—and the still-existing potential for public disclosure and humiliation. "And the media. I thought—"

"It can't be held as a military tribunal, but it'll be done as privately as possible," the general assured her. "All information about Alpha Force will be treated as classified to the extent permitted by law."

"And Simon and Grace will be fine," Quinn added, sounding happy. "Instead of being murdered during the next full moon, as Olivante had planned—after he murdered another innocent tourist or two, or maybe more cops, with his wolf-weapons collection, then blamed it on Alpha Force. He'd have gone public then about its existence, its shapeshifting members and its mode of operation. That was why he kept Simon and Grace captive instead of just killing them."

"As for Kelly and Holt." General Yarrow shook his head. "They were handpicked by Olivante to handle the official investigation until the next full moon. He fed them what he wanted to about Alpha Force—that it existed, and that rumors about its members being shapeshifters were greatly exaggerated in the interest of creating a diversion that allowed the unit to accomplish its missions. Plus, he claimed he wasn't the source of their orders but the conduit from a higher-up. Those guys followed orders well when it came to attacking Kristine and using other means to try to get more information. And undermining Alpha Force, whatever it was? That was first on their agenda, and they obeyed with little question. They weren't exactly the sharpest tools in the DSPA's shed."

"And," Drew Connell added, "Olivante also informed the local authorities about how the existence of murderous wild animals had been greatly exaggerated. That was why a couple of cops were sent out originally to watch the murder scene without expecting to trap the animals that killed those tourists. They remained curious and under orders to keep watching—so Olivante could set them up, too, and claim that the missing honeymooners were definitely the killers, and that his guys would capture them momentarily."

"So…" Kristine said, trying to digest all this information. None of it was surprising, though. "It sounds as if everything worked out okay for Alpha Force, right?" She loved the unit as much as she adored the camaraderie and rules—and unpredictability—of being in the military. Even more.

"Better than okay," the general said. "In fact, we're currently in recruiting mode again, assuming we find the right kinds of soldiers to fit with Alpha Force—both shifters and members for their support teams."

Kristine couldn't help grinning as she turned to look at all the other members, and supporters, of Alpha Force in that room. But when her eyes met

Quinn's, she couldn't read his expression. Was he glad, too? Was he sorry?

From the first, he had made it so clear that he didn't like following orders and respecting the chain of command. That the investigative assignment they'd been on together was important to him, but that staying in the military wasn't his first choice, especially considering the combative nature of his initial experiences.

Would there be an empty position in Alpha Force soon because he was resigning early? He had strongly hinted at the possibility.

Kristine understood, at least somewhat. She hadn't been happy, either, that Quinn and she had had to appear to ignore a lot of orders to come out with the good result they'd achieved. But Major Connell had understood. Despite the positions he'd had to take, he had protected them within Alpha Force and even beyond.

He was like family. Alpha Force was definitely family.

And Quinn? As much as she cared for him, she had to make her emotions stand down or risk being tremendously hurt.

As if she wouldn't already be, when he left.

The meeting ended a short while later, with the general and Major Connell promising to keep Quinn and Kristine in the loop.

It was over. And Kristine felt sad, as if the meeting had more significance than a recap of all that had occurred. Especially when Quinn said goodbye right away. "Got to run," he said. "I'm meeting my new aide."

Quinn knew the staff change was right. It had been the short time frame, plus necessity, that had given him the amazing opportunity to have Kristine as his Alpha Force aide.

Now, he met for the first time with Staff Sgt. Noel Chuma, who had been assigned as his new assistant.

Chuma was a short but well-toned guy who should have no trouble watching his back and supplying his elixir and light. Seemed nice enough, too, as they met for coffee to get acquainted at the Ft. Lukman cafeteria, near the middle of the base. His deep-toned skin was highlighted by his smile as he told Quinn his limited, but exciting, experiences so far with shapeshifters.

He'd do. But he wasn't Kristine.

It had only been a few weeks since he had met her. Worked with her. Fallen for her, and that gorgeous, sexy body, so deeply that it had taken him by surprise.

He should have acted on it before. Now, they'd run into each other on the base but there would be no official reason for them to get together except at group Alpha Force meetings.

He hadn't wanted to join the military in the first place, but Simon, and his talk of the special elixir and the support behind Alpha Force, had convinced him to join.

And now?

He wasn't pleased about how some things had been handled. His commanding officers hadn't backed him up. The best they had done was turn a blind eye as Kristine and he essentially went AWOL. Would he be able to stay at the base, follow orders, act like a good little soldier?

On the other hand, they *had* turned that blind eye, at least for a while. His discussions with other Alpha Force members since his return had confirmed that not all military protocols were demanded of Alpha Force members—since it was such a unique and covert unit.

Well, his tour of duty wouldn't be up for more than a year. After a lot of reflection, he had decided not to resign early but to wait and see how he enjoyed his military stint once the excitement of the recent few weeks had died down.

After that…well, it depended.

And part of what it depended on was something he could start pursuing.

Now.

And further testing Alpha Force's position about military protocols.

A lot depended on the answers he found.

The basement of the main Alpha Force building at Ft. Lukman was where the supersecret elixir formulations were always being experimented on further. Kristine had nothing to do with them, but Grace's husband, Simon, had been working on his own formula before joining Alpha Force, and she had sent Kristine down there to retrieve something from the lab.

But it wasn't Simon she saw there, nor the other primary elixir creator, Major Drew Connell.

It was Quinn.

He stood waiting outside the elevator door in the dim hallway. Kristine saw no one else around.

"What are you doing here?" she demanded gruffly, trying to hide the bittersweet pang of pleasure at seeing him again.

"Waiting for you."

"How did you know— Oh, I get it. You got your family members to set this up. Well, hi, and bye." She pushed the button to get the elevator to rise once more.

"No, just hi," he said softly, joining her in the elevator car. "See this?"

She noticed that he held a backpack nearly as large as hers. "Are you taking that to your new aide?"

"Nope. I was hoping that you would join me. I'm going to be trying out a new version of the formula that Simon has been working on with the major."

"Don't they have to conduct controlled experiments?" she asked dubiously.

"Sure, but it's a lot more fun to choose to shift when you're the one watching me."

The elevator stopped and the door opened again. Kristine sped out, trying hard to ignore the tightening within her body that signaled how much she was attracted to this man. Again. Still.

He kept up with her. "If you don't want to use the excuse of a shift, I'd still like you to spend the night with me."

She stopped and looked at him. "Look, Quinn." She tried to make her tone cool, but it sounded plaintive, even to her. "We had some good times, and it didn't hurt to have our adrenaline flowing because of the investigation we were conducting. But that's over. We're back here, on duty. If you decide to fulfill your tour of duty, we'll see each other now and then. But I'm still military, here for the long haul. I—"

"I love you, Kristine." She watched his golden-brown eyes widen in shock, as if he hadn't expected that any more than she had.

She swallowed. Closed her eyes. Opened them again.

He was waiting for her reaction. He looked so vulnerable…

"I…I'm not a shifter, Quinn," she began. "You know that. Your brother married Grace, and she's a werewolf just like he is. You and I—well, we're so different. We can't really have a relationship."

"You want me to count off the other Alpha Force couples who are mixed shifters and humans?" he demanded.

"No. I know that, but you're an officer and I'm a noncom. There's the military's nonfraternization policy—"

"You think I care? Look, we'll find a way around it. Alpha Force isn't the usual military unit, and I've gathered, in offhanded discussions with Drew Connell, that not all protocols applying to the rest of the military are enforced around here. What we've had so far is only the beginning. I can't guarantee it'll last forever, but we can see where it does go. I'll even stay in the military. Hell, I've come to really like Alpha Force. Only…do you care about me, too, Kristine? Even a little?"

It was moving to hear this strong, macho lone wolf, who liked so often to tease, sound so earnest. And caring. Definitely caring.

But love?

Hell, yes!

She had thought before that she would never want a real relationship with a shifter. A permanent one. One that might even someday lead to little werewolf offspring.

Nor would she be interested in a guy in the military who so obviously chafed at following orders.

And now?

Now the idea intrigued her. A lot.

Quinn's failure to follow orders might even have allowed him to save her life. Plus, she'd done a bit of that herself.

And the werewolf part ?

"Tell you what," Kristine said. "Let's try a marathon tonight. Your place or mine. Lots of down-and-dirty sex, even more than before. Then, if you feel like it when we're done, I'll watch your back while you shift here on the base—and I'll also watch your butt, and your—"

"I get it," he said with a laugh. Kristine found herself in his arms, pressed hard against his body that was reacting overtly to his suggestion.

"Until you shift," she said against his lips. "After that, you're on your own—till you shift back again."

Their kiss was hot. And so sexy that Kristine wondered if they could even make it back to her place, or his, before tearing off each other's clothes.

"It's a deal," he whispered against her mouth.

"Good." She pulled back and grabbed his hand. "Let's hurry. Oh, and for the record?"

"What?" he asked as he smiled sexily down at her.

"I love you, too."

And as Kristine knew, werewolves mated for life.

* * * * *

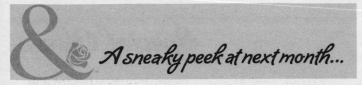

A sneaky peek at next month...

NOCTURNE™

BEYOND DARKNESS...BEYOND DESIRE

My wish list for next month's titles...

In stores from 19th April 2013:

❏ Keeper of the Moon – Harley Jane Kozak

❏ Beauty's Beast – Jenna Kernan

In stores from 3rd May 2013:

❏ Lord of the Beasts – Susan Krinard

Available at WHSmith, Tesco, Asda, Eason, Amazon and Apple

Just can't wait?

Special Offers

Every month we put together collections and longer reads written by your favourite authors.

Here are some of next month's highlights— and don't miss our fabulous discount online!

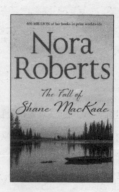

On sale 19th April   On sale 3rd May   On sale 3rd May

Save 20%
on all Special Releases

Find out more at
www.millsandboon.co.uk/specialreleases

Visit us
Online

0513/ST/MB414

The World of Mills & Boon®

There's a Mills & Boon® series that's perfect for you. We publish ten series and, with new titles every month, you never have to wait long for your favourite to come along.

Blaze

Scorching hot, sexy reads
4 new stories every month

By Request

Relive the romance with the best of the best
9 new stories every month

Cherish™

Romance to melt the heart every time
12 new stories every month

Desire™

Passionate and dramatic love stories
8 new stories every month